I0780938

RIVER IN THE SAND

ALSO BY AJ PARK

Seven Rivers Series

Forgotten Rebellion

River in the Sand

Guardians of the Horsemen Series

Silver Song

War's Ending

The Exiled Horseman

Sea and Iron

Stand Alone Novels

The Ring Keeper

Poisoned Splinter

RIVER IN THE SAND

AJ PARK

StarTree Press

River in the Sand - Seven Rivers Book Two

Copyright ©2024 AJ Park

Cover Design by StarTree Press

ISBN: 9781962564076 (trade paperback) 9781962564069 (epub)

StarTree Press 1706 N 1200 W, Unit #2012, Layton, UT 84041

N
Izana Cave
Kallah
Saarin
Niaz
Ashkan's Canyon
Seven Rivers
TYAR

PROLOGUE

CROWN PRINCESS TAHLEA

THE ROYAL STEWARD ARRIVED in Tally's sitting room, red-faced and breathing hard, interrupting what had been a quiet moment. She sat comfortably holding her baby, a small, warm weight, soft against her shoulder. Tally brushed her fingers against her infant daughter's downy hair. Despite his obvious haste, the man attempted to be quiet.

With a gesture, Tally invited him forward. "What is it?"

He hurried forward to kneel beside her chair. "Crown Princess, a messenger just arrived from Ondari province. Governor Gathan is dead."

Her muscles tightened in alarm. "What happened?"

"The messenger said he succumbed to a sudden illness."

Tally's eyes widened. "But he was no older than my father, and in perfect health the last time I saw him. Is there more information about what happened?"

"His son Conall is here. He brought the news to you personally. Perhaps you'd like to meet with him?"

Tally nodded. "I would. Immediately. Please have him wait for me in the council chamber. I'll join him there shortly."

"Yes, Crown Princess." The steward got to his feet, bowed, and departed.

As he closed the door behind him, Nita appeared from the next room. "Shall I help you dress, my lady?"

It was inevitable. Tally couldn't attend a meeting in the soft robe she wore here in her rooms. She stood, her baby cradled close against her. "Thank you, Nita, I would appreciate it. I'll just put her down."

Tally kissed her daughter and lowered her to rest in her cradle, covering her with a soft blanket. Her dark lashes brushed against her fair skin. A warm rose flushed her cheeks. "Sleep well, Kyjia."

Beside Tally, Nita looked down and smiled. "I'll watch over her while you're gone."

"Thank you."

A short while later, wearing a gray velvet gown appropriate for a princess and a silver crown on her head, Tally entered the council room. At her appearance, a stocky young man jumped to his feet and bowed. He wore the fine tunic of a nobleman, dusty from his ride. His shoulders slumped in weariness and grief.

Tally came forward and took his hand. "Conall, I'm so sorry about your father."

"Thank you, Princess." He closed his eyes, taking a deep breath as he attempted to master his emotion. He brushed a hand across his eyes. "I felt I had to come to Namradan myself."

"I'm glad you did." She gestured to a chair. "Please, sit and tell me what happened."

Conall sank into the chair. "My father has been governor for many years, and, lately, he began to think that it was time to turn leadership over to someone else. His good friend was the obvious choice; they'd worked together for a long time. But another man—Theron—has gained great power in Ondari during the last several months. Theron has positioned himself to take leadership. My father grew ill very suddenly, and his second in command suffered the same malady soon after. When they both died of it, Theron was named governor."

Tally's stomach tightened at the news, but she met Conall's gaze directly. "Do you believe it was an ordinary illness?"

Conall slowly shook his head. "How can I, Princess? The timing was too convenient, and I've never seen anything like it. They suffered a sudden high fever and were unable to see. They were both blind during the last few weeks of their illness."

"Was anyone else surrounding them affected?"

"No," Conall rubbed a hand across his face. "Only the two of them."

"Do you suspect it was some kind of poison?"

"Perhaps." Conall's voice was uncertain. "I've never heard of anything like it. My father had a strange injury, a cut on his arm. Perhaps the wound allowed the toxin into his body. We have a mystic in our household, but he was unable to identify the cause."

"We must investigate this further," Tally said. She looked up toward the door as the steward opened it.

His eyes were wide. "Princess, I wouldn't disturb your meeting, but I just received news that the delegation from Tyar is approaching the city."

"They're arriving now?" Her eyebrows shot up.

The Seven Rivers hadn't had official contact with their desert neighbor in many years. It had been a surprise when her guards had reported the group entering her lands. The two nations shared common roots, and had never been exactly at war, but Tyar had refused to set up trade or to maintain any sort of friendly relationship. They must have had some strong motivation that compelled them to break their silence now.

The steward nodded vigorously. "They are nearly at the gates. I had to tell you!"

Tally nodded. Her father remained in stonesleep. If he'd been awake, he would certainly have more information that would help to handle this situation, but she would have to do her best alone.

She kept her expression impassive and her voice calm. "Thank you. How many are there? I was told they appear peaceful. Is that still the case?" Tally needed to discover what this visit meant. It would be up to her to begin negotiations, and she wanted Tyar as an ally, not an enemy.

"There are a few dozen people, Princess, and, so far, they have made no attempt to harm anyone."

"As they arrive, please escort them to the throne room," Tally instructed. "Make sure our guards are in place and on the alert. Let General Kylith know they're here. Keep an eye on them." She didn't know what to expect.

Tally got to her feet, turning back to Conall. "I'm very sorry to cut our meeting short. I want to know more about this strange illness. Please, have something to eat, rest, and we will talk again soon. I will send someone back to Ondari with you to learn more."

Conall stood up, taking her hand and kissing it. "Thank you, Princess." He drew back, shaking his head. "I fear the news I brought means trouble for the Seven Rivers."

Tally agreed. She needed to learn more about Theron, the man now leading Ondari Province. Two guards took positions flanking her as she headed toward the throne room.

Outside the large, heavily carved doors, the familiar tall figure of her husband stood waiting. Flint wore a slightly dusty, blue military uniform and armor. His face lit up as he saw her, and he bowed, kissing her hand, his gaze meeting hers.

"You look stunning, my princess. And where is Kyjia?"

"Asleep." At least, Tally hoped she was. She returned Flint's smile, looking up into his dark eyes, savoring the warmth she saw there. "Where have you been?"

"Helping Gerran train a group of new soldiers, but, since we finished, now I am free and completely at your command." His mouth turned up in a slow smile.

Too bad she wasn't free to spend time alone with him at the moment. Ruling a kingdom reduced the amount of time she had to herself. Time with Flint would have to wait.

Instead, she nodded toward the door. "We have visitors from Tyar. If you would care to join me?"

"As you command, Princess." He offered his arm. She took it, and they entered the throne room together.

Several members of the court had arrived already. Another messenger hurried up to them to report that the delegation had arrived at the palace.

"Show them in," Tally instructed.

Flint escorted her to her chair at the front of the room beside her father's ancient throne.

Though Tally had ruled the Seven Rivers for nearly two years, she still refused to sit on the throne. It belonged to her father, and he would resume his rule soon. She occupied the smaller, plainer chair she'd always used, while Flint stood at her shoulder.

She wanted him to sit with her, but no matter how many times she asked, trying to convince him, he flatly refused to sit in the throne room beside her. "No one in your kingdom will ever question who rules the Seven Rivers," he'd said. "It's not me. You are Crown Princess, and someday you'll be queen."

Just as the doors at the far end of the hall opened to admit the visitors, General Kylith strode in through the side door and took his place standing on Tally's other side. His well-built form and stern face with its long scar looked intimidating, as always, but Tally appreciated his solid support.

At the doors, the delegation from Tyar appeared. With graceful steps, a tall, slender woman led the group across the hall. Her hair fell in soft, snowy white waves around her shoulders. A glittering gem hung on her forehead, and more sparkled around her throat. Her gown was of fine silk, deep blue, intricately embroidered at the neckline, hem, and cuffs.

As the woman drew nearer, Tally met her piercing, dark eyes. Though lined with age, her skin was as pale as Tally's own, her complexion contrasting sharply with the rest of her dark-haired, olive-skinned companions.

At the foot of the dais, the woman curtseyed, her movements graceful. "Crown Princess Tahlea, daughter of King Allenthal. I am Tillian."

Her words were spoken in the accent of Tyar, noticeably different from the speech Tally's people used, but still understandable.

"My son is King of Tyar," Tillian announced. "I'm your grandmother."

Only years of training to maintain her composure kept Tally's mouth from falling open. Her grandmother? She'd never known any of her mother's family, though she knew her father had attempted to reach out to them many times. Her father hadn't been very specific when he'd mentioned it, not explaining the reason. He'd certainly never told her anything that might have prepared her to meet a grandmother she'd never known.

No one else in the room moved or spoke as Tally got to her feet. She stepped down and stood facing Tillian. She was nearly as tall as Tally, and she wore an unreadable expression.

"Welcome to the Seven Rivers, Lady Tillian," Tally said.

Slowly, a smile spread across the old woman's face. With a start, Tally realized that tears welled in Tillian's eyes as she gazed at Tally.

"You look very like her. My Kyjia, my beautiful daughter. I'm so happy to see you. I came with urgent news and to see the new child who bears my daughter's name."

For a moment they looked at each other before Tally stepped forward to embrace her grandmother. With a sob, Tillian returned the hug.

"After all these years, I must beg your forgiveness, Granddaughter."

Tally drew back to look at her. "Why?"

Tillian wiped her eyes. "All this time, I have stayed away, when I might have been part of your life. I regret that very much, and I didn't have a good reason. Only that I was angry at Allenthal. The last time I came here was during Kyjia's final illness. When she died, I couldn't bear it. I'm afraid, in my grief, I blamed your father. It was never his fault. I see that so clearly now."

Her father had always told Tally that her mother had died of an illness. How could something like that have ever been his fault? "What happened?"

Tillian bowed her head. "There is so much to tell you."

"Then perhaps we need someplace to speak more comfortably? Your companions may wait here." She turned to take Flint's arm. "Lady Tillian, this is my husband, Flint. Will you join us?"

"Yes, thank you." Tillian turned toward her guards. "We will return shortly." Then she noticed Kylith, where he stood beside her chair. A sudden smile of recognition lit her face, and she hurried to embrace him. "Kylith! After all these years, it's so good to see you. You will join us, of course?" He nodded and offered her his arm as Tally led them from the room.

Soon, they were settled in a comfortable sitting room with food and drink spread before them. Tally had taken the sofa, Flint beside her, while Tillian and Kylith settled into chairs opposite them. For a long moment, no one spoke.

"It's been so long," Tillian said, breaking the silence. "For years, I thought I would never speak of those events again." Her eyes strayed to Kylith, glancing at the scar on his face. "But now, I feel I must." She reached into the small bag she carried over her shoulder and took out a slender shard of green crystal encased in clear glass.

At the sight of it, Kylith jumped to his feet. "Why would you bring that here?"

Tillian drew in a deep breath. "I had to. All those years ago, we tried everything in our power to destroy it. When we failed, we surrounded it in a protective coating to prevent its evil from harming anyone else."

"But the poison!" Kylith protested. "You shouldn't touch it."

Tillian looked up at him. "I have handled it like this many times. The toxin cannot penetrate the glass," she assured him.

Kylith stood stiffly for a moment, staring down at the crystal. "Forgive me. Even though it's been many years, I'll never forget that Allenthal nearly lost his life to its poison. And Kyjia..." His voice trailed off, and he slowly settled back into his chair.

Tillian turned back to Tally. "This is a rhan stone, containing powerful dark magic. It once belonged to a man who attempted to seize power in Tyar, a man who embraced evil and used his powers against our people. The poison of the stone causes illness, blindness, and death.

At the words, Tally's muscles tightened. "Blindness?"

Tillian nodded, her expression grave.

Sudden illness and blindness, exactly like the two deaths in Ondari province.

"I would never have brought such an evil thing here," Tillian said, with a quick glance at Kylith, "except that we have discovered that someone in Tyar is using a similar stone again. When we attempted to learn more, we discovered that this person is not acting alone. I fear another servant of dark magic has arisen here in your land."

A moment of silence fell.

Tendrils of unease wound through Tally's stomach. She needed to decide how best to combat this new threat to her kingdom. Reviewing the information in her mind, she nodded slowly. "News just reached me of two men in positions of power and influence, dead of a mysterious illness, blind in the last few weeks before they died."

Tillian's eyes widened. "So, it's true! Many years ago, when this evil showed itself in our land, it nearly gained power over our entire kingdom. We did everything in our power, but our people suffered battle and bloodshed before we could stop it. Once the evil sorcerer was dead, we searched for a cure for the poison but never found one. When your mother died, it broke my heart." She paused, wiping her eyes. "I'm sure, now that you are a mother yourself, you can understand how I felt. In my grief, I blamed Allenthal, thinking he should have found a solution. I know he tried..."

Shock flooded through Tally. "Are you saying this poison caused the illness that took my mother?"

Her lips tight, Tillian nodded.

Her father had never told Tally this. Flint's strong hand tightened around hers, and she held onto him. "Please. Tell me."

CHAPTER 1

CROWN PRINCE ALLENTHAL

Twenty-Two Years Ago

ALLENTHAL GRIPPED THE STONE railing of his balcony as he looked out over the great river. Despite the lingering chill of night, sweat drenched his body. He took long, even breaths, attempting to slow the wild pounding of his heart. When he closed his eyes, he saw his brother's face, his eyes glazed in pain, his body broken and bleeding. The dream had felt so real. It had taken him back to that terrible night five years ago when he'd fought so desperately to save his brother's life.

Now all was quiet. The first hint of dawn glowed behind the mountains. Raising his eyes to the bright dome of stars, he drew in another deep breath, attempting to find peace. The quiet murmur of the river filled the air. Trying to regain a sense of calm, he paced the balcony.

At the soft sound of the door opening, he turned to see his father. Still dressed for sleep, King Valteron wore a loose tunic and pants, his feet bare. He came to stand beside Allenthal. For a moment, they watched the river in silence.

"You're up early," his father observed.

Allenthal nodded. "You too."

His father put a hand on Allenthal's shoulder. "Was it another dream?"

Allenthal drew in a deep breath, rubbing his forehead, as if that would wipe away the memory. "No matter how I try, I can't get the images out of my head."

Valteron nodded. "I understand. Sometimes, the most vivid memories are the ones we most want to forget. The events of that day have stayed with you. I want to help."

What could anyone possibly do to help? No one could change the past. Allenthal looked back silently at his father.

Valteron's gaze was kind. "I won't try to minimize your feelings by saying I know how you feel. I wish there was more help I could offer. In my own life, I have relied on the Goddess during my most difficult moments. I hope you will turn to Her. She understands our struggles and knows more than we do. Earlier this morning, I spoke to Divine Namradill. About you."

Allenthal's eyes widened. Since the day five years ago when his older brother had died, he'd suffered from nightmares, unable to move past what had happened. He was now heir of the Seven Rivers, but it would be many years before his time came to rule. What interest did the Goddess have in him now?

"Allenthal, you've been the best son anyone could ask for. You've always done whatever was needed." His father's words trailed into silence, and he took a slow breath. "Sometimes I worry that you're making an extra effort to serve because you're trying to make up for—"

"Please don't say it," Allenthal interrupted, holding up his hand. "Please. It's not because of Alvaren. You raised me to do my duty to our kingdom, and I respect you too much not to do whatever

I can to help." He looked away, out across the river to the distant mountains. The morning light touched the peaks.

"What happened to Alvaren wasn't your fault," Valteron said, laying his hand on his son's shoulder. "I've never blamed you."

"You weren't there," Allenthal ground out through clenched jaws. His hands gripped the stone balustrade in front of him.

His father's voice was quiet, calming. "I didn't have to be there to know that you boys loved each other. You would never have done anything to harm each other. It was simply an accident."

All Allenthal's muscles were rigid. "An accident that took his life."

"Alvaren loved you," the king said. "He wouldn't have wanted you to spend your life grieving for him. I want you to know how proud I am of you. Our kingdom will be in excellent hands when your time comes to rule."

His father's words helped a little to soothe the ache inside Allenthal. His older brother, Alvaren, had spent his entire life preparing to be king. Allenthal hadn't been anyone's first choice...until he became the only choice.

Valteron's voice broke the stillness. "Divine Namradill requested that you go on a journey—to Tyar."

Allenthal's eyebrows shot up. "Tyar? No! I can't do that. Father, my place is here. You have no other heir. It's my responsibility to be here. I can't just leave our kingdom to travel."

"Our Goddess wouldn't have asked you to go if it wasn't the right thing to do, Son. Give it some thought." Valteron gripped his shoulder. "We'll talk about it more later."

He went back through the door, leaving Allenthal alone with his spinning thoughts.

At the end of the long day, when Allenthal finally went to bed, he lay tossing for hours, thinking about his conversation with his father. Why would he want to send Allenthal away? Maybe he was more disappointed in him than Allenthal had realized. But he was the only heir. His family and his nation needed him to maintain communication with Namradill. It made no sense for him to travel to another nation. Tyar was a desert land, a harsh and violent place.

Despite his worries, eventually Allenthal dozed.

A slender girl with dark eyes and long dark hair struggled to pull her arms free from two men gripping her from both sides. Though she twisted and fought, she couldn't escape. Fury was plain in her expression, and she lifted her chin defiantly. The light was dim, the rough stone walls of a cave surrounding them.

A man faced her, his expression dark with menace. "Tell me where the tablet is!" he demanded. "This is your last chance."

She struggled again, her eyes meeting his directly. "No!"

The guards dragged her around, turning her back to the man. As she fought against them, he tore her cloak away. With his knife, he cut through her tunic, ripping the fabric aside to expose the pale skin of her back.

He raised his hand, holding a sharp sliver of green stone. When he pressed the edge against her skin, blood flowed down her back. She screamed as he carved a symbol into her flesh.

Allenthal sat up gasping, his heart pounding. Another nightmare. By now, he expected the dreams of his brother, but this had been something entirely new. He was certain he'd never seen the girl before, but he wouldn't easily forget her.

He spent the rest of the night pacing his balcony, in his mind seeing the brave tilt to her chin and her determination to fight, despite the odds.

Eventually, morning came, and it grew late enough that his father might be awake. Allenthal dressed and went down the hall. He knocked quietly before slipping inside his father's chambers, hoping to have a quick word with him. Instead, he found the room quiet and empty. His father was usually here at this hour, but perhaps something had come up. He glanced inside the bedchamber and saw no one.

A bright blue light shone from an open chest in an alcove at the far end of the room. The pulsing glow intrigued him, and he moved nearer. Namradill. He had not touched the stone since the ceremony when he'd been a baby. Maybe he was never meant to. It had always been Alvaren who had planned and prepared to make a connection with the Goddess on behalf of all the Seven Rivers. The blue light drew Allenthal nearer.

He paused, entirely still, staring at the light. Would She speak to him?

Allenthal looked around. Still finding himself alone, he walked quickly toward the chest and looked inside to see the glowing stone. Reaching in, he put his hand against the cool, hard surface.

Allenthal, son of King Valteron. I greet you.

He gasped, pulling his hand away. She didn't sound angry, but should he even try to talk with her? Was he worthy to ask Her his questions? She must have far more important matters to attend to. He drew in a deep breath and replaced his hand. "May I speak with you, Divine Namradill?"

You may. Though it is not yet your duty to speak on behalf of all your people, speaking with me is the privilege of your bloodline. One day, we shall speak often. One day, you will be with me completely.

Was She referring to the stonesleep? Or did She mean he would be with Her at the end of his life? "Why do you want me to go to Tyar?"

Much good will be accomplished if you go. My brother Karineth was God of the land of Tyar. Once, He guarded and cared for His people. The royal family of Tyar was tightly connected to Him, just as your family is with me. But Karineth is lost. As He failed to care for His people, the rains fled and the land dried up into a harsh desert. His people are scattered, and the man possessing the sacred tablet of Karineth, who should be King of Tyar, is nothing more than a poor wanderer attempting to feed his family. I ask you to find him, to help him and his family.

"Why would they want my help?" Allenthal asked. "When I tried to help my brother, I failed."

Is one failure enough to prevent you from attempting the good you might do with the rest of your life?

Allenthal stood still, shocked. Maybe he had allowed himself to think that he had nothing to offer anyone. "Does the king of Tyar have a daughter?" The images from his dream were burned into his memory.

Yes. You have seen her already; the dream showed her to you clearly. She is Kyjia, daughter of Ashkan, and she needs your help.

"The tablet they spoke of," Allenthal said, "it's the symbol of the royal family? Their line of communication with Karineth?"

It's the most valuable thing in Tyar. A symbol of royalty. Everyone in Tyar would recognize it, though it isn't large, a small slab of gold engraved with the symbols of Karineth. The location of the tablet is a closely guarded secret. At the moment, it is kept by a man named Ashkan, uncrowned and unknown to his people, but by his lineage, King of Tyar. Will you find him and help him?

All his muscles tightened, but Allenthal couldn't refuse Namradill. He would have to trust that if She sent him on this errand, She would help him find a way to succeed. He would put himself in Her hands. "I will go, Divine Namradill."

Good. I will give you such guidance as I can. Karineth, God of Tyar, has slept for generations. If he is to care for his people again, he must be woken by an heir of the royal family. This prophecy speaks of his awakening: "While I sleep, my land is buried in sand. The people of Tyar must rise again. Hold the tablet aloft and speak my name three times, and I shall hear and answer. A new ruler shall rise in the desert, and a light in the night sky from the ancient city of kings shall proclaim their coming. My power shall be in their hands and a river shall flow out of the sand."

In his mind, Allenthal repeated the prophecy, committing it to memory.

Allenthal found his father on his balcony, looking out over the great river. He came to stand beside him. "I'll go."

"Good," Valteron replied, "but not alone. You'll need someone you can trust along the road. Take Kylith with you. He'll guard you and watch your back."

Allenthal smiled in agreement. Kylith was a skilled fighter, his ability far surpassing any of the other soldiers. And he was already a good friend.

He found Kylith at the edge of the training field, gathering up his weapons after a practice session. "Am I late?" he called.

Kylith looked up and smiled, offering him a blade, hilt first. "Yes, but if you still want to practice, I'm ready."

"Today, it's something more serious than that," Allenthal admitted.

Kylith stood up and faced him, his arms folded across his chest, waiting for an explanation.

"My father asked me to do a little traveling. Will you come with me?"

Kylith's eyebrows rose. "Just me, or a whole troop of men? Don't tell me King Valteron is sending his only heir out of Namradan with *one* guard?"

Swiftly, Allenthal laid out the details of the journey to the desert. "Our errand is a secret. Divine Namradill asked me to go," he said. "I'm only a mortal, and I trust in my faith that She knows what She's doing. We plan to stay out of sight. No one outside our own lands will know who we are."

Kylith raised one eyebrow. "It's true you are mortal, don't forget that. Anonymity is no guarantee of safety."

"I know," Allenthal admitted. "But it will help."

"But... Tyar?" Kylith's eyes widened. "It's hot there. And from everything I've heard, it's a difficult place to survive."

"True enough." Allenthal grinned at his friend. "I understand. If the journey would be too *demanding* for you, I can see if one of the others—"

Kylith narrowed his eyes. "I didn't say I wouldn't go."

Allenthal smiled, clapping him on the shoulder. "Good. We'll leave in the morning."

With his plans made, Allenthal packed the few belongings he would take with him. He'd never been away from home for more than a few days before, but he trusted Namradill that some good would come of this. There was no way to know what would happen. With his packing finished, he went to bed. Pushing worry to the side, he closed his eyes.

Her body lay crumpled and still on the rough floor of the cave. The dim light illuminated her pale skin; the blood on her back was now dried and darkened. She was alone. With a groan of pain, she stirred.

She inched her way along the floor. With agonizing slowness, she crawled along the passageway toward a swift-flowing stream running along the cave floor. When she reached the water, she rolled over to immerse her injured back in the water. The lines of pain smoothed from her face.

For a time she rested, until her body jerked suddenly, and she cried out in pain and fear. When she pulled her arm close to her body, fresh blood ran down her skin. Something had attacked her, something out there invisible in the dark. Her eyes were wide in terror, her expression tight with pain. Dragging herself up, she struggled to her feet, leaning heavily against the wall. A hiss came out of the dark. Still leaning on the wall, she stumbled away. Hidden in the dark, something followed.

He was already out of bed, half standing, reaching out to help her. Allenthal had to do something to protect Kyjia. His hand searched for a weapon to defend her against the invisible danger lurking there in the dark. The dream had felt so real, as crystal clear as if he had watched the events with his own eyes. The Goddess said she was Ashkan's daughter and that she needed his aid. He had to find her. Was she even now lost in the dark? He prayed to Namradill that the events he saw hadn't happened yet and there was still time to help her.

At dawn, Allenthal met Kylith in the stables. They loaded their gear into saddlebags and strapped on their bedrolls. Allenthal met his friend's eyes. "Last chance to speak up if you don't want to go."

Kylith grinned. "It'll be more interesting than guard duty."

The spring sun shone clear and bright as they followed the road over the ancient stone bridge out of Namradan. For miles outside the city, the road wound between well-tended farms and little patches of woods. They took the path leading up the valley of the River Edri. Villages and fields gathered all along the river. It took them several days to reach the end of the valley. Beyond the city of Edrithil, the way wound northward, up into the mountains.

Allenthal had traveled this road before, but it had been five years. In the intervening time, he'd flatly refused to go anywhere near this place. Did Divine Namradill understand what it would cost him when she asked him to come this way again?

Riding cautiously through the rocky terrain, they came up over a rise into a narrow, rocky valley. Giant boulders stood at the feet of the cliffs above, standing guard over a slender path winding along one side. Below the narrow trail, the land fell sharply downward.

This was the place. Allenthal recognized it at once. Every landmark had been burned into his memory. This was where the accident had happened. A rockslide had come down the steep slope above and would have taken Allenthal off the edge, except that his brother had shoved him out of the way only to fall himself.

Allenthal sat frozen on his horse. All this time, he'd avoided this place. Now, he had to come this way. There was no other reasonable route to Tyar. His horse snorted and tossed its head uneasily, sensing its rider's discomfort.

Ahead of him, Kylith stopped and turned in the saddle. He knew a little about what had happened but not everything.

"Are you all right?"

Allenthal nodded stiffly, his jaw clenched. "I need a moment."

Cold dread washed over him as he looked at the unforgiving rocks. He had to go on. There was no other choice, unless he wanted to go back and tell his father he couldn't continue the journey. Valteron would understand. Somehow, Allenthal knew that would be even worse.

"I can do this." He gritted his teeth and urged his horse forward.

He rode on, following Kylith at a steady pace. When Allenthal passed the place where Alvaren had fallen, he stopped, rigid in his saddle, beads of sweat forming on his forehead. If he dismounted and looked off the edge, he'd be able to see the exact place where his brother had landed. If he didn't look, he could pretend he was anywhere else in the world but here.

They'd rushed to Alvaren's aid, finding him badly injured but alive, wedged between the rocks. Today, the spring weather was soft as they rode, with no trace of the bitter chill of the day he remembered so well. Now, the sun warmed his back, and the breeze was pleasant, not the biting wind that had roared down the valley that night. It had been so cold. He'd done everything he could to keep his brother warm, but, by morning, Alvaren had been gone. With all his might, Allenthal tried not to remember.

Did the Goddess know how hard he had worked to avoid coming this way? Had part of Her reason for this journey been to encourage Allenthal to face what had happened? A wave of anger surged through him at the thought. His fury helped get him moving again.

He stared straight ahead, following Kylith until they traveled over another rise in the land and passed out of sight of the little valley. They crossed a small stream cutting through the path and paused to water their horses.

Kylith dismounted and turned to him. "I'm ready to rest a little."

Allenthal nodded, dismounting. He knelt beside the water, scooping up handfuls of the clear cold liquid. He splashed water onto his face and rubbed it through his hair.

Beside him, Kylith asked, "That was the place?" He motioned back down the trail.

Wordlessly, Allenthal nodded.

Kylith met his eyes. "Do you want to talk about it?"

Allenthal's stomach clenched. "No!"

Kylith shrugged. "Maybe a good fight would be better."

"Are you volunteering?" Allenthal growled, clenching his hand into a fist.

"Only if you're desperate," Kylith replied grinning. "If you think you're angry enough to take me."

Allenthal eyed his friend. Kylith was an inch or two shorter but broader and heavier in build. He could also defeat any man in the Seven Rivers. They had trained together enough during the last few years for Allenthal to know that he probably wouldn't win.

"I'll wait until we find a better fight," Allenthal said. One corner of his mouth lifted. "But thanks for offering."

They rode on. As they got further away from the narrow valley, Allenthal gradually relaxed, able to concentrate on where they were again. The icy dread in his limbs thawed. Hours later, with the terrible place far behind them, they made camp.

As they brought water and firewood and began to prepare a meal, Kylith didn't say a word, accepting Allenthal's silence and not pressing him.

Allenthal broke the quiet at last. He glanced over to find his friend watching him. "After it happened, we had to take him home," he said. "When we finally got back to Namradan, I couldn't do it. I couldn't face my father. I stopped outside the city and refused to go any further. Late that night, I was still there when he came to find me."

Kylith shook his head in sympathy. "I'm sorry. It must have been terrible."

Allenthal nodded. "Everyone in the kingdom loved Alvaren, my father especially. I couldn't stand to be there, watching them tell him the news, seeing his face when he looked at Alvaren's body." Allenthal took in a long breath. "Back then, I expected him to be angry at me, to demand why I'd let this happen to my brother. I thought he'd wish for a way to tell me that I should have fallen instead. He needed Alvaren. All of the Seven Rivers needed him. He should be their king."

Kylith put his hand on his friend's shoulder. "He wasn't angry at you, was he?"

Allenthal shook his head slowly. "He never was. So many times, I wanted him to be. I was so angry at myself, it only made sense that he would feel the same."

"King Valteron is a good man. A good father. I know he loved both his sons," Kylith said. "He didn't really wish that you had died and Alvaren had lived. No one could ever make such an impossible choice."

Allenthal drew in a long breath, staring out into the gathering darkness. "Maybe that was me too. I'm the one who wished it had been me. I loved my brother. All my life, I thought that he would be a great leader. He should have been."

"Can't you live your life to be the kind of leader he would have been, in his memory?"

Allenthal's throat tightened. It was a good idea. Years had passed, and Alvaren was gone. Maybe attempting to honor his brother's memory would help him to move forward. He nodded.

"You took on this quest," Kylith pointed out. "You did it to serve the Goddess, your father, and people in a nation you've never even visited before. Maybe you can allow this act of service to make up a little for what happened to your brother?"

Was that the real reason he'd agreed to this journey? Allenthal couldn't be sure. It had felt like the right thing to do in the moment. Maybe his friend was right. He looked up to meet Kylith's steady, gray eyes and drew in another long breath. "Then let this be my way forward."

CHAPTER 2

KYJIA

THE RED DESERT SUN slipped slowly behind the distant hills. In the fading light, Kyjia gathered the last of the rala nuts into her bag. The remains of the day's heat still radiated up from the sandstone beneath her boots, but the cool of night began to spread across the land. Darkness came quickly. Slinging the bag over her shoulders, she slipped through the rocks, climbing swiftly down toward the cave where her family made a temporary home.

A faint glow of white light silhouetted three dark shapes where they had gathered for an evening meal. Kyjia entered the shallow cavern and set down her bag.

"Come and eat," her mother, Tillian, said. She looked tired.

As Kyjia met the eyes of her family, she saw worry in all of them, especially her father, Ashkan. Some of the lines on his face had appeared recently. It wasn't hard to know the reason. They all saw their dwindling store of supplies.

Every morning, Kyjia rose before dawn to gather fruit from the cactus and every evening, nuts from the hardy rala trees. Every scrap of food she could gather from the harsh landscape would help them survive a little longer. The tiny seep at the back of their cave provided enough water for four people and a camel to survive.

"I'm leaving tonight," her father said, staring out across the dunes.

"Do you have to go?" Kyjia asked.

He turned to meet her gaze, but didn't answer, only took a bite of food.

She shouldn't have asked, when she knew the answer already. He had waited as long as he could to travel to Niaz and sell his carvings to buy more supplies. If he didn't go now, they wouldn't have enough provisions to survive until he returned.

Kyjia couldn't name the reason she was so worried about him this time. It was only a feeling. Her father knew what he was doing. He was an expert at navigating in the desert, and he'd made the trip many times before.

"I can go with you, Father," her younger brother, Terjan, offered. "I'll be your guard."

Her father smiled, gripping Terjan's shoulder. "Not this time. I need you here to protect your mother and sister."

Terjan nodded, sitting up a little straighter after this charge.

It didn't take them long to finish their meager meal. They had only a few slivers of dried meat and a fast-dwindling sack of grain remaining. Kyjia reviewed the landscape surrounding the cave in her mind. Maybe, if she walked farther each day, she could reach more trees or find more fruits that would help sustain them. She could pick the seeds from the stalks of desert grass, but it would take a long time to gather enough to be useful.

Kyjia rose, gathering their worn wooden bowls to be cleaned.

"I'll take those." Her mother took the stack of dishes. "Will you take this water to your father?"

"Yes."

Kyjia picked up the two full, heavy waterskins and carried them to where her father was loading his camel. It had taken them two days of gathering extra water from the tiny seep to fill them and provide enough liquid for the animal to drink its fill before going out into the barren lands.

Her father lifted carefully wrapped bundles and secured them to the animal's pack frame, while it sat patiently. He took the water and carefully placed it with the other things.

"Thank you, Kyjia."

She put her hand on his shoulder as he bent over his work. "I'm sorry to be worried, Father, but it's almost time, isn't it?"

He got to his feet and looked down at her. "Yes," he admitted. "But I can't say whether there's actually any truth to that old legend. Our God has slept for a long time now. Maybe the whole thing is only a story. It's hard to imagine Divine Karineth returning and suddenly making water flow where now there is only empty sand."

"But the story says He will wake and speak again, that He will crown a new ruler in Tyar."

Her father laughed bitterly, shaking his head. "No matter who our ancestors were, I can't imagine myself as a king with a palace, a crown, and a shining sword. I've never done anything but provide food for my family, barely."

She hugged him. "You've done so much more than that!" she insisted. His arms surrounded her, pulling her close. He had always sheltered them, loved them, protected them.

"You give me too much credit, Daughter," he murmured. "But know that I love you, and I would do anything for you. I only want to keep you safe. Why else would we live out here, so far from anywhere? I hope that everything will be different soon. I have to find a way to change things for us. You and Terjan don't deserve this kind of life."

"We'll find a way. We can do anything as long as we're together."

He took a step back and met her eyes. "Do you remember the words I taught you?"

How could she forget? They'd spent years going over them, searching the simple words for any additional clues.

While I sleep, my land is buried in sand. The people of Tyar must rise again. A new ruler shall rise in the desert with my power in their hands and a river shall flow out of the sand.

How could a few simple lines be enough to change the fate of Tyar? It didn't seem possible.

"Kyjia," her father's voice broke into her thoughts. "I want you to keep it for me while I'm gone."

A sudden shiver ran down her back despite the warm night. "I can't do that!"

He took her hand and gripped it. "You can." His voice was firm. "Just keep it safe for me while I travel. I'll be back before you have a chance to miss me."

Tears welled in her eyes. He reached into an inner pocket and took out the tablet. The gold gleamed faintly in the moonlight. Slowly, she reached out her hand, and he placed the tablet on her palm. It felt surprisingly heavy for its size, the gold surface smooth against her skin as she closed her fingers around it.

He met her eyes. "I trust you to guard it for me. You must keep it safe."

"I will, Father," she promised. "But only until you get back."

CHAPTER 3

CROWN PRINCE ALLENTHAL

A FEW MORE DAYS of riding brought Allenthal and Kylith to the border of the Seven Rivers. The trail climbed up out of the valley. They crossed the sharp, stony ridge marking the boundary of their nation.

"I've never been outside before," Allenthal said, pausing to look back at the green valleys and snow-capped mountains of his homeland.

"That's good," Kylith replied, "we're hoping no one out here will recognize you. Our way will be much more dangerous if anyone finds out who you are."

Allenthal nodded. "Who should we tell people we are?"

"We're just two simple travelers looking for work. The less we say, the better."

They both wore ordinary clothes, nothing that would identify them, but they were well-armed. The open road between nations could be dangerous. They passed other groups on the road, mostly merchants with long trains of heavily laden pack horses guarded by several armed men.

For three weeks, they followed the long ridge until it dwindled into a line of hills. The weather grew drier and hotter every day. To the southwest, the snow-capped mountains of the Seven Rivers faded gradually into the distance behind them. To the north and east, the hills sank into a vast expanse the color of sand, the desert land of Tyar.

Allenthal savored the opportunity to see new places. Perhaps if Alvaren had lived, Allenthal might have been allowed to travel more. In his youth, his father had visited Tyar, and a few of the Seven Rivers ambassadors had gone as far as Ischar. Now, with Alvaren gone, Allenthal was Crown Prince, and this might be his only chance to see more of the world.

On the day of the accident, Allenthal had lost much more than a beloved family member. Much of his freedom had disappeared as well. Now, the Seven Rivers had Allenthal's future planned out for him in detail. He would stay near Namradan, receiving the daughters of noblemen or visiting princesses, sifting through the crowd of young ladies until he chose one of them, married her, and started a family. It was his responsibility to produce an heir to the royal line.

He had accepted his duty and tried to find a companion that suited him, but, somehow, none of the women he'd met thus far seemed right. His father hadn't pushed him too much—yet. But he couldn't wait too long. If Alvaren had been alive, their father wouldn't be so worried about Allenthal. Now it was up to him to continue their family. If their line failed, who would converse with Namradill? Could She simply find someone else? One of the mystics perhaps? If their communication was lost, would their land become like Tyar without the protection of a goddess? Would the Seven Rivers disappear entirely?

Allenthal walked through a market bustling with people buying and selling wares of all kinds. A man sat cross-legged; a collection of wood carvings was displayed before him. His face was care-worn, his dark hair and beard just beginning to gray. Another merchant passed by the man, waving a greeting.

"How's business, Ashkan?" His words were spoken in the accent of Tyar.

The man nodded and shrugged in response.

Further down the street lay a building crowded with people eating and drinking. An inn, perhaps? When Allenthal entered, he noticed the clothing of the people inside didn't belong to the Seven Rivers. Many of them wore long cloaks the color of desert sand and had their heads or even their faces covered. They ate and drank, talked and laughed, and played a game of dice.

To one side of the wide, busy room stood a door. Unnoticed by the crowd, a man in a cloak with the hood drawn down over his face slipped quietly through. He descended a flight of stairs. Allenthal followed him into a large room that appeared to be used for storage. Barrels and crates filled much of the space. The cloaked man waited. After a little while, another man entered, and they spoke together.

They were too quiet for him to hear their words, but instinct insisted to Allenthal that this was an important conversation. He needed to hear what they were saying.

As Allenthal rolled up his blankets, the strange dream still occupied his thoughts. Had the woodcarver he'd seen really been Ashkan? If so, maybe Divine Namradill really intended him to find the man, and She had sent him a little help. And the cloaked man in the basement? It felt significant.

Kylith was already awake, sitting with his back against a rock, looking out at the vast expanse of sand lying east of them. He turned to look at Allenthal.

"What's wrong?"

Allenthal rubbed his hand over his face. "I saw Ashkan."

Kylith's eyes widened in surprise. "Where?"

"In my dream; I saw him in a market." He stared at his friend. "You can tell me, honestly, if you think I'm losing my mind."

For a long moment, Kylith returned his gaze. "No more than before."

As soon as the horses were saddled and packed, they rode on. Throughout their day of travel, Allenthal reviewed the vision in his mind, focusing on every detail that might prove important. As the afternoon shadows lengthened, they came around a rocky outcropping to look down into the valley holding the town of Niaz. It was the only settlement of any size they'd seen since they'd left the borders of the Seven Rivers. The buildings, constructed of stone or adobe, blended into the color of the desert background.

There were many people, some wearing long desert cloaks, others dressed as Allenthal and Kylith were, in linen shirts and riding pants lined with leather. Their jackets had long ago been packed away. The crowd contained a mix of people from several nations, many of them obviously here to trade.

Groups of armed men in white tunics emblazoned with the symbol of a golden sun appeared to oversee the town. Tyar had no official king, but someone was obviously in charge here.

They made their way along hard-packed dirt streets to the market at the center of Niaz. The wide area was clear of buildings. Instead, tents, booths, carts, and wagons filled the space. Everyone here had something for sale, from spices and fabrics to jewelry and foods of all kinds.

Allenthal's mind raced back to the dream he'd had this morning. The exactness of it chilled him. Tying their horses, they wandered through the stalls, looking at everything.

Niaz had been built at the edge of the desert. Most of these people belonged to the kingdom of Tyar. As a rule, they were cinnamon-skinned and dark-haired. They wore long cloaks, with lengths of cloth wrapped to cover their heads and sometimes their faces. Many of the women wore veils, concealing their features except for their striking dark eyes.

Had the girl from his dream looked like them? Allenthal wasn't sure. When he'd seen her, the light in the cave had been dim, and he hadn't gotten a clear look at her face. He had seen her skin, pale and creamy. Maybe she wasn't one of the desert people at all.

As they wandered through the market, Allenthal watched carefully, and, after a while, spotted a display of woodcarvings. They drew nearer until Allenthal recognized the merchant from the dream. He bent to examine the carvings. The work was exquisite. He picked one of them up and dug in his pocket for a coin and held it out.

"Is this enough?"

The man nodded and took the coin. Allenthal met his eyes. "Are you Ashkan?"

For a long moment, they stared at each other.

Ashkan's eyes were guarded. "You're not from Tyar, a riverman from your speech. Why would you be asking?"

Ignoring the fact that the man had not confirmed his identity, Allenthal pressed on. "I urgently need to speak to you. I have a message from the King of Seven Rivers."

Ashkan raised his eyebrows, laughing derisively. "That's one I've never heard before. Did Zhandar hire you to say that? Leave me alone."

"I don't know Zhandar," Allenthal protested.

Getting to his feet, Ashkan turned away. "You will. Nothing that happens in Tyar escapes his notice. Do yourself a favor and get out of the desert."

"But the king sent me to find you," Allenthal protested.

Ashkan shook his head. "That's ridiculous. The river-king has no idea who I am. I've never had any dealings with your people. Now, leave me alone. Don't follow me."

"But—"

In a single fluid motion, the man drew a blade and stepped nearer to place the point of it against Allenthal's chest. "I said, *don't follow me.*"

Allenthal stepped back, saying nothing more as the man gathered up his wares, picked up the bundle, and disappeared into the crowd.

Kylith looked after the merchant. "Do we follow him?"

Even if Ashkan didn't want their help, Allenthal couldn't give up on his quest so easily. As discreetly as possible, they followed the man toward the edge of town. They watched him slip away into a narrow draw between two rocky hills.

CHAPTER 4

CROWN PRINCE ALLENTHAL

As they walked along the main street of Niaz, Allenthal reviewed his brief conversation with Ashkan in his mind. There must have been a more diplomatic way to handle it, something else he could have said that would have gone better.

He looked up to see an inn across the street. There was no doubt that this was the place he had seen in his dream.

"That's it," he said to Kylith.

"Let's go in," Kylith said. "I'm hungry."

With a strange sense of familiarity, Allenthal entered a room he'd seen in detail but never entered before. People from several nations crowded the room. Only a few empty tables remained. Taking a seat at one, they looked around. Allenthal couldn't help but look across the room, toward the door he knew would be there. He saw no sign of the man in the cloak yet, but he needed to get through that door before the man came.

A woman approached their table. She was tall, her lush figure set off by a blue dress with a low neckline. Her dark eyes were framed by heavy lashes. She stood beside their table, her gaze roaming boldly over them.

"Do you want food," she glanced back to Kylith, "or something else?"

"We'd like food," Allenthal said firmly.

Looking a little disappointed, she disappeared.

Allenthal kicked his friend under the table. Kylith watched her go, his eyes on the departing view of her curves, until finally turning back to face him. She was undeniably attractive, but she would be trouble for sure.

"Don't get distracted," he reminded his friend.

Kylith grinned. "Of course not." He glanced toward the kitchen door where she had disappeared, then back at Allenthal. "But you need a distraction so no one notices you making your exit."

That was true.

A moment later, she was back, a tray balanced in one hand. Just as she passed the next table over, a man reached out and grabbed her backside.

She took three more steps to set the tray on their table and whirled furiously to face him. "Put your hand on me again, and I'll cut off your fingers," she snarled.

His friends laughed uproariously. A moment later, she had a blade in her hand, and, as she pressed it against his throat, he stood slowly. He was short, and his head barely reached her chin. Kylith stood up at her side.

"May I offer my assistance?" he asked politely.

She took another long look at him, her eyes lingering on his muscled shoulders. Everyone in the room had turned to watch the scene.

It was time. Allenthal moved between the tables to the door, glancing behind to make sure no one was looking at him. He slipped through the door. Beyond the door, a staircase descended, and he followed it, turning a corner to find the storage room exactly as he had seen it hours ago. No one was there. He needed to get out of sight, quickly.

The room was stacked high with boxes and barrels. He lifted the lid of a large crate near the back and saw that it contained the remains of a huge pile of potatoes. Now it was nearly empty. Hearing the sound of the door opening at the top of the stairs, he climbed inside and pulled the lid closed, leaving just a crack so he could see.

A moment later, a man in a gray cloak appeared. After a quick survey of the room to confirm that he was alone, he stood silently, waiting.

Allenthal remained still and silent, watching the man through a crack between the crate and its lid. The space was much too confining, and Allenthal realized he hadn't completely thought his plan through. But he couldn't reveal himself now. He needed to hear the conversation the man was about to have. He drew in a long, slow breath. Sweat beaded on his forehead, and his heart raced. The wooden sides of the crate pressed in on him from all sides.

There wasn't enough air inside, making breathing difficult. Panic threaded through him, causing his breath to become rapid and shallow. He had to get out. He couldn't stay in here.

In the room, a small door opened and shut, and the second man from his dream appeared.

"You're late," the first man hissed from under his hood. His face remained hidden.

The other man was of medium height and stocky. "Sorry. It took longer than we thought to find him."

"Where did he go?" the cloaked man asked.

"He was in the market selling his wares until a couple of foreigners stopped to talk to him. One of them bought something from him, gave him a coin, and they talked. They must have threatened him, because he pulled a knife. After that, Ashkan got out of the market. He's already left town."

Allenthal held his breath. They were after Ashkan. Why?

"Did you send someone to watch him?"

"Of course," the stocky man replied. "We can find him easily."

"You'd better be able to," the cloaked man said. "Finding one man in the desert can be difficult. He knows about the prophecy. If he has the tablet, he could be planning to claim the throne. We cannot let that happen. Zhandar will be king. He already has great power, and the people are loyal to him. We will not bow to some penniless merchant. Ashkan needs to disappear."

The stocky man rubbed his chin. "We can take care of that, and we know how to find him. He won't get far."

The cloaked man nodded. "Go immediately. You know where to meet me."

In a moment, the cloaked man returned up the stairs, and the other man disappeared.

Allenthal put a hand against his chest to still his pounding heart. He couldn't move. He was stuck inside a crate, and he couldn't get out.

No. This panic was completely irrational. He knew it, but he couldn't help it. Not after watching what had happened to Alvaren. Ever since that day, tight spaces terrified him. So far, he'd managed to hide his fear. Now, Allenthal forced himself to breathe, in and out. Slowly. He looked out at the room again, confirming that it remained empty. With shaking hands, he opened the lid slowly. Awkwardly, he clambered out and stood up straight.

He drew in great breaths of the free air.

Brushing the sweat from his face, he stood, waiting for his breath and heartbeat to slow. He wasn't in danger, but the merchant Ashkan was. And they needed to help him. He climbed the stairs and slipped back into the common room.

Whatever had gone on in the intervening time must have been exciting. People were shouting and laughing. The short man who had put his hand on the waitress lay on the floor, while his friends bent over him. Kylith sat at their table finishing a plate of food. The woman stood behind him. As he took the last bite, she put her arms around his neck and slid onto his lap.

"I hope you're planning to stay in Niaz," she purred, running her fingers through his hair. She bent her head to kiss him.

Allenthal headed for the main door, and despite the distraction, Kylith's gaze flicked to him. He must have done a good job with the kiss, for a moment later when he slipped out of her gasp and headed for the door, she stayed where she was, looking after him, her gaze unfocused.

Together, they left the noisy crowd and slipped back into the street. Outside, the light was dim, with only the moonlight and a few lights in windows and doors.

They crossed back through town.

"We have to find Ashkan," Allenthal explained as they went. "They're planning to kill him. We need to warn him."

They hurried toward the rocky draw where Ashkan had disappeared. The place was empty now, but he might have left tracks. As soon as dawn lit their way, they could follow him.

Allenthal stared out into the empty desert. "We don't know what's going to happen if we go out there. Are you sure you want to follow me?"

Kylith raised his eyebrows. "Your father ordered me to guard you. That's what I intend to do."

"But that doesn't mean you can't tell me my choice is unwise, if that's what you think."

Kylith met his eyes. "I'll be sure to let you know, if that should become necessary. We should find Ashkan and his family."

A short while later, they had traded their horses for two of the desert-dwelling animals they learned were called camels. The trader showed them how to instruct the tall, long-legged beasts to kneel and then sit down, so a rider could easily get on or off.

"Rivermen aren't used to the desert. If you see any snakes, don't go near them," the camel trader warned. "All poisonous. And the scorpions. Their sting can be deadly. Always shake out your boots before you put them on."

Allenthal didn't dare admit that he didn't know what a scorpion was.

"And whatever you do, stay away from the azarim." Seeing their blank looks, the man rolled his eyes. "They are lizards, four or five feet long. Big teeth." He pointed to his own mouth. "Meat eaters. Scavengers. And they never move alone. If you see one, there are more around, watching you. They wait for unwary rivermen like you to collapse from thirst. If they bite you, their venom will paralyze you. They want you to lie still on the sand, so they can eat you. And they don't care if you're all the way dead before they do."

"Thanks for the warning," Allenthal said. He looked at the man intently, trying to decide if he was telling the truth or only having a little fun at their expense, but his serious expression didn't waver.

By dawn, they had loaded their supplies, mounted the camels, and followed the merchant's tracks into the barren land. In the tradition of the desert, they wrapped themselves in long cloaks to protect themselves from the sun.

The dawn light painted the sand pink. Allenthal scanned the land in all directions. He saw no buildings, roads, or signs of human habitation. Rocky hills and outcroppings broke up the expanses of sand, but he saw nothing green and no sign of water anywhere.

He exchanged a glance with Kylith. They were strangers in a harsh and dangerous land. They couldn't afford to lose their way, and they couldn't go too far if there wasn't any water. Even the camels must eat and drink, and the heat would swiftly destroy any lost human with no supplies or shelter.

The sun climbed higher. It grew hotter. Allenthal wiped the sweat from his face with the back of his hand. He squinted into the distance, the heat causing the air to shimmer. Nothing else moved. They traveled on through a long, burning day.

When the sun sank behind the distant hills, it became so much cooler that they pressed on until the middle of the night. As days passed, they adjusted their travel to move more at night and find shelter from the harsh sun during the heat of the day.

They had traveled for nearly two weeks, when Allenthal pulled his camel to a halt and Kylith drew up beside him. Finally, the sun was sinking. Allenthal nodded toward a ridge of rock jutting out from the sand.

"I want to climb up there and take a look around before it gets dark. From the high ground, maybe we can see which way the merchant went. I think we're still on his trail, but I'd like to know how far ahead he is."

Kylith nodded and slid to the ground. "Go, I'll stay here with the camels."

Allenthal climbed swiftly up through the rocks. When he reached the ridge, he kept his body low so he wouldn't stand out. He crept to the edge and looked out, expecting to see nothing more than miles of empty desert.

Far away, he saw a large caravan moving. There were many camels and wagons, but the distance made it difficult to tell anything else.

Directly below Allenthal, a narrow canyon wound through the rocks. A bit of motion drew his eye to a camel, its brown coat blending well with colors of sand and rock. Only the movement had made it stand out against its background. The animal moved at a slow, measured pace. The man walking beside it in a sand-colored cloak was barely distinguishable. It was Ashkan. They had caught up to the merchant, though he wasn't going to be pleased to see them. He'd made it very clear when they parted that he didn't want to see them again.

What could Allenthal say to him? He needed to come up with a better explanation, something that wouldn't cause the man to reach for his knife again.

As Allenthal stared down, several dark shapes appeared from different directions, converging on Ashkan. They attacked, attempting to seize the merchant. He fought surprisingly well, his movements quick. He had his knife in his hand, holding back the attack of three similarly armed foes. Already two of them had been hit and were bleeding. But there were more. A moment later, they had pulled him to the ground, still fighting desperately.

There wasn't time to make a decision. Allenthal found himself running and sliding back down the rocks to Kylith. "Ashkan has been ambushed—just around those rocks." He mounted his camel. He had not yet attempted to make the animal run, but, as he urged it forward, they achieved a surprising pace. He gripped the saddle tightly, directing the beast into the canyon.

Allenthal and Kylith came around the rocks to see a small open space and several attackers. Some of them held Ashkan down, searching carefully through his clothes. A man in a gray cloak bent over him, a blade in his hand.

"Tell me where it is!" he demanded.

Allenthal slid to the ground, Kylith close behind him.

"I don't have it," Ashkan protested. "Someone must have lost it generations ago. I never saw it."

"Lies," the man snarled. His blade fell, and Ashkan grunted in pain. "Tell me where it is."

Desperate to stop what was happening, Allenthal yelled and charged toward them. The men turned to defend themselves. Allenthal and Kylith struck them like a storm. It took only a moment for the attackers, those who were still able, to flee.

As the men disappeared into the rocks, leading Ashkan's camel with them, Kylith followed, while Allenthal jumped to the ground beside the merchant. His jaw was clenched, sweat beading on his forehead. Blood poured from a wound on his chest.

Allenthal applied pressure to the wound, attempting to stop the bleeding. "I'm sorry. We tried to help. I saw them attack—"

The merchant clutched at him. "It's too—too late for me. Please, my family—"

"Kyjia?"

He nodded. "My daughter. I knew they were following me. I tried to get away—I'm sorry I thought it was you who wished me harm."

"They tried to get the tablet from you?"

The merchant nodded. "They seek power, and they thought I had it."

Allenthal's mind spun. "You're the king of Tyar?"

"Tyar has no king," Ashkan ground out the words. "I'm no leader, just the latest member of an ancient family. Karineth doesn't care about any of us. I gave the tablet to Kyjia. And they will do anything to get it from her. Please help—" His body shook all over. "With me gone, they will hunt her down to get it."

Allenthal grabbed a piece of cloth from his pack and pressed it against the wound to slow the bleeding. There must be something more he could do.

Moving with great effort, the merchant lifted his hand to trace a figure into the sand. Allenthal watched him carefully, but when he finished, it didn't look like anything meaningful.

"What is it?" he asked, desperately trying to decipher the drawing.

"Go east from here until you see a mountain that looks like that. When you reach it, turn south into a canyon so small it looks like nothing is there. Find my family there. Please warn them. They aren't safe. They need to hide." His dark eyes were desperate.

Allenthal put a hand on his shoulder. "I will do what I can to help them, Ashkan. I promise you."

"Please! Don't let them harm my family. They are everything to me, Tillian, Terjan, and my beautiful Kyjia—"

"I'll help them."

Ashkan nodded. His grip on Allenthal loosened; his eyes closed.

Kylith returned, dismounting beside them. "They're gone. Is he—?"

Allenthal examined the merchant, searching for any sign of life. He found nothing. "Dead."

He stared down at the blood covering his hands. Namradill had sent him to find and protect this man, and he'd failed. Just as he'd failed to help his injured brother five years ago.

"I tried to stop it, but we were too late." He bowed his head.

Kylith gripped his shoulder. "We still have a chance to aid his family."

He was right. Allenthal couldn't let his failure prevent him from attempting to complete his quest. He turned to the drawing in the dust. Now that he knew it was a mountain, it helped. Two peaks with a third summit to one side, flat topped.

He pointed to the drawing. "Look at this, Kylith."

His friend went to one knee, examining the figure.

Allenthal looked down at the still form of the merchant. "He told me to go east until I saw a mountain that looked like this."

Kylith met his gaze. "What did he want us to find there?"

"His family."

The last rays of the sun faded fast. Allenthal bent over the fallen man, checking again for any sign of breath or heartbeat. The dead merchant held a scrap of fabric in his hand, a piece that might have been torn from the hem of a tunic or a cloak. Had he gripped it in his last effort to defeat his foe? The murderer would not have intended to leave the piece behind. But the attacker had jumped back, startled, and fled, killing Ashkan rather than allowing anyone to rescue him. The fabric might be a clue to discover who had done this. Allenthal put the piece carefully in his pocket. He wrapped Ashkan's cloak around his body, pulling a fold over his still face.

The Goddess had sent Allenthal here to protect the lost king of Tyar. So far, he hadn't accomplished much. But, Kylith was right. This wasn't over yet.

They dragged the two fallen bandits a little distance away from their makeshift camp. The light faded into a dark desert night, silent except for the whisper of the breeze across the sand. They had no wood to start a fire, and Allenthal didn't feel like eating anything. The evening's violence had driven such ordinary concerns from his mind. He sat down with his knees drawn up, his back resting against the rock wall of the canyon. One by one, bright stars came out in the black expanse above him.

Two stars shone in the dark across the canyon from him. Allenthal blinked, but the two points of light remained. As he stared at them, another pair of lights appeared beside the first. No, not stars. They were eyes. He jumped to his feet, drawing his knife.

Some living creature waited out there in the dark, watching them. The camels shifted uneasily while Kylith attempted to soothe them.

The foremost of the creatures crept nearer, its glowing eyes fixed on Allenthal. It stopped before it reached him. Ashkan's body lay between them. Allenthal picked up a rock and threw it at the eyes. An angry hiss marked the impact of the stone. He gripped his knife, holding it ready, and jumped back as a sudden hiss sounded behind him.

From the direction of the camels, a yell and a curse sounded. "Kylith?"

A sudden glow of light illuminated Kylith, holding a torch. "One of them bit my leg." Blood soaked through the torn fabric of his pants, just above the top of his boot.

The sudden torchlight revealed several large lizards with long jaws and sharp teeth, two of them already biting into Ashkan's body. These must be the azarim the camel trader had warned them about. The creatures hissed and retreated a little, avoiding the light. They must have followed the smell of blood to this place.

Kylith threw a rock, and, in the light, his aim was good, hitting one of them on the head. It retreated, disappearing into the darkness. He stood, swaying slightly on his feet. His hand fell to his side as if he couldn't hold the torch up anymore.

"I—I—" He sank to his knees, then collapsed onto the sand.

Quickly, Allenthal stepped forward and picked up the torch. The lizards had begun to advance again. Some of them crept toward Ashkan, while another charged forward and bit into Kylith's leg. He remained still, not responding at all to the attack. Allenthal drove them back, shouting and throwing stones. He picked up the precious torch before it went out. The azarim didn't like the light, they moved back when he approached, staying outside the brightest glow. But when he moved forward, the dark advanced behind him, and they were ready.

Kylith hadn't moved at all since he fell. Allenthal examined him in the torchlight. His eyes were open.

"Can you hear me?" Allenthal asked.

Kylith looked at him, but apparently couldn't answer, his only motion a slight twitch of his head.

"Blink if you can hear me."

He blinked.

"Is there anything I can do? Blink once for yes, and twice for no."

Two blinks.

Allenthal helped him onto his back. Kylith was always so strong and capable. Now, his body felt limp, every muscle slack. If he'd been alone, the lizards would already be dining on him. Allenthal shuddered. He gripped his friend's shoulder.

"I'll keep watch."

A sudden hiss warned him of a lizard creeping up behind him, way too close. He kicked it as hard as he could. His stomach churned. If he was bitten too...

During the endless night, he kept the torch burning, guarding Kylith and driving back any lizard that drew too near. When the first light of dawn lit the canyon, Allenthal searched the area for lizards but saw none. They had disappeared, but they'd probably be back as soon as darkness fell.

Kylith groaned, and Allenthal bent over him. He moved his arms and legs, only slightly at first, but his mobility improved gradually. Finally, he managed to speak.

"Allenthal?"

"I'm here. Are you all right?"

"That was the worst thing that's ever happened to me," Kylith exclaimed. "I felt everything, but I couldn't move. I'll owe you forever. If I'd been alone, they would have eaten me. A slow horrible death."

Allenthal gripped his friend's shoulder. "Try not to think about it too much. I don't see any more of them. Hopefully, the lizards are gone. As soon as you're ready, we'll get out of here."

Kylith sat up, examining the bites on his leg. Allenthal found a piece of cloth from their pack and tore it into strips. He used a little of their precious water to clean the wounds and then wrapped them.

"Here, rest and have something to eat. I'm going to make sure there's nothing else nearby."

Just around the corner from their camp, Allenthal came across what was left of the two dead bandits. His stomach twisted, and he struggled not to vomit. The azarim had been efficient. Much of the flesh had been torn from the bodies, leaving white bone exposed.

His mind went back to the warning they had received in Niaz. At the time, he'd thought the man was exaggerating or teasing them. In actuality, his cautionary words had not been strong enough.

There was nothing else they could do for Ashkan and the two bandits except prepare some place to lay them to rest. The burning sun was high in the sky before they finished. A simple rock cairn was a humble resting place for a king, but what else could they do? They couldn't carry him with them. When they finished, they packed their things onto the camels and rode on.

Relief flooded him as they left the canyon behind them. They headed east, sweating under the desert sun. They traveled five more days before they sighted the mountain Ashkan had described. As they looked east, the setting sun illuminated its distinctive profile against the faded sky. He'd said his family would be there.

CHAPTER 5

KYJIA

A SMALL SERVING OF grain provided them each a sparing breakfast. Kyjia dared not add any more of their rapidly dwindling stock to their bowls. As it was, they had only enough for a few more meager days. They sat together in silence as they ate, avoiding meeting each other's eyes.

The time had come to make a decision. If they didn't, they would starve here. Kyjia's foraging had extended their meager supplies, but, alone, it wasn't enough to keep them alive. She had hoped their provisions would last until her father returned. He should have been back several days ago, but travel in the desert could be unpredictable. There were a dozen reasonable explanations for his tardiness. Maybe his camel had gone lame. That might have delayed him. Perhaps customers for his wares had been scarce, and it had taken him longer than usual to sell his work. Reviewing excuses in her mind didn't ease the tension building in her belly or the lines of strain on her mother's face.

"I can travel to the city and find work," Terjan said. "There must be lots of people wanting to hire someone."

At seventeen, he had grown tall but remained lanky. He would continue to grow bigger and stronger. His offer was brave, though he sounded unsure. They all knew that they had to do something. They had remained hidden in the desert as long as they could.

"No," their mother said, brushing back a strand of his dark hair. "No one will travel anywhere alone. We must stay together. It wouldn't be safe, and we don't have enough supplies to split up."

"Father will be back any day," Kyjia said. "We need to give him more time."

Her mother put her hand to cover her daughter's and gripped it. She shook her head. "I'm afraid there is no more time."

She got to her feet and went to the nook in the stone, which served as a storage area, and took out a small, ornately carved wooden chest.

"No," Kyjia protested, watching the reverent way her mother held it. "It's the last thing you have from grandmother." Kyjia had watched her mother sell off her heirlooms, one by one, until they were all gone but this.

Her mother opened the box and held up a glittering bracelet. She smiled sadly as she admired the sparkling gems. "I've kept it all these years. But jewelry does us no good if we starve. We'll go to Niaz and sell it."

"You probably won't find anyone there with money to pay what that's worth," Kyjia said. "Wouldn't it be better to find a buyer in Saarin?"

Her mother shook her head. "If there's any chance we might find your father on the road, we must go that way. We can buy provisions in Niaz, maybe even find work of some kind there. I will attempt to sell the bracelet to one of the clan chieftains, someone who already has money. I will make the best bargain I can. We must go soon. We can't wait any longer for Ashkan." She looked at Kyjia and Terjan. "Gather your things."

As the others packed, Kyjia slipped from the cave up into the rocky draw behind it. She had grown to know this place well in the years they'd lived there. The narrow canyon felt like a haven of safety, though a lonely one. She knew every stone of this draw by heart. Coming to a small notch between the rocks, she found a sheltered flat space. It was quiet. No one would see her or hear her.

Kyjia reached beneath her tunic to draw out a golden tablet a little larger than her palm. With a reverent finger, she traced the sacred symbols carved into its surface. She pulled the chain over her head and held the ornament up to the morning sun. The gold shone in the bright light.

She knelt on the flat rock, looking up at the pale desert sky. "My Lord Karineth, God of the Desert, please speak to me. Our people are scattered, striving to live in this land that becomes harsher every season. We need your words, and we need your care. Please! Are you there?"

Kyjia remained still, waiting for a long time. She heard nothing. The tablet grew heavy in her hand, but she felt no sign of the presence of any god. Maybe He was dead. Maybe Karineth had only ever been a myth.

She stared at the tablet in her hand. Even if God didn't answer now, she couldn't abandon her faith. Her father had charged her with keeping the tablet safe, and she'd promised him she would. She must never let it fall into the hands of anyone outside her family. The journey they were about to make was dangerous. She needed some place safe to hide the tablet.

Taking out a piece of cloth, she carefully wrapped the bright, golden medallion. Walking a short way from the flat area, she found a loose stone that revealed a small space behind it. Tucking the cloth-wrapped tablet inside, she replaced the stone and stepped back to examine her work.

She'd left no sign that the rocks had been disturbed. It looked exactly like a thousand other nearby stones, yet this entire area was very familiar to her. She had no doubt she could find it again. They would leave the canyon and hopefully meet her father soon. When they found him, they could all return here together, and she could give it back to him. In the meantime, there was no risk of it being lost or taken.

Kyjia returned to the others, quickly stowing her few belongings in a bag. She filled water skins from the tiny seeping spring. There wasn't enough to fill them all at once. She had to wait for the pool of water to refill slowly.

It didn't take long for them to hide every trace of their presence. They each carried a share of their belongings and water. It would take two weeks to walk to Niaz, if not more, and there were no wells in between. They would have to ration their water carefully.

As they walked away, Kyjia looked back into the draw that had been their home for years. Besides the tiny hidden spring, there was nothing special at all about the place. Only the presence of her family had made it important. Where was her father now? She missed the solid comfort of his presence.

Wrapping her hood over her head, she tucked the ends around to cover her face. Slightly bent under the heavy pack, she followed the others out into the open. The sun had baked the ground so hard that her boots left no sign of her passing.

They walked for hours until the sun blazed directly overhead. A few small clumps of boulders provided a tiny sliver of shade. They took off their packs and huddled gratefully into the shelter, each allowing themselves a small drink of precious water.

"We'll rest here until sunset," her mother said.

They sat with their backs against the rock, keeping every part of themselves in the shelter of the shade. Nothing moved except the shimmering of the hot air.

The setting sun offered welcome relief from the heat. As the air cooled, they prepared to move again. After a small meal, they shouldered their packs and continued to head west. The sun sank ahead of them, and the stars came out. Her cloak, which had protected her from the burning rays, now provided warmth as the heat vanished with the sun.

Many of the desert creatures were more active at night. She saw scorpions skittering across the earth and the undulating track of a snake across the sand. Once in the distance, she saw the sets of glowing eyes that belonged to a pair of azarim, but the lizards came no nearer.

They walked all night. By the time the sun rose again, they were all exhausted and eager to huddle into another small patch of shade. They took turns watching while the others slept.

By the fourth night, they knew someone was following them. Just visible in the faint moonlight, several camels moved behind them. Tillian changed direction, and they moved as quickly as they could. That day, they hid in the shelter of a ridge of rocks. While the daylight lasted, they saw nothing moving. When they set out again in the evening, it wasn't long before they saw several people following.

Were they bandits?

Kyjia felt a rush of relief that she'd hidden the tablet and also a sharp pang of worry. She gripped the hilt of the knife at her belt. Maybe they were simply thieves who had crossed their path at random, ready to attack any travelers who didn't have a troop of guards. No one should have known of their journey, but someone had; otherwise, they wouldn't be following. Kyjia could only hope that it was coincidence and not because of the tablet.

CHAPTER 6

KYJIA

ALL NIGHT, THEY HURRIED on as quickly as possible. It didn't matter if they were tired, hungry, and thirsty. They needed to reach safety. Kyjia's hand returned constantly to the hilt of her knife. If someone attacked them, she needed to do what she could to protect her mother and brother. A line of rocky hills lay ahead, and, if they could reach it, there would be places to hide. They'd have a chance of slipping away.

An hour before dawn, they reached the edge of the hills, eagerly moving into a draw that would hide them from sight of anyone behind them. A short way in, her mother took out the precious bracelet. If the thieves stole it, they would have nothing left to bargain with when they reached Niaz. She wrapped it in a piece of cloth and hid it carefully among the rocks.

"Remember," she instructed them.

Observing every detail, Kyjia formed a picture in her mind of the exact rocks that surrounded the place. With the image imprinted on their memories, they moved on quickly. Farther along the draw, they found a slender crack in the rock. From a distance, it didn't look like anything, but when they examined it closely, they found it wide enough for a person to slip inside.

Kyjia was the shortest, and she slid in first. Terjan followed her. There wasn't room to move at all with the stone pressing in on them from both sides. Their mother moved to stand beside them. She could see out of the opening, at least. Behind the others, Kyjia couldn't see anything. She felt Terjan's hand and gripped it.

"They're coming," their mother hissed.

Fear twitched in Kyjia's belly as they waited, still and silent. Men's voices came from outside, several of them, talking and laughing raucously. Dawn had not yet come, and the darkness would hide them. After what felt like a very long time, the sounds grew fainter, and she let out a breath of relief.

They waited until it had been silent for a while before they moved. "Come," their mother whispered.

Terjan and Kyjia followed her. They didn't have much time. Moving almost at a run, they moved along the rocky path until they came to a fork.

"Which way?" Their mother looked from one route to the other. She chose the left way, and they hurried on.

Dawn was breaking, and the light grew brighter every moment. Kyjia clenched her teeth to hold back a curse. In the growing light, she saw that their chosen route came to a dead end, leaving them trapped against a sheer, rocky cliff.

Shouts from behind made Kyjia drop her pack. She drew her dagger. They stood, side by side, with their backs against the stone wall. They had knives but no other weapons. A chill seeped into her, making her shiver all over, but she held her blade ready.

The bandits came quickly. Several men moved to block the entrance to the draw. They slid down off their camels and moved to face their victims. Their faces were covered except for dark eyes. They were all armed with deadly scimitars, the long, curved blades pointed at Kyjia and her family. There had to be a way out of this. She needed a way to protect her mother and brother.

"Don't move," one of them hissed, holding the blade against her mother's throat while he took her dagger.

One of the men, apparently their leader, stepped forward. He was tall, and the scarf pulled across his face didn't hide a thick scar running all across the middle of one cheek and over the bridge of his nose.

"There you are," he said, his hand twirling something bright. With a sick feeling, Kyjia realized it was her mother's bracelet, the last valuable thing they had to bargain with.

The bandit lowered the cloth covering his face and smiled. "Watching you turned out to be *very* worthwhile. This little bauble is worth a lot of money. And I'm betting that a person who owns something like this will have more treasure hidden away somewhere."

Kyjia's stomach dropped. The bandit was sure they had more to offer, and he wasn't going to be kind as he attempted to force it out of them. He'd never believe that the bracelet was the last valuable thing they had. They were in serious trouble.

"Now, put down your weapons, unless you want us to cut her throat," he nodded toward her mother while she stared back at him, furious. No trace of fear showed in her face.

Kyjia wished she could be so brave. She wanted to run from these men and never stop running. But they had her mother. Slowly, she bent to set her knife on the ground. Beside her, Terjan did the same. As soon as they released the blades, bandits surrounded them, seizing them from all sides.

The leader with the scar strolled forward to face Kyjia, his eyes roaming offensively up and down her body. His large hand gripped her arm hard. For a long moment, he stared down at her, then ripped her hood from her head. Icy terror twisted through her belly as she met his gaze. His eyes were flat and cold, without a spark of compassion.

He stared at her appraisingly. "You're too pale to belong in the desert. Pretty though." He dragged her hard against his body and kissed her.

Kyjia struggled fiercely, fighting to pull her mouth away from his, but his arms held her immobile.

Finally, the bandit drew back. He looked down at her and smiled. Kyjia spat in his face, and his grin widened.

"You could bring a high price to the right buyer. Unless I decide to keep you for myself."

Fury burned through her. She hated the way he looked at her, as if she were nothing more than a possession, an object to be bought and sold.

"Leave her alone," Terjan yelled, dragging himself free of the hands that held him. He seized the hilt of a scimitar sheathed at one of their belts and drew it, attacking them.

Kyjia twisted in the bandit's grip and brought her knee up hard into his crotch. Cursing, he sank to his knees, dragging her with him. She fought, landing several more good blows, but he was big and strong, and two of his friends stepped forward to help him. A line of white-hot pain struck her arm. As she fought to escape their grip, one of the men struck her with a large fist. Pain exploded along one side of her face and she crumpled.

Blinking away the white lights in her vision, she saw attackers surrounding Terjan, preventing him from reaching her. He moved quickly, swinging his blade to block their assaults, but there were too many of them. One of them raised his scimitar and struck him from behind. With a cry, he pitched forward, going to his knees in the sand.

The pounding of horse hooves against the hard ground rang out around them. Cries and shouts came from their attackers and most of them quickly disappeared as a group of men charged into the narrow draw. They dismounted, moving to confront the remaining bandits.

A moment later, one of the riders held the point of his blade against the bandit holding Kyjia. "Release her," he demanded.

Moving very slowly, his eyes on the sword aimed at his throat, the man let go of Kyjia and got to his feet. Instead of their leader, it was one of the others. The man with the scar was nowhere in sight. Two of the newcomers came up behind the remaining bandit, seizing him and dragging him away. The rider bent to one knee beside Kyjia. He took a piece of cloth from his pocket and held it firmly against the wound on her arm.

She gasped in pain, but the pressure would slow the bleeding. Looking up, she saw eyes dark as midnight. He pulled down the cloth covering his face, revealing a firm jaw and a strong, slightly hooked nose. "I am Zhandar, Chieftain of the Sunfire clan. May I offer my assistance?"

Kyjia nodded, relief flowing through her. She had never met Zhandar before, but everyone had heard of him. By reputation, he was a decent man, and powerful. A large portion of the people of Tyar offered him allegiance. He wouldn't harm them.

She let out a breath of relief. "My brother is hurt."

"We will help him," Zhandar promised. He offered his hand, and when she took it, he gently assisted her to sit up.

Terjan lay on the ground with their mother beside him. When she applied pressure to the wound, he let out a strangled yell.

"He needs help," Zhandar said. "May I offer you the hospitality of my camp? I have a mystic there who can tend his wound."

"You're very kind," her mother said. "We accept your help gratefully, but if you have water and supplies, I will tend to him myself."

"As you wish, my lady." He turned to one of his men. "Find more cloth. We need to wrap the wound before we move him."

He turned back to her mother. "We have no extra horses. Will you consent to ride with one of my men? With your permission, I will assign someone to transport your belongings."

Zhandar's men lifted Terjan into a saddle, and one of them mounted behind him, holding him steady as he slumped in the saddle. Another man offered his saddle to her mother, and she mounted, allowing him to sit behind her.

After the fight, Kyjia was still trying to catch her breath. Her head throbbed from the blow that had knocked her down. She felt her cheek and jaw already swelling. The knife cut on her arm burned, and she wasn't sure how well she could use her arm.

At least the bandits were gone. Relief flooded through her. Zhandar's men would help them. They would care for Terjan's injury, and he would be all right in time. They would all be all right.

Zhandar stood quietly beside her as she attempted to collect herself. He was tall, his large frame towering over her, but his expression was kind.

"Thank you for your help. We're very grateful." She looked up to meet his dark eyes.

He nodded in acknowledgement. "I'm relieved that I arrived in time to help you. Did you see a man with a scar on his face?"

Kyjia nodded. She wouldn't soon forget him. Her mind replayed the image of his grin as he casually twirled the precious bracelet. And the way he'd looked at her. He felt he had every right to kiss her, with or without her permission.

She'd never kissed a man before, and now the moment of intimacy had been stolen by a man who was cruel and selfish. He would have taken whatever profit he could from her, not caring if she suffered.

Zhandar had saved her from a dreadful fate.

"His name is Hakkir," Zhandar said. "He's proven difficult to catch, very skilled at robbing people and then disappearing into the desert."

Zhandar picked up the reins of his horse and led it nearer to where she waited. The animal was powerful and sleek, with a dark gray coat. She'd ridden camels before, but never a horse. She stood staring at it, still gripping the cut on her left arm.

The adrenaline remaining after fleeing through the dark hours of the night and the panic of the confrontation was wearing off, leaving her exhausted and overwhelmed.

"May I help?" he asked gently.

She nodded, putting one foot in the stirrup. Zhandar gripped her waist and lifted her easily into the saddle while the horse stood patiently. He mounted behind her, reaching around her to take the reins. He guided the animal, turning it and sending it to follow the others out of the ravine. She and Zhandar now sat very close together. After Hakkir's embrace, being so near a man made her uneasy.

Still, she felt his strength, and she was grateful not to have to go any further alone. Her own energy had been exhausted.

When he spoke, his voice was close, just behind her ear. "Will you tell me your name?"

"Kyjia."

"I will keep you safe, Kyjia."

His promise brought relief from the fear that had followed her since they'd discovered the bandits on their trail.

Chapter 7

Kyjia

THE MORNING BRIGHTENED AS they rode, the day already getting hot. She needed water, shade, and most of all, rest. First, they needed to tend to Terjan's injury.

Out in the open, the horses settled into a steady rhythm. They were much faster than camels, but they would need water. Sitting this close to Zhandar, it was obvious that he was used to riding. His body moved easily with the animal. Somewhere in the middle of their ride, she straightened up with a start, realizing that exhaustion had lulled her into leaning against him.

She saw nothing of the camp until they came over the crest of a small hill and entered a hollow where many men, camels, horses, and tents had congregated. Zhandar dismounted, turning back to help her. She lifted her leg across the saddle, and his hands grasped her waist, lifting her down. Was it only her imagination, or had he held onto her a little longer than necessary?

She took a step away but turned to face him. "Thank you."

He nodded, offering his arm. "My servants are preparing a tent for you."

Kyjia took the arm, wishing that she didn't need the support but grateful for it. He led her to a tent, shouting orders as he went.

They were carrying Terjan inside with her mother walking beside him. Only a few moments later, they had all been given water, and Terjan lay on a pallet on the floor. Zhandar's servants worked quickly, and soon, there was clean water, cloth, herbs, and other supplies for the treatment of injuries.

Kyjia hurried to help. Gently, their mother removed Terjan's cloak and peeled away his bloodstained tunic to reveal a long cut that ran from his shoulder, across his shoulder blade, nearly to his spine. Kyjia's stomach clenched at the sight of it, and she tried not to picture what might have happened. There had been several of the bandits, and he'd been trying to defend her.

Her mother leaned close and put a hand on her son's uninjured shoulder. "I need to stitch it."

Terjan said nothing, did not even open his eyes, but he nodded.

It was a long process. Slowly and carefully, their mother brought the edges of the cut together. Kyjia wondered if Terjan would yell. His jaws were clenched tightly shut, and he let out nothing more than a groan. When she finished, their mother covered the whole area with a healing salve and wrapped it. She coaxed him to drink a cup of dark liquid.

"Rest, my son," her fingers brushed strands of his dark hair out of his face.

She raised her gaze to Kyjia. "And you."

"I'm fine," Kyjia protested. But when had that ever worked? At a stern glance from her mother, she sat down, allowing her to examine and clean the cut on her arm. She'd want to stitch it, of course. There was no way out now. Kyjia would simply have to endure it bravely.

Kyjia attempted to prepare herself. It didn't help much. The needle going through her flesh hurt at least as much as the cut itself, and she wanted to wail like a baby. Terjan hadn't wailed. Neither could she.

She thought her teeth might crack from clenching them, and sweat beaded on her forehead as her mother worked, her hands steady and sure. Kyjia felt another hand take hers, and desperate for comfort, she gripped it. Zhandar. He sat beside her, his dark eyes holding hers.

At last, it was over.

Two of Zhandar's servants entered the tent with trays of food. Zhandar released her hand and got to his feet. "Please, eat and sleep. You are well-guarded here. Rest, and we will speak later."

Kyjia rose to her feet and faced him. "Thank you for everything you've done to help us," she said sincerely.

He nodded in reply and went out, leaving the three of them alone in the tent.

Kyjia looked at her mother. "Are you all right?" she murmured, keeping her voice low enough that it wouldn't carry through the thin fabric walls.

"I'm fine." Lines of worry lingered between her brows. "For now, we will do as Zhandar suggests. There will be time later to decide what to do next." She bent over Terjan. "Can you eat, my son?" He shook his head but didn't open his eyes. "Then rest. The medicine will help you sleep."

Kyjia sat beside her mother, and they each took a tray on their lap. Her mouth watered as she looked down at the food. They'd been hungry for a long time as they waited for her father to return with fresh supplies. She hoped wherever he was, he'd found food, water, and rest.

She ate roasted meat and bread, slices of sweet melon, blood red pomegranate seeds, and roasted nuts sweetened with honey. They didn't talk to each other while they ate everything on the tray. Kyjia took a long drink of water. She turned to her mother.

"Is it... safe to sleep here?" she whispered.

"I hope so, my daughter. Rest."

Kyjia curled up on a soft pallet, her head on a pillow, and allowed exhaustion to claim her.

When Kyjia opened her eyes, she had no idea where she was. The woven wall of a strange tent moved slightly in a light breeze. She lay on something soft. A twinge of pain from her arm reminded her. They'd been attacked. Terjan was hurt. They were in Zhandar's camp.

Her mother sat nearby. She rose when one of the servants came to the door with water for washing. Such a luxury was a surprise so deep in the desert, but they quickly took advantage. They washed themselves and put on clean clothes from their packs. They brushed out their hair and braided it.

Terjan still slept.

A short while later, the servant girl returned. "Lord Zhandar invites you to join him for dinner." She nodded to another girl beside her. "I will guide you, if you choose, and my friend will stay here to watch your son in case he wakes."

"Very well," her mother accepted for them.

They followed the servant girl between the tents until they reached a large one in the center. She held back the tent fabric to allow them to enter. Inside, Zhandar stood, waiting for them.

He bowed. "Welcome, Lady Tillian and Lady Kyjia. Please, join me."

His imposing frame appeared even bigger inside the tent. He had washed and changed into fresh clothing, a magnificent, embroidered tunic, and a jeweled belt. If Kyjia had taken that to sell in the city, it would have brought a sum large enough to feed their family for a long time.

Their own clothes were simple and well worn. She felt his gaze survey her, and she looked up to meet his eyes, seeing no judgment there, only welcome.

"Please, come in and sit down," he invited.

They moved forward to seat themselves on cushions around a small table.

"You are very kind to invite us here," her mother said.

He nodded graciously. "It's my pleasure. I wanted a chance to speak more with you."

On silent feet, servants came in with trays of food, placing them on the table and departing. Zhandar smiled at Kyjia and Tillian, extending his hands in invitation. "Please, eat."

Kyjia tried to not let her eyes widen at the trays of beautiful food. She'd never seen anything like it. There appeared to be enough to feed a dozen people.

They began to eat. Zhandar was a kind host, inviting them to try all the different dishes, explaining the unfamiliar ones. "How is your son?" he asked.

"He's still sleeping, Lord Zhandar," her mother replied.

He nodded. "We wish him a swift recovery. You're very lucky it wasn't worse. Often, when people meet Hakkir, they end up as nothing more than a meal for the azarim."

Her muscles tensed at that thought. They were very fortunate he had arrived in time to help them. She suppressed a shiver.

For a long moment, silence fell. Zhandar broke it by clearing his throat, "Travel in the desert can be very dangerous. Do you mind if I ask what you were doing out there?"

Her mother nodded, but her face remained impassive. "My husband, Ashkan, traveled to Niaz to trade for supplies. We intend to meet him when he returns. Did you come from there? Maybe you have had word of him on the road?"

He lowered his brows in concern. "Yes, I came from Niaz myself. My people and I are returning to Saarin. Before I left, some of my men reported that they'd seen Ashkan speaking with two rivermen. They must have had some sort of argument, and he left town very soon after that. I wanted to be sure he was safe, and I sent some of my people to look for him. I'm afraid I have not heard anything from them yet, Lady Tillian, but they should be meeting us any day. We will stay here for a few days to see if they return. You are welcome to remain here as my guests. I can send someone to search."

"Thank you, Lord Zhandar. I would be most grateful. And your offer is very welcome. My son is not ready to travel. In fact, I should return to him now." She got to her feet.

Zhandar rose as well and offered a hand to lift Kyjia. "Of course, my lady. We hope he is well. With your permission," he bowed to her, "may I ask Kyjia if she would walk with me for a short while?"

Kyjia met her mother's eyes. Her expression was unreadable. The decision would be hers.

She gave a small nod of consent. "Your invitation is gracious, Lord Zhandar. Perhaps you would show me around the camp?"

"It would be my honor." He offered his hand, and she took it. Her fingers felt small inside his.

They strolled slowly through the camp as the sun set against the distant hills. He led her to the base of a small rise a little way beyond the last tent. They climbed it together. When they reached the top, the sky arched wide above them, the bright colors of the sunset shining through a few slender, distant clouds.

"It's beautiful," she murmured, lost in the view.

"Yes," he replied. "Though we live in a difficult land, it's still beautiful. I believe, one day, Tyar will become great again. Our people will grow strong, and our nation will regain the power it once had. Generations ago, only the dry edges of our land were desert. The rest was green fields and orchards."

Kyjia nodded sadly. "I've heard the stories of how the King of Tyar ruled in wisdom and power from a graceful palace in a city of white stone. His windows looked out over a wide river that flowed through a fertile green valley. Our people were merchants and artisans, musicians and poets."

Zhandar smiled. "Not many remember our history so well. Most of us are too occupied now with trying to stay alive while the burning sun grows stronger each year and the rains become ever rarer. I want to help them."

"I do too," Kyjia agreed. "What do you intend to do?"

He smiled down at her. "The first step is to find a way to get them all to cooperate. We are stubborn people, and our kingdom has disintegrated into small bands fighting with each other. We can't afford war with ourselves. There are too few of us left as it is." Zhandar lifted his eyes to the distant horizon.

Kyjia looked away into the sunset. "We need the blessing of our god."

He turned to focus on her. "I agree. For many years, the mystics have told us that our god sleeps. Mystics are rare these days, but I have been lucky to have Jaro with me. He plans to find a more powerful way to communicate with the divine. Through his many years of service, he has gathered the influence to help our people. I've seen it already."

Kyjia sat up, looking back at him with interest. "I've never met a real mystic."

"It is a unique experience. They are the descendants of deity here, living among us." Zhandar smiled. "I'll be happy to introduce you when he returns."

Kyjia found herself smiling back. "Thank you, Zhandar. You saved my family today."

His gaze fixed on her. "When I rode into the canyon this morning and saw that man strike you, I couldn't stand it. I had to help." He brushed his fingers along her jaw, below the dark bruise on her face. "I'm very grateful you're safe now."

His dark eyes held more than simple kindness. She could sense his attraction, and her own body heated under his gaze.

CHAPTER 8

KYJIA

BY THE TIME THEY'D been a week in Zhandar's camp, Kyjia had spent time with him on several occasions. He'd been kind and courteous to her and her family. While he hadn't spoken of it directly, the way he looked at her revealed his interest in her.

Though she felt grateful for his help, Kyjia remained determined to move slowly. She'd spent much of her life living in isolation, aside from her family. She hadn't spent time with any man besides her father for a long time. It would take more time for her to completely trust Zhandar, but for now, her family's position was precarious, and they needed his protection.

As the days passed, they began to heal and regain their strength. Terjan remained weak, and his wound was very painful whenever he moved, but he improved steadily, day by day. One evening, a servant came to their tent. "Lord Zhandar is coming with a message. He'll be here in a few moments."

Kyjia's stomach clenched. Was there word of her father?

When the chieftain arrived, they invited him to sit. For a long moment, they waited in silence. Zhandar drew in a long breath. He reached out to take her mother's hand. His expression was grim. "I'm very sorry, Lady Tillian. The news I bring is not good. My men brought word of Ashkan."

Her mother's other hand clutched Kyjia's, and she closed her own around it.

"I'm very sorry," Zhandar repeated. "Your husband is dead."

Her mother stiffened beside her. All the color drained from her face, leaving her deathly pale. "No," she gasped.

"Where? When?" Kyjia asked. They needed more information. What had happened to her father?

"Some of my men just returned with the news. They left Niaz hoping to find him and make sure he traveled safely. When they found Ashkan, two strangers were attacking him, both big men, skilled fighters. Hurrying to help, they got to him as quickly as possible and drove them away, but not before one of them had inflicted a mortal wound."

A flood of hot rage swept through Kyjia, and she fought to keep her voice steady. "Who were these strangers?"

"They must be the same two who were seen speaking to him in Niaz. Now they ride camels and wear desert cloaks, but beneath that disguise, they are rivermen."

None of it made sense. What reason could foreigners have to attack her father? Why would they even enter the desert at all?

"Where are they now?" The words escaped between jaws clenched in anger. They had to find the men who had murdered her father.

"I will know very soon. I have sent three groups of my men to search for them. They can't have gone too far. I will find them for you." Zhandar got to his feet, shifting uncomfortably. "I'm sorry it fell to me to bring this news. When I know more, I will let you know." He slipped out, leaving them alone with their grief.

They held each other and cried. Her father wasn't coming back.

Grief lay like a heavy weight on their shoulders, but by the next day, they felt compelled to discuss what they would do next. They sat close together, their voices low enough that no one could overhear them. "The last thing he asked of us was to keep the tablet safe," Kyjia whispered. "No matter what happens, we must do that much."

"Your father's death wasn't a random event," their mother said firmly. "Someone killed him for a reason. I fear someone found out who he was, who all of us are. And if that's true, with him gone, they'll come after us next."

"Do you think those two strangers are looking for us?" Kyjia asked.

Her mother gave a slight shrug. "I can't imagine why men from another nation would be concerned with the fate of Tyar or how any of them would know who your father was. Perhaps someone from inside Tyar hired them as mercenaries. Or assassins."

Kyjia shivered at that thought. She and her family weren't soldiers. They had no formal training to fight. What chance would any of them have against men who had been trained to kill?

Kyjia exchanged a glance with Terjan. "If that's true, what can the three of us do about it? Zhandar's protection has kept us safe here, but that can't last forever. I don't think it would be wise to go out alone again, not if we're being followed before we start."

"We must protect each other," Terjan said. "It's the only thing we can do."

"You're both so brave. No mother could ask for better children." Her mother put an arm around each of them, pulling them close. "I know your father was so proud of both of you."

Tears welled in Kyjia's eyes at her words. She missed her father so much, and she was determined not to fail in his last request to her. "We won't let him down. But if we find the strangers who did this, they need to pay for what they did."

Her mother took in a long breath. "I know how you feel, my dears, but revenge is not the answer. We must find out why this happened. More killing will not bring Ashkan back. He rests now with Karineth in the unseen world."

A flood of questions rose up in Kyjia. She couldn't ask them all, so she asked the first one. "We have already asked our god for His blessing so many times. If Karineth is real, why doesn't He hear us?"

"He is real," her mother said firmly, "and I still believe He will help."

Kyjia sat alone on the crest of a dune just outside the camp as the red sun sank slowly out of sight behind the vast expanse of desert. Inside her head, thoughts swirled in a tangled mass. Her grief shaped itself into a tight pain in her chest. Father had always been there. Now, she missed his voice, his smile, and she'd never see him again. He had been there all her life to teach her and care for her.

She gasped and whirled around as a shadow fell over her. Zhandar stood beside her. She hadn't heard him approach.

"I didn't intend to startle you," he said, his tone contrite. "May I join you?"

A breath of relief escaped her, and she nodded as he settled onto the sand beside her.

"It must have been a very difficult day for you. I'm sorry." His voice was quiet.

"None of it was your fault," she said. "We appreciate your help very much. It's only that... we need to decide what to do."

He nodded. "Yes." He rubbed his chin. "I know this isn't the right time to ask this, and you don't have to answer now. I watched how Tillian cared for your brother's injury, and it's obvious she is a skilled healer. I will soon be returning to Saarin, where many of my people live. It would be a great help to me if she would consider settling there. If she would be willing to assist the sick or injured, I would make sure you and your family have everything you need."

"That's a very generous offer," Kyjia said.

"Perhaps it is," he admitted, "but we have urgent need of her ability. Often, my men are injured when they are forced to defend the people. Sometimes others living in Saarin become ill. Her skills would be most welcome."

Kyjia didn't want to admit what a relief it would be to have an option to earn a living. Her family had struggled for a long time, but recent events had made it obvious that her father had good reason to remain hidden. Kyjia and her family couldn't afford to assume that the danger had passed. Whoever had killed her father was still out there, and they might try to do the same to the rest of them.

"I will discuss your offer with my mother," Kyjia said.

"Don't rush her. I understand she'll need some time," Zhandar said. "I will make sure you have what you need while you take time to grieve."

It was kind of him to help them when he got nothing in return. She turned to meet his eyes. "Thank you."

A slight smile lifted one corner of his mouth. Slowly, almost shyly, he reached out to take her hand. His hand was large and warm, callused from riding and handling weapons. For a long time, they sat watching the fading colors of the sky.

Before she'd met Zhandar, she'd never held a man's hand before, other than her father's. Their canyon had been a lonely home. Now, Zhandar's hand felt good in hers. It was comforting to feel that someone else shared the burden of taking care of her family.

CHAPTER 9

CROWN PRINCE ALLENTHAL

ALLENTHAL LOOKED AROUND THE bare canyon with its stark sandstone walls. All was still and silent. "There's no one here."

Kylith shrugged in response, and they widened their search.

This was the right place, Allenthal was sure of it. He'd followed Ashkan's directions exactly. There must be some sign that someone had been here. It didn't take long to search the place. They found the tiny hidden spring and drank all the water they could hold. They refilled their water skins and let the camels drink.

As they searched, they found a few, nearly invisible signs of habitation: a track in the sand which the wind had failed to erase completely and stones inside the cave that had been worn smooth.

Allenthal looked at the desolate rocks and sand, picturing people living here in this remote place. The people of Tyar must be as tough as old tree roots. Kylith had finished his search and turned to look at him. "I'm sure this is the place, even though they were careful to erase any sign of their presence. They're gone." Allenthal shook his head.

How would they find a small group of people in this vast desert? From here, Allenthal had no idea where Kyjia and her family would have gone. They could be anywhere. Searching the vast desert would be futile without some clue.

"We might be able to find some tracks," Kylith suggested. "At least to get a direction."

From the mouth of the canyon, they searched the ground, much of it entirely smoothed over by the shifting winds, but here and there, they were able to locate small signs of tracks. They followed them.

For several days, they followed the tiny hints of a trail. They'd seen no people, no sign of habitation. How far would they go? Their water was already running low. They would be fools if they kept going without knowing where they might find more water.

As the sun sank, they searched for a place to stop for the night. From behind a small, rocky outcropping, a strong company of men on horses charged out to surround them. The horses were much faster and more maneuverable than camels. There wasn't time to run.

The horsemen wore desert clothing, and they were well-armed. Several had bows, their arrows nocked and drawn, pointing at them. Now wasn't a good time to fight. Allenthal raised his hands, palm out. Maybe these men could give them more information, though they weren't friendly at the moment.

For a breath, no one moved.

"Get down," one of the desert men growled.

Allenthal coaxed his camel to sit and then got off and stood, facing the newcomers. Beside him, Kylith did the same. One of the desert men dismounted and came to face them. "Who are you?" he demanded in the accent of Tyar. He was tall, nearly as tall as Allenthal, and well-muscled.

"Only travelers," Allenthal said. "We mean no harm to anyone."

"No one travels here," the man said, his dark eyes boring into theirs. "I want to know what you're really doing."

Allenthal took a deep breath. "Very well. I am carrying a message."

The man laughed harshly, and took a step nearer, his body stiff with anger. "That's ridiculous. There is little contact between Tyar and the outside world. Who is it for?"

Allenthal wasn't sure if it was wise to tell the truth, but what other answer did he have? "My message is for Kyjia, daughter of Ashkan."

At the name, the man's face darkened with fury. "What message could you possibly need to give her? You will not go anywhere near her. She has no need to speak to a stranger."

"Then you know where she is?" Allenthal should have thought before he said that.

The man's brows lowered in anger, and he gripped the hilt of his scimitar. "Tell me what you want with her."

"Only to deliver a message," Allenthal insisted.

A short, slight man came to stand with his friend. His dark eyes fixed on Allenthal with a chilling stare. "These two are the ones. We saw them arguing with Ashkan in Niaz. They found him alone in the desert." He spoke with finality and looked from one to the other with his icy gaze. "They killed Ashkan, and two others who tried to defend him."

At those words, the ranks of men closed in surrounding them, holding them immobile.

"No!" Allenthal protested. "We didn't kill Ashkan. We tried to help. Several men attacked him, and we tried to stop them. We were defending him. By the time we drove them off, it was too late."

"Lies," the big man barked. "You were seen. We already knew that he'd been murdered by two men, strangers in the desert."

"That's not true!" Allenthal argued. "What reason could we possibly have for killing him?"

"I intend to find that out. Take them back to camp."

This wasn't going well at all. They dragged Allenthal's arms behind him and tied them. One man shoved him onto a horse, the reins tightly gripped by another rider. He might still have tried to escape, but he needed to find Kyjia and help her. Maybe she was also a captive of these men.

They rode only a short distance before they came upon a large, busy camp. The riders drew up and dismounted. Dragging Allenthal and Kylith from their horses, they took them into one of the tents. Allenthal didn't fight as they tied them back-to-back with the tent's central pole between them, shoving them down to the ground. They needed answers, but he wasn't sure this was the best way to get them.

For some time, they sat still, alone for the moment, except for a crowd of guards outside. "Sorry, Kylith," Allenthal spoke quietly over his shoulder. "I got us into this."

"What else could we have done?" Kylith answered. "We're not here to start a fight. And she is here. I hope there will be a diplomatic way out of this. You're good with words. Talk them out of it."

There had to be a way. If there wasn't, Allenthal had just made the biggest mistake of his life not fighting harder while they still had a chance.

A shadow appeared in the door of the tent, and someone entered. When she took a step nearer, Allenthal recognized her at once, even with her face covered. Only her dark eyes were visible, now blazing with fury as she glared at him. "Why would you do it?"

Allenthal met her eyes directly. "Kyjia, we didn't kill your father, I swear it. We tried to help him."

She shook her head. "Of course, you would say that now that you've been caught. Anything to save your skin. I want to know *why* you did it." She took a step nearer.

He returned her gaze steadily. "I *did not* kill Ashkan. I came to Tyar to help him. Please, Kyjia!"

"You have no right to use my name," she hissed. "How do you even know who I am?"

That last question was difficult to answer. He ignored it for the time being. "I have only one clue to the identity of the real murderer. Your father tore a section of fabric from the killer's tunic. If you find the garment with a missing piece, you'll know who killed him. Ashkan had the piece in his hand when he—"

"Lies!" But she took another step nearer as she said it.

"Don't let anyone else see it," Allenthal pleaded. "Whoever it was had a reason for killing him, and they might intend to harm you and the rest of your family."

Her brows rose and her eyes widened. "How do you know anything about us?" she demanded.

That was a long story, and he couldn't tell it now. "There isn't time to explain everything. Come and take the piece of fabric." He nodded toward his shirt pocket.

For a long moment, she just stared at him. Did she believe him? She still looked furious, and he couldn't blame her. Her father had been murdered, and she believed that he had done it. It was only natural for her to be angry.

From outside, the sound of voices approached the tent. Kyjia darted forward. With quick fingers, she took the scrap of fabric and backed swiftly away from him.

Several men entered the tent, led by the big man who had confronted them earlier. He placed a hand on Kyjia's shoulder. "My lady, you shouldn't be here. These strangers are dangerous."

"I wanted to see the men who killed my father." Her voice sounded cool now, controlled.

"I promised you we would find them," he said.

She stood with her back very straight and bowed to him. "Thank you, Lord Zhandar."

The name was familiar. Allenthal had heard it during the secret meeting he'd observed in the inn at the edge of the desert. So, this was the man they said would be king. Whether he knew about the murder or not, someone close to Zhandar had killed Ashkan. Allenthal couldn't say anything about what he'd heard. It would not improve their situation, and would likely make things worse.

Zhandar cast a dark look at Allenthal. "I will make sure justice is done for you and your family."

Justice? The word sent a chill down Allenthal's back. Someone was determined to hide the truth, from Kyjia and from everyone. He didn't detect deceit in Zhandar's eyes, but someone intended to use himself and Kylith to take the blame. Not good. They needed a way out of this situation.

Zhandar's men took them to the center of camp, where several lanterns burned. The stars had come out above them. All the people from the camp gathered around. Kyjia went to stand beside another woman, her mother? A boy stood beside them. They must be her family. There wasn't enough light to see them clearly.

Now, Allenthal stood in the center of the group with the lamplight shining directly into his eyes, making it difficult to see the faces in the crowd. From what he could see, they didn't look happy.

Zhandar's loud voice was easily heard, and the crowd quieted. "These strangers entered our land and were seen killing one of our people. They killed two more in the fight that followed. We must judge them, here tonight. They will have a chance to speak."

Well, at least Allenthal would get to tell his side of the story. Not that anyone would listen.

Zhandar went on. "They found Ashkan traveling alone and brutally attacked him." The crowd murmured angrily. "A party of our men saw them and rushed to aid Ashkan, but, by then, it was too late. The strangers fled, leaving two men dead and Ashkan dying." He turned to Allenthal. "Why did you kill him?"

"We didn't kill Ashkan," Allenthal said, loudly and clearly. "We were traveling, that much is true, and we saw a group of several men attacking him. We tried to defend him. They fled, leaving him to die."

The short man they'd seen earlier with Zhandar stepped forward. "Who were they? Did you see any of their faces?"

"No," Allenthal admitted. "After only a short fight, they ran."

"Your people don't travel the desert," Zhandar said. "You have no honorable reason to be here. Why did you come to Tyar? Your lie about carrying a message is preposterous. We want to know why you're really here."

Allenthal couldn't tell them the whole truth. They would never believe him. What should he say? "We spoke to Ashkan. He felt he was in danger, that someone wished him harm, and asked me to take a message to his daughter."

"Why would he give such a personal message to a riverman?" Zhandar demanded.

"There was no one else," Allenthal said.

Zhandar walked back and forth in front of them. "You're asking us to believe that you came all this way, bought camels, supplies, and journeyed into the desert, simply to deliver a message to someone you'd never met before?" The big man's eyes were wide.

When he said it like that, of course it sounded ridiculous. Allenthal shook himself internally. Maybe he had made a serious mistake. Even though today was the first time he'd actually met

Kyjia, he'd seen her before. He already felt he knew her. They were all staring, waiting for his answer. "Yes. I promised Ashkan I would."

"And what message could be so important?" Zhandar demanded. He turned to Kyjia. "Lady Kyjia, do you want to hear his message?"

"No," she responded, her expression stiff, her voice angry. "I've never seen these men before you brought them here. I don't want to hear anything from them."

So much for sympathy from her.

The short man stepped forward again. He looked around at the crowd and then pointed to Allenthal and Kylith. "We saw these two outlanders when I, and several others, were riding. They attacked Ashkan. They are both skilled fighters, and what chance would a simple merchant have against two of them? They killed two of our guards when we tried to intervene. That one," he pointed at Allenthal, "had a knife in his hand." His eyes darted to Kyjia and her family, and he paused as if he couldn't bear to discuss the details in front of them. "When we got to Ashkan, it was too late."

"No!" Allenthal protested. "That is not what happened. We tried to help him."

For several moments, confusion covered the crowd as everyone spoke at once. "Quiet!" Zhandar's voice boomed out over the noise, and silence fell. "Three men have been killed," he said, bowing his head. "Justice must be done. Is there anyone here who has anything else to say?" He looked toward Kyjia and her family, but they didn't speak.

"Very well," Zhandar said. "Our laws are simple but clear. We can't let this deed go unpunished. These men will be taken to the rock. We will allow the desert to claim them."

Allenthal's stomach clenched, and he looked desperately toward Kyjia. Back in the tent, he'd told her the absolute truth. He'd given her the only real piece of evidence he had, and she hadn't believed him. In her mind, they were guilty. She wasn't going to try to stop the others from harming them. They were in serious trouble.

As soon as the decision had been made, Zhandar's men seized them, dragging them away from the camp. Hands held Allenthal from all sides, and though he struggled, he couldn't escape. After a short walk, they came to a ridge of rock. The slope was gentle, and they all walked up it, emerging onto a flat shelf of rock.

They cut the ropes binding his hands and stripped off his cloak and tunic. He knocked several of them back, but there were too many. It was too late now to decide to fight. They wrestled him to the ground and pulled his arms over his head, trying them to a boulder. They pulled off his boots, tying his ankles to another point, leaving him lying full length against the unyielding stone.

Zhandar knelt beside him, checking carefully that all his bonds held him securely. "We give you to the desert. This land is cruel, and what it takes, it keeps. It will kill you soon enough. None of our people will return to this place. If the sun doesn't kill you tomorrow, by nightfall, the azarim will find you, and they will. You should never have come to Tyar." He got back to his feet.

Was Kyjia here? Was she part of this crowd who wished them to suffer and die? Allenthal couldn't spot her. Zhandar deliberately turned his back on them. Slowly, they all went away, leaving the strangers in dark and silence.

They lay alone on the rock. Allenthal turned his head to see Kylith bound exactly as he was. "Are you hurt?"

"No," Kylith growled, "but I wish I was. I'd rather die fighting than like this. We should have..." His voice trailed off.

They should have made a good fight of it back when they still had a chance of escaping. Giving themselves up had been Allenthal's decision.

Kylith struggled against the ties, his muscles bunching and straining against the restraints. "Help me find a way to get free before the sun comes up."

Both of them jerked and pulled at the ropes until the raw skin of their wrists and ankles bled. While the lines loosened enough to make them marginally more comfortable, they failed to escape.

The cool hours of darkness passed all too quickly. The first light of dawn found them still struggling to free themselves. Allenthal paused and lay still, turning to his friend. "My choices got us killed, Kylith."

"No one is keeping score. And we're not dead yet," Kylith protested. "Maybe we'll still find a way out."

When the sun rose, the heat quickly intensified, burning against their exposed skin. "We'll be nicely roasted by tonight," Allenthal said. "I'm sure the lizards will enjoy their meal."

"We'll get out before that happens," Kylith insisted stubbornly.

Under the harsh sun, the rock heated beneath them, gathering the rays until Allenthal felt like he was being fried on one side and baked on the other. Desperately, he wished for shade or any other source of relief. For some time, sweat rolled off his body. Then, the last of his sweat burned away, leaving behind a dry, deadly heat.

As he blinked into the blazing sun, he began to see shapes and colors moving. In the brutal heat, he was losing his mind. Despite Kylith's optimism, they weren't getting away, and they wouldn't last the day like this. In his mind, he saw his father and other family members back home. What would his family do when he didn't come back? What would the Seven Rivers do with no heir?

Then, he saw Kyjia. In his dream, she lowered the cloth to reveal her face, full lips, and a delicate chin. No anger remained in her expression, and she smiled at him. The warmth in her heavy-lashed dark eyes caused a strange feeling in his middle. She was beautiful.

Too bad the real Kyjia wanted him dead.

CHAPTER 10

KYJIA

KYJIA SAT IN HER favorite spot at the crest of the dune, hiding in a tiny scrap of shade beside a rock. Overhead, the harsh sun burned. Had she done the right thing? Last night, she could have tried to speak up for the strangers. But the mystic Jaro had actually seen them kill her father. There was no reason to doubt, was there?

Meeting the stranger face-to-face, it had been hard not to believe him. He had looked her straight in the eye and told her that he hadn't killed her father. Some part of her wanted to believe him, but he had come from far away, from the river country, and how could she trust him? They said he was a skilled fighter. She had no way of knowing if he was simply a skilled liar as well.

She took out the torn scrap of fabric. Had her father really held it in his hand as he died? She didn't know if anything the stranger said was true. Either way, it made her feel a little closer to her father. She knew of only one reason anyone would want to kill him. He hadn't been rich or powerful, only a merchant trying to earn enough for his family to survive. Had someone discovered the secret of the tablet? If they had, why wouldn't they leave him alive to demand he tell them where it was?

Her father had entrusted the sacred artifact to her before he left. He would no longer have known exactly where it was. The whole thing made no sense. Why would two young strangers enter the desert and kill him? The tablet belonged to Tyar. It wasn't something another nation would value, except for a bit of gold, much more easily obtained elsewhere. If they were skilled with weapons, maybe someone had hired them to do it.

"I thought I might find you here." Zhandar's voice broke into her thoughts.

Quickly, she tucked the bit of fabric out of sight.

He sat down beside her. "You've had such a difficult time. I know it doesn't ease the grief, but you must feel a little satisfaction knowing that his murderers didn't escape."

No. She felt no satisfaction. The pain in her heart remained sharp and fresh. Suddenly, it was all too much, and she realized, horrified, that she was crying. Her father was never coming back.

Without expressing any judgment, Zhandar put his arm around her and pulled her close. The kind gesture dissolved what little remained of her control.

"I'm sorry," she gasped, fighting to quell the sobs that wracked her body.

"You don't have to apologize," he murmured. "You are not alone. It will be all right."

How long had it been since anyone had offered her such comfort? He had already done so much for them. She leaned against his shoulder and cried. He didn't try to stop her. Instead, he let her cry, rubbing his hand lightly along her back.

After a time, her sobs stilled, and the sun had grown even hotter, burning down on the top of the dune. "Are you ready to go back?" he asked. "I'll get you some water, and you can rest."

He stood, offering his hand to assist her to her feet. She took it, and he didn't release it as they walked back to camp. They were nearly to the door of her tent when Jaro appeared. "Lord Zhandar." He bowed. "I must speak with you."

"Very well," Zhandar replied. He turned to look down at Kyjia, brushing a tear from her cheek. "Will you be all right now?"

"Yes, thank you," she replied. "I'll do as you suggest and get some rest."

He smiled slightly and nodded, releasing her hand to turn toward Jaro.

Kyjia's eyes flew back to the mystic as he put a hand on Zhandar's shoulder. The hem of his tunic was torn. All her muscles tightened at once. The two men walked slowly away from her, already deep in conversation. She took a few steps after them, her eyes examining the damaged garment. A small scrap of cloth had been torn away. The shape and pattern matched exactly.

Barely able to draw a breath, she stumbled back toward the tent, her whole body numb with shock. Her fingers found the small scrap of fabric in her pocket and clenched around it. The riverman hadn't been lying, and she'd left him to die without even trying to help.

She entered the tent and found Terjan alone inside. He jumped up immediately. "What is it?"

"I've been so wrong." She kept her voice low so no one would overhear, but she felt like shouting. She held out the piece of cloth and realized her hands were shaking. "The riverman gave me this. He said father gave it to him, that he tore it from the man who killed him. I just saw a tunic with a piece torn off, and they match exactly."

Her brother came near and put a hand on her arm. "Who?"

"Jaro. Zhandar's advisor, the mystic."

Terjan's eyes opened wide. "How? Why?"

"We'll find out later," Kyjia interrupted. "There's no time now. We left those men to die, and I have to help them."

"I'll come," Terjan said.

Kyjia couldn't help feeling concerned. "Will you be all right?" He still wore bandages over the healing wound on his back.

"I can do it," he insisted.

With forced casualness, they strolled through the camp, until one at a time, they slipped behind one of the wagons and out of camp to hide between the stones. They paused, panting. "Did anyone follow us?" Terjan asked.

Kyjia peeked around the edge of the rock. "I don't think so. Most of them are resting in the shade." For good reason; the sun was high and blazing down. This was the hottest part of the day. Moving stealthily through the rocks, they hurried away.

They found the ridge of rock where they had left the men. No one was in sight now. Kyjia climbed up the rock until she reached the top. The two men remained where Zhandar had left them. Neither of them had managed to get free, though from the dried blood on their wrists and ankles, they had tried. Neither of them moved now. Was she too late?

Kneeling beside one of them, she looked down at the face of the man who had given her the scrap of cloth. He had called her by name, insisting he hadn't killed her father. She should have believed him. Putting her fingers to his neck below his jaw, she still felt a faint pulse. Pulling out a waterskin, she spread the liquid over his face and head, drizzling a small amount on his cracked lips and dry mouth.

Taking out her knife, she began sawing at the bindings. Terjan did the same for the other man. It felt like it took hours to part the tough fibers, and when they finally came loose, his arms fell limply to the rock.

She moved to his feet. When they were free too, she shook him, trying to rouse him. He didn't respond at all, his head lolling to one side. She tried to lift him, but his dead weight yielded only a little. "Terjan!"

He came to help. With their combined efforts, they dragged the unconscious man into a narrow patch of shade in the shadow of a stone.

"Where can we take them?" Kyjia asked.

"I saw a hollow down at the base of the ridge," Terjan said. "Maybe even a small cave. At least they'd be out of the sun there."

Leaving one man in the slight shade of the rock, they dragged the other down the ridge. "Why are they so heavy?" Terjan groaned. "They must have plenty of everything in their land if all of them grow so big."

They were sweating and panting by the time they dragged the unconscious man into the opening. The cave was deeper than it had looked at first. It was also much cooler inside, and there was even a tiny bit of moisture at the back.

Kyjia was already tired and hot, but they had to do it again. Back up the slope they went, to drag the second man to rest beside his friend. They drizzled more of the precious water over the men's parched lips.

Kneeling beside one of them, Kyjia dripped a little of the water onto his hot forehead, spreading the droplets out. She took the end of her head cloth and moistened it, trying to cool his face and head. The back of the cave held a tiny seep, not even enough to pool, but some of the rocks were wet and cool. Kyjia gathered several of them and stacked them against the man's hot skin.

She dripped a little more water into his mouth, as much as she dared while he was unaware. Aside from the sunburn, his skin was pale, nearly as white as her own. Her complexion was an oddity, a shocking spectacle to the rest of her olive-skinned people. Even

Terjan, though they looked quite a bit alike, had the usual brown skin of Tyar. Her mother had passed her pale skin to her. Every time she'd asked about it as a child, her mother had simply told her it was a family trait and that her grandmother had been the same way. "Why?" But her mother had never been able to answer that.

These men both had fair skin, their hands and faces tanned, but where their bodies were usually covered, the brutal sun had left their skin red and blistered. She'd never even met anyone from the river country before. Why had they come to the desert? They were both young. The taller one, the one who had given her the fabric, looked only a few years older than her. The other, who Terjan was tending now, was shorter, broader, and a little older. Though his hair was dark, she'd seen earlier that he had strange gray eyes.

The man who had given her the cloth had brown eyes. She'd seen them when they'd spoken the night before. Now she knew that he hadn't been lying. She should have believed him before Zhandar had done this to him. She laid her hand on his forehead. His skin blazed with heat.

CHAPTER 11

CROWN PRINCE ALLENTHAL

ALLENTHAL'S HEAD THROBBED AS if it might explode at any moment. The hallucinations had grown worse. Maybe it was a sign that the end was near. He felt too weak to fight anymore. Around him, everything had gone dark. He couldn't even see the sun anymore. Had night fallen? Were the lizards coming out to eat them? He couldn't help but recall the grisly sight of the two bandits after the azarim had finished with them. Were he and Kylith destined to look like that by morning?

Still remembering the lizards, he started as something brushed against his forehead. Instead of pain, the touch was soft, leaving a life-giving coolness behind it. The damp cloth swept over his chest and shoulders, easing his burning skin. He blinked, seeing only dim light. The dream remained with him. He saw Kyjia with her face uncovered and the anger gone from her eyes. He stared up at her, mesmerized. It was the first time he'd really gotten a good look at her when she wasn't angry, and she was breathtaking. Heavy lashes surrounded her beautiful dark eyes. Her skin was pale, even lighter than his own. He'd always been told the desert folk were dark complexioned. Still, in his vision he'd noticed her pale skin when he'd seen her bare back.

How odd that he should see her when he was about to die of heat under the burning desert sun. "You're so beautiful," he murmured. At least he could die thinking of her. He had given everything to try and help her. Still, he'd failed. Perhaps that moment in the cave was still ahead for her, and he wouldn't be there to stop it. Maybe he wouldn't have been able to stop it anyway.

"Why would you say that?" she asked, looking down at him, her dark brows drawn together. "Have you lost your mind from the heat?"

Allenthal thought he had. He nodded slightly.

She dribbled a few drops of liquid onto his cracked lips and parched mouth. He swallowed, opening his mouth to plead for more. Another bit of water entered his mouth, cooling his dry tongue. "More, please," he begged, opening his mouth.

She lifted his head and held the mouth of a water skin against his lips. He drank desperately, trying to pull the life-sustaining liquid into his dehydrated body as quickly as possible. After a time, the water disappeared, and his head rested back on the stone.

Allenthal blinked, opening his eyes all the way to look around himself. Kyjia was still there, bending over him. Was she real? Was he still hallucinating? He lifted a shaking hand to circle her wrist. Expecting not to feel anything, surprise flooded through him as he felt a real flesh-and-blood person. Her eyes widened at his touch, and she stared at him warily, as if trying to decide if he were dangerous.

"You're real," he muttered, dropping his hand. "I thought I was dreaming."

"No." Her voice was smooth and calm.

Something must have happened to get her to change her mind. Earlier, she'd wanted him dead. She'd said nothing as they condemned him and Kylith to death. Now, she was here, helping him.

"Kyjia," he whispered.

She looked down at him, holding the waterskin. "Are you ready for another drink?"

He nodded eagerly.

She cradled his head, lifting him again so he could drink. When he finished and lay back, she dampened a cloth and held it against his throbbing forehead. The coolness brought a measure of relief.

"Thank you."

She brushed the cloth over his face and then his shoulders and body. The sensation of cool and damp felt wonderful.

"What happened?" His body and throbbing head were gradually cooling, allowing Allenthal to think more clearly. He realized now that they were inside a cave. It was still day outside with the vicious sun beating down on the sand. He turned his head to one side to see Kylith lying nearby, a young man helping him drink.

Allenthal's voice sounded scratchy. "How did we get off the rock?"

"My brother and I brought you here. This cave lies at the base of the ridge." Her eyes held sorrow he had not seen before. "I'm sorry I didn't believe you yesterday. But I found the man with a piece ripped from the hem of his tunic. When I saw it, I knew you were telling the truth, that you didn't kill my father."

Allenthal shook his head. "I'm sorry we didn't get there in time to save him. Do you know why they might want him gone?"

She looked away, shaking her head.

The men who ambushed him had been looking for the tablet. They had searched Ashkan, and demanded that he tell them where it was, right before Allenthal and Kylith had attacked, trying to stop them. The men who had plotted to kill him intended to make sure he could never try to claim the throne. They had killed him rather than allow him to be rescued. But they still wanted the tablet, and if they were willing to murder for it, no wonder Kyjia didn't want to talk about it. Either she, the boy, or their mother must know where it is. They were all in danger.

"Don't trust any of them," Allenthal murmured. "They didn't get what they wanted from Ashkan. They will try again. Your family is in danger."

She gripped his shoulder. "How do you know that?" Her piercing eyes bored into his. "How do you know my name, my family? You're not from Tyar. Why should you care about any of this?"

That was a long story. But she deserved some explanation. He drew in a breath, trying to gather his scattered thoughts to explain. "I came from the land of Seven Rivers. I received a... message that you were in trouble. My father sent us to try and help you."

Her eyes widened in incredulity. "Why would you travel so far, risk yourself, risk everything, to help someone you don't even know?"

Because the Goddess had asked him to. But how to better explain? "I serve the Goddess Namradill. She is the guardian of my homeland. She is the one who sent me to find the king of Tyar and his family. They are connected to Karineth, the god of the desert. We think they hear His voice, as we hear Namradill's."

All expression and color had drained from her face. "Then you knew who my father really was." Her gaze fixed on him. "You knew he should have been king of Tyar?"

Allenthal nodded. "I'm very sorry I failed you. But you must know that if they hunted him to try and find the tablet, they will come after you next."

She pressed her fingers over his lips to stop his words. "You must never speak of it again."

Wordlessly he nodded.

She removed her hand. "It is hidden. No one must know about it."

"I'm sorry," he answered. "We heard them asking him where it was. Why else would your father be a target?"

He could see it in her eyes. She already knew that or suspected it. There was no other logical reason for a poor merchant to be pursued. Ashkan must have suspected it too. Back in Niaz, he'd been suspicious of them, as if he already feared someone was hunting him. He must have given the tablet to someone for safekeeping: one of the three people he loved and trusted.

After giving Kylith another drink of water, the young man got to his feet and disappeared out of the cave mouth. He returned a short while later, his arms full of their clothes and boots. He set them in a pile in the middle of the floor.

"Thank you, Terjan," Kyjia said. "Please go back to camp, and try to make it look like neither of us is gone."

The young man nodded, slipping soundlessly away.

Turning back to Allenthal, Kyjia laid a cool hand across his forehead. "How are you feeling now?"

Though his head still pounded, the deadly heat of his body gradually eased. He lifted one side of his mouth in half a smile. "Much better than I would be out there." He nodded toward the top of the cave. "You saved our lives. Thank you."

She nodded. "I'm sorry I didn't help sooner. I should have believed what you told me the first time." She poured more water into the cloth and held it against his forehead. After a moment, she added more water and applied it to his arms and chest.

He must be recovering, because in addition to the cool sensation of the cloth, now he noticed the soft brush of her fingers against his skin. A shiver ran through him.

She took his hand, lifting it. With great care, she slid her knife between the remaining bindings and his torn skin. She cut through it, tossing away the cut ends. Gently, she cleaned the damaged skin of his wrist. When she finished, she repeated the process with his other hand before moving to work on his ankles.

He lifted his head to look at her as she worked. Her touch was soft against his skin, and he closed his eyes when she was finished, savoring the relief she had offered.

Allenthal didn't realize he'd dozed until he roused to feel her touch his shoulder. "Will you drink again?"

He nodded, attempting to sit up on his own. His whole body felt weak, his dehydrated muscles sore. She put her arms around him, and, with her aid, he managed to sit up, though moving his aching head had been a mistake. He slid himself closer to the cave wall where he could rest against it.

She smiled when she saw him upright. "Better?"

Despite the condition of his abused body, he couldn't help but return the expression. "Better." When she offered him the water, he drank deeply.

Waving off her offer of help, Kylith dragged himself up too.

"I need to return to the camp," she said. "No one must discover that I freed you. I'll leave the water here. If we can slip away without attracting notice, we'll come back after dark with food."

In a moment, she was gone.

CHAPTER 12

KYJIA

THE MESSAGE FROM ZHANDAR arrived only a few moments after Kyjia had returned to the tent she shared with her family. The chieftain wanted to have dinner with her. How could she refuse?

She washed herself and brushed and braided her hair. Her clothes, a threadbare tunic and worn pants, at least were clean. It had been a very long time since they'd had enough money to buy new clothes. These would have to do. Zhandar had asked to spend time with her, knowing that she had no possessions. He must have genuine interest in her as a person.

But he was close to Jaro. Did Zhandar realize what the mystic had done? They were old friends, and Zhandar appeared to trust him. He believed Jaro's story of the two strangers attacking Ashkan. Either Jaro had lied or Zhandar was part of the plot to destroy her father. She needed to be careful.

A sharp twist of shame gripped her. She'd been so angry at the strangers, enough that she felt justified in standing by while they were sentenced to death. It had been foolish. Someone had been trying to place the blame on the rivermen while the real killer remained hidden.

When she arrived at the entrance to Zhandar's tent, a servant pulled the flap back for her. Inside, he was seated comfortably on a pile of cushions. He rose when she entered and offered his arm. "Please join me."

They sat down, side by side. "I've been thinking about you all day," he admitted. "I confess that it disturbed me to see you cry. Are you feeling better than before?"

Heat rushed to her cheeks at the memory. She hadn't meant to break down, especially not in front of him. "Yes, Lord Zhandar. I apologize for my display."

He waved off her apology. "It's only natural, given the painful experiences you have endured lately." His eyes met hers. "I'm grateful I was able to assist and that you felt you could turn to me when you needed someone. The whole experience caused me to consider my life from a new angle."

She looked up at him. "What do you mean?"

He took a deep breath. "For most of my life, I've worked very hard to achieve my goals. The last few years, it felt like there was always one more important task ahead, gathering people, establishing trade, driving back the bandits who prowl the desert, building wells and expanding them. But having you with me reminds me that through all of my work, I have been alone." He paused and took her hand, his dark eyes meeting hers. "It made me envision a different kind of future. One where someone stayed with me, and we worked together to make Tyar great again. With the right companion at my side, we could do anything. I want our kingdom to be what it once was."

Excitement suffused his features, and he gripped her hand. "Can you imagine what it would mean to our people if we could usher in a new era of prosperity? They would have everything they need, not just scrape a bare living from the desert soil."

It sounded wonderful, of course. Too good to be true. "How do you plan to do this?"

"We think there might be a way to build a canal that would direct water here from the mountains. If we could only get more water here, we could grow crops. It would mean everything to us, food, prosperity. All I need is for our people to work together. Not everyone in Tyar sees my vision yet. It will take time—and the right partner working with me."

He looked at her when he said it. What did he actually mean by that? He wanted her help and cooperation. That was very clear. But did he envision a much closer relationship between them? She couldn't rush into anything with him.

"I want a better life for our people," she agreed. "It's hard to survive in the desert. I have always wanted more for them. For all of us."

He smiled, the expression lighting his handsome face. "Then you understand what I'm trying to accomplish here. Not everyone does."

"And what role does Jaro play in all this?" she asked, keeping her expression innocent.

"I couldn't have come this far without him," Zhandar said. "He's been by my side since I was a boy, and he's worked just as hard as I have to unite our people. He wants the same things I do. We want to see Tyar become powerful again. He's a good man who cares for our people as much as you and I do."

A servant arrived with a tray of food, setting it on the table before them. The food appeared exquisite, and all over again, Kyjia felt embarrassed by her worn tunic and scuffed boots. Zhandar had obviously given care to the preparations.

He gave no sign that her humble appearance bothered him. Instead, he smiled. "Please, eat."

It was the finest meal Kyjia had ever tasted. At the end of the evening, he lifted her hand to his lips and kissed it. "Thank you for spending time with me, Kyjia. I will count the moments until we can be together again." There was no mistaking the warmth in his eyes or the way his hand lingered against hers.

"Thank you, Lord Zhandar." She bowed to him and slipped away into the night. No matter what he wanted, she wasn't ready to move forward. Not until she knew the truth about his plans, and Jaro's.

Back in her own tent, she collected a bundle of food and as much water as she could carry. The others weren't there, so she gathered up everything and slipped out into the night. Moving silently through the tents, she made it to the edge of camp without meeting anyone. In the starlight, she slipped away through the rocks.

Staggering under the heavy water and supplies, it took longer to reach the cave than she expected. When she came to the mouth, all was silent, except for a solitary azarim that croaked at her and scurried away to disappear between the rocks. She crept to the mouth of the cave. It was dark inside, and she'd gone only a step through the opening when she ran into something.

She would have stumbled back, but a hand gripped her arm to steady her.

"I'm sorry," the riverman's voice came through the dark. "That was my fault. Are you hurt?"

Now that he was standing, he seemed so much bigger. Her nose had run directly into his bare chest. "I'm fine," she murmured awkwardly, heat rushing to her cheeks. Her eyes began to adjust to the dark inside the cave. A little starlight came in the entrance.

"Let me help you." He took one of the waterskins. "These are heavy," he said, taking another one from her shoulder. "How did you carry everything by yourself? I should have found a way to help you."

How was she supposed to answer that? She'd lived in the desert all her life, and carrying water was inevitable. His concern caused warmth to blossom inside her.

"Thank you for coming back for us today," he said. "We'd be dead by now if you hadn't."

She felt sincere gratitude behind his words. "Neither of you deserves to die for a crime you didn't commit," she said honestly. "I brought something to put on your burns."

"Thank you."

She searched by feel through her bundle, taking out a small jar and opening the lid. Her fingers dipped into the contents and smoothed a little of the gel onto his shoulder. A shock raced through her as she touched him, and she became acutely aware of the sudden intimacy of feeling his bare skin beneath her hand there in the dark.

"Here," she stepped quickly back, placing the jar in his hand.

From somewhere further back in the cave, the second riverman cleared his throat. "I'm going outside to make sure no one followed you." His quiet footsteps passed her in the dark.

Now, she was alone with the riverman. Sudden awkward silence filled the cave. What should she say to him? The spicy scent of the ointment surrounded them.

"What is this stuff?" he asked. "It helps."

"My mother makes it from kir leaves. It's very good for burns." She paused, and silence fell again. "Will you tell me your name?"

He chuckled in the darkness.

The unexpected sound was pleasant and sent a shiver running through her.

After a moment, he spoke again. "Before I do, you should know that my people, and my family in particular, have a fondness for elaborate names."

She took a step nearer to him. "Now I *am* curious."

"My name is Allenthal."

What a strange name. "Allen-?"

"Allenthal," he repeated. "If you don't want to bother with the whole thing, you can just go with Al. In fact, that would be better. It's safer if no one here knows my real name."

She wanted to ask why that was, because he didn't strike her as the kind of man who would be fleeing from the law or something like that. What reason could he have for keeping his name a secret?

"Al?" she laughed under her breath. "That's quite a difference. Thank you for telling me. I know things haven't gone well for you here in Tyar, but I appreciate your attempts to assist us, especially my father."

"I tried to help." He cleared his throat. "I hope you believe that, even though I couldn't save him."

He sounded so sad as he said it that she felt sure the weight of another failure lay heavily on him. What had it been? She wanted to know, but they barely knew each other, and it didn't seem the time to ask such a question. "You put yourself at great risk trying to help," she said. "That kind of effort is never a failure, Al."

He was silent for a long moment. "Thank you."

"You must be hungry." She knelt by the parcel of food she'd brought. "I brought food for you." In the dark, their hands brushed together as she passed him the bread and meat.

He took a bite, mumbling a thank you as he chewed. For several moments, he ate and drank. Then, he sighed. "I'm very grateful for everything you've done today. That's so much better. Kylith is right. It's not a bad idea to keep watch. Maybe you would be willing to watch with me for a while?"

She felt a sliver of warmth as he asked. "Yes."

His hand found hers in the dark, and they moved toward the entrance. Outside, there was more light, and the stars hung like points of crystal in the black heavens. On the rocks above the cave entrance, they saw the outline of his friend, dark against the sky as he sat looking out over the silent desert.

"Kylith?" Allenthal whispered.

Silently, the other man got to his feet, climbing down the rocks to face them. "There's food inside for you. And take this." He handed Kylith the jar of ointment. "It helps the burns. Go get something to eat. I will keep watch for a while."

Kylith nodded in response and headed back toward the cave.

They climbed up to the place where Kylith had been sitting. Out here, she saw a little more in the starlight. She couldn't see the blisters on his cheeks and chest, but she saw the smooth contours of his body, the hard muscle and strength of him. In the dark, he wouldn't be able to see the heat rush to her cheeks either. In the daylight, her pale skin would display her blush for anyone to see.

He held a shirt in one hand, and he pulled it over his head with only a slight hiss of pain as the fabric brushed against his burned skin.

"In the desert, we learn to hide from the sun," she said, sitting down on a wide rock. "I'm sorry for the pain I caused you."

"You saved our lives. There's no need to apologize." He sat beside her. "I'm sure leaving us to bake in the sun wasn't your idea."

Her stomach clenched at the thought of what she had almost allowed to happen to him. "No, it wasn't, but I didn't stop them. I was angry about my father."

"You have every right to be angry," he said. "But I'm glad it's no longer directed at me."

"You must think the desert is a cruel place. I'm sure things are very different in your home." She felt suddenly aware of his closeness beside her, the strength and solidness of him.

He gave a low laugh. The sound filled her, making her want to laugh too, happy and carefree.

"It's true that my homeland is very different. Sometimes, it's very cold, and even when it's warm, if you get too hot, all you have to do is jump in a lake to cool off."

"A lake?" She'd heard of them in old stories, but she'd never had the opportunity to travel the world, and she truly wondered if they were only a legend. "You mean water? So much water all gathered together? I've never seen anything like that."

He was silent for a long moment. "You've never seen a lake?"

She shook her head. "Never."

"A river?"

"You mean water flowing across the land? It flows every day? Even after the rain has passed? I've never seen one. Here in the desert, there are rumors of a hidden river flowing beneath the surface. Somewhere in the Izana Cave, there is a hidden well, and the water flows from it in three different directions. I've heard that's where the water for all the great wells comes from."

"Izana Cave? Where is that?" he asked.

"Northeast of Saarin, I think. I've never been there before."

"You've never just wanted to go for a swim?" he asked.

"What is a swim?"

"Well, I guess you'd have to find a lake or a river to find out. Swimming is moving through the water."

What an outlandish idea. She'd never heard of anyone doing that. She couldn't help but laugh at the strange image it brought up. Water was precious in Tyar, and wells were jealously guarded.

She couldn't imagine anyone jumping into one. "I would like to see more of the world someday," she said. "I'd like to see your lakes and rivers."

"You'll see them someday," he replied. "When all this trouble is over, you'll have a chance to travel. You will see the world. Imagine sunlight sparkling on the surface of the water. It's beautiful."

In her mind, she tried to picture it. They sat in silence, watching the stars glitter overhead. She reached out and took his big hand in both of hers. He didn't try to resist. "I'm glad you're not dead."

"Me too. I owe my life to you."

"You are a kind man, Allenthal," she said. "You have given everything to try to help us. If I am not asking too much of you, can you tell me about my father's last moments?"

He shifted uncomfortably beside her in the dark. "I know you loved him," he said quietly. "I wish to spare you all the details." His hand tightened around hers. "But I understand why you have to ask me. In truth, there isn't much to tell." He took a deep breath. "I climbed to the top of a ridge of rock. From there, I saw several men ambush Ashkan. He fought well, but several of them came at him from different directions. We hurried to help and tried to stop them. We fought. After a few moments, they fled. When I reached Ashkan, he was badly injured. He didn't last long after that, but he begged me to find you and help you. He thought that his own murder was a sign of danger to you and your family. I promised I would warn you. We laid him to rest in as much honor as we could."

Sorrow twisted through her, but at least she knew a little more about what had happened. "Thank you, Allenthal."

"I wish I could do more to help."

"You've already done so much," she murmured. "Zhandar's men all believe you're dead now. If our people leave someone to the desert, they will not return to the place again. This is your chance to escape. Take the provisions I brought you and the extra water and go back to Niaz. If you drink only a little each day, there should be enough. Get yourself and your friend to safety. Keep your faces covered, don't speak to anyone, and you'll be safe. Hide in the daylight, and walk at night. You'll need less water that way."

A sharp pang rushed through her at the thought of never seeing him again. She didn't want him to go, but she wanted him to be safe, and he never would be out here, especially not with the false accusation of murder.

"If any of Zhandar's men find you, they will kill you." She brought his hand to her lips and kissed it. "Stay safe, Allenthal." Releasing his hand, she climbed back down through the rocks, and slipped away into the night.

CHAPTER 13

KYJIA

I T WAS LATE WHEN Kyjia crept past the guards and into the camp, moving silently between the tents until she reached her own. Inside, her family lay on their pallets. Her mother sat up as she entered.

"Terjan told me where you went. Are they safely away?"

"They will be soon," Kyjia said. "I told them to go back to Niaz. They're good men, and I believe them when they say they tried to help father."

Terjan sat up as well. They huddled together into a small, tight circle.

"What are we going to do?" Kyjia asked.

Her mother's arm came around her shoulders, and Terjan's hand gripped hers. "We're in serious trouble, no matter which way we go now," he said.

Their mother pulled them close. "I'm sorry, dear ones. Your father and I always did what we could to keep you hidden, to keep our secrets so you could live a normal life. I'm afraid that's impossible now. We have guarded the secret of your lineage all your lives. Now, someone has discovered who we are. None of us is safe until we find out who it is and what they want."

"It's pretty clear that they intend to find the tablet," Kyjia said. "Once they have it, they'll try to use it to gain more power. We should get as far away from Jaro as we can."

They were silent for a moment. Their mother broke it. "That would be my first impulse as well," she admitted. "But if we go another way now, we'll just have to run, waiting for them to pursue us. I don't know where we could go to find safety. So far, Zhandar has helped us."

"I don't think he realizes everything Jaro has done," Kyjia said. "If we stay with them for a time, maybe we will have a chance to find out."

If they stayed with Zhandar's party, Jaro wouldn't be far away, and that was dangerous. Still, it wouldn't be wise to leave the caravan here in the middle of the desert. They had already experienced the dangers of traveling alone. They needed to remain under Zhandar's protection.

"We need his help to reach Saarin safely. At least when we get there, we will have more options," Kyjia said. "We can't afford to completely trust Zhandar, but we need to stay near enough to find more proof that Jaro killed Father, and we need to discover why."

The next day, Zhandar and all his people broke camp, preparing to resume their journey to Saarin. Everything was packed up and loaded into wagons and onto camels. Zhandar invited Kyjia and her family to ride on horseback beside him. Kyjia had ridden camels all her life, but she'd never handled a horse before. With a smile, Zhandar explained the basics.

He brought a horse, saddled and ready. Once Kyjia had mounted, he showed her how to hold the reins and direct the animal. "Good," he praised her, as she rode in a small circle. "You have a natural talent."

Kyjia doubted that was actually true, but she appreciated the compliment. In a surprisingly short time, nothing remained of the camp but empty sand, and the caravan moved into the desert. They rose before dawn each morning and traveled for a few hours. During the worst of the day's heat, they stopped to rest and shelter from the sun, resuming their journey late in the afternoon as the sun began to sink.

On the evening of the sixth day, they came over a rise in the land. Kyjia gasped at the view. The shallow, brown valley before them held a beautiful city built of white stone. A line of pale stones marked the path of an ancient riverbed. Water had once flowed through this valley. Any sign of moisture was long gone, leaving only bare stone, sand, and dust.

Zhandar paused beside her, pointing toward the city. "Kallah," he said, shading his eyes with his hand to gaze across the distance. "Once, it was the royal city of the king of Tyar. Before the river dried up, this valley was filled with fields and gardens."

"I've heard stories about it," Kyjia said. "I've never seen it myself before." She stared at the beautiful city, silent and still in the shimmering heat.

While the sun sank, they rode nearer. As the stars came out, the caravan stopped to make camp just outside the ancient walls. Dismounting, Zhandar offered Kyjia his hand. "Would you like a closer look at the city?"

She couldn't deny she was curious. So, as the others cared for the animals and made camp, she took his hand, and they walked past the ruined gates into the ancient streets. Some of the buildings remained nearly intact, while others had crumbled to rubble. Zhandar led her down what must once have been a magnificent thoroughfare. Now, only the soft sounds of their footfalls and the whisper of sand against stone broke the silence.

Tyar must have been a great nation once. Looking at the beautiful architecture of the city, Kyjia understood Zhandar's passion to restore what had once been.

"Does anyone still live here?" she asked, as they walked along the utterly silent streets with the soft sound of their footfalls echoing in the stillness.

He shook his head. "No. There is no more water."

Only the ghosts of the past remained here.

They climbed a long flight of stairs and up a street with a steep incline, coming out in a flat space that allowed them to look out over the rest of the city. Beside her, Zhandar pointed to a circular building. "That's the temple of Karineth, right in the center of the city."

Tall columns stood at its outer edge. It was a beautiful building. Surely their ancestors wouldn't have gone to all the effort of building a temple to a god who wasn't real. "He wasn't always asleep, was He?" Kyjia asked suddenly. "We've all heard the stories, but do you believe Divine Karineth will really wake and help us?"

Zhandar was silent for a long moment. "I believe He will."

He sounded very sure of it.

Kyjia looked out at the old temple. "We've waited for such a long time, but if the prophecy is true, then the time for Him to awake is soon. It's time for a new ruler who will lead the people and cause water to flow in the desert sand."

That seemed impossible. Kyjia had never seen that much water in her life. There might be rivers far away, but not in Tyar. Not anymore. She turned away from the view of the temple, the last rays of the sunset illuminating the white stone.

They came to the wide steps of the royal palace. Kyjia's dusty boots looked out of place against the smooth white stone. The roof of the great room had fallen long ago, leaving only the evening sky above them as they walked slowly down the long hall. A row of tall window openings looked out. The glass was long gone.

Perhaps these windows had once looked out onto a valley filled with growing things. Where had Karineth been while His land dried up and His people scattered?

"It's a sad sight." Zhandar stood behind her and placed one hand on her shoulder.

The contact was a symbol of their growing closeness. Kyjia wasn't sure she felt ready. It was clear that Zhandar wanted more than friendship from her. Was she willing to give it? She wanted time to consider.

She nodded slowly. "I understand why you want to fix this. I do too."

He smiled. "I'm so glad you understand. I know it must seem like a lost cause, but I believe it can be done." He paused, taking in a breath. "We talked before about my vision for Tyar. Do you think you might be willing to help me?"

"I'll try," she agreed. "I love Tyar too, and our people."

The light faded. Out beyond the edge of the city, the last rays of the sun disappeared.

Zhandar looked down at her and smiled. "Are you ready to go back now?"

They turned away from the view and walked back through the abandoned palace. This was where the king had once lived. Kyjia had never even tried to imagine her father as a king before. Now she looked back along the room to the place where a throne would have sat. What would it have been like to see him there, in power and prosperity?

The last king had been her ancestor, but there was nothing here now. Her father was dead, and she couldn't imagine a king returning to this desolate place.

Outside the palace, the city looked different in the gathering darkness. The ghosts of what had once been felt more real in the dark. Every breath of wind sounded like a whispering voice.

Kyjia gasped as two glowing orbs appeared in the dark between the buildings, down one of the deserted streets. Azarim. "I hate how their eyes glow in the dark."

Zhandar found her hand and gripped it. They hurried back through the streets. Ahead of them, three more sets of eyes shone out, this time blocking their route out of the city.

They paused, watching warily as the creatures hissed, creeping nearer. Kyjia drew her knife and Zhandar drew his sword. One of the lizards sprang forward. With a powerful stroke from his curved blade, Zhandar sliced its head off. Another azarim came a moment later, and he struck it down as well. The third must have fled, for the eyes disappeared and did not return.

Everything grew quiet again. Drawing in a breath, Kyjia realized she was clutching Zhandar's arm. "I'm sorry," she said, embarrassed, loosening her grip. "I hate them." She shivered.

"You're wise to be cautious around them," he said. "They'll eat anything that lies still for too long. One of my men got bitten once. By the time we found him..." His voice trailed off, as if deciding the story was better left untold.

Kyjia shivered again, swallowing hard as her stomach turned over uneasily. The images her mind brought up weren't pretty.

Zhandar put his arm around her. "I'm sorry. I shouldn't have said that."

A few moments later, they came back out into the light and bustle of the camp, and the eerie feeling dissipated.

CHAPTER 14

KYJIA

KYJIA WATCHED A GROUP of men moving at the edge of the camp. It had been more a feeling than a sound that had disturbed her sleep a few moments ago. Slipping out of her blanket, she crept to where Terjan slept and woke him. She put a finger to his mouth, warning him to stay silent.

"Zhandar and Jaro are leaving camp," she whispered. "They're headed into the old city."

Terjan nodded, immediately understanding. He buckled his knife around his waist. Together, they crept silently through the camp. Zhandar and the others carried several torches and had a group of guards with them. What could they be doing in an abandoned city in the middle of the night? Kyjia intended to find out.

With silent steps, Kyjia and Terjan followed, taking care to stay outside the light of the torches. The old city lay silent and empty, eerie in the moonlight. They walked a long way, following as Zhandar and Jaro went down through the old buildings toward a dark corner of the city. The light of their torches vanished suddenly.

Beside her, Terjan gripped her arm as they came to the edge of a wide depression. Before them, the ground fell away sharply. A stone staircase led steeply down. The other men climbed steadily downward. Kyjia watched as they arrived at the level ground below and walked through a narrow passageway.

Moving carefully in the dark, Kyjia felt her way down the stairs, making sure each step was secure. At her side, Terjan did the same. When they finally reached the bottom, nothing else could be seen. Feeling their way along the passageway, they moved forward.

They emerged from the end of the passage into a circular space. Tall stones stood, apparently at random, blocking the sound of distant voices. Slipping forward, Kyjia hid behind the nearest stone. The guards with their torches stood in the center of the space, surrounding a mysterious building with a black door. It looked like a shrine or a crypt. The structure appeared more intact than the rest of the city.

Terjan stood beside her, watching.

Jaro walked forward to face the strange door, placing his hand flat against the surface.

They were too far away to hear what the men were saying. Kyjia exchanged a glance with her brother and then dashed forward into the shadow of another standing stone.

The ancient hinges protested as the door swung slowly inward. "Wait here," Jaro ordered the others.

Zhandar's tall form stood beside him. "You will go in alone?" He didn't sound happy about it.

Jaro turned toward him. "We are about to receive a vital part of the power we need to save Tyar. Are you still here to support me?"

Power? What power did Jaro mean?

For a long moment, the two men faced each other silently.

"I will support you," Zhandar finally answered.

"Good." Jaro nodded, turning back toward the door. "I must complete the next step alone. It won't take long. Wait here for me."

He turned to enter the doorway. The light of his torch faded as he walked further inside. After a moment, only blackness remained.

Kyjia and Terjan stood watching, hardly daring to breathe. The moments stretched as they waited. Zhandar remained where he was, his guards beside him.

Several times, Kyjia thought she heard voices from inside, but she couldn't make out any words. Was there another voice inside? In the doorway, she saw a flicker of green light, very different from the warm orange glow of a torch.

As they waited, the time grew longer. Zhandar shifted his feet. Beside him, his guards waited silently for his orders.

Finally, a glow of green light approached the doorway from the inside. Moving very slowly, Jaro came back out into the light. He no longer held the torch. Instead, his hands were clasped around something that glowed green between his fingers.

Zhandar stepped forward to help his friend. Jaro moved stiffly as if he were injured. "Are you all right?" Zhandar asked.

Jaro stood still, looking up at him. "It is done. We have obtained power which was out of our reach before now." He looked down at the glowing object in his hands. "This is a rhan stone, a rare crystal imbued with power."

"But what is it? How—"

Jaro waived his questions aside. "Now is not the time for questions. We have a great work to do together, you and I. The fate of our nation is at stake, and we must work together. Everything depends on your loyalty. Are you with me?"

Zhandar met his gaze. "I am with you." His voice sounded confident.

Jaro nodded. "Good. We have placed a great deal of faith in each other. We will succeed or fail together. You must never forget that. Our path to glory will be a difficult one, and you must be prepared. There will be sacrifices to be made along the way. Are you ready to make them?"

Zhandar nodded. "I will do what I must for my people and my kingdom."

"Good," Jaro said. "Then we are ready to leave this place. There is much to be done."

Gathering the guards around them, they headed toward the stairs. Still and silent in the dark shadows, Kyjia watched them pass.

She waited until everything was quiet before she and Terjan made their silent way back through the city to their camp. Only a single azarim came forward to confront them. Terjan threw a fist sized rock at it, striking a solid blow. With an angry hiss, the lizard vanished.

CHAPTER 15

CROWN PRINCE ALLENTHAL

BEFORE THEY LEFT THE cave, Allenthal and Kylith used a layer of dust to darken their skin. As long as they kept their faces covered it would help them blend in. They practiced imitating the accent of the desert people when they spoke. It would be essential to hide the fact they had come from outside. Traveling at night should also help. They shouldered their packs and walked away into the gathering darkness.

Kyjia had told Allenthal to go home to his own land, but he couldn't do it. All his instincts told him this wasn't finished yet, and he couldn't leave it that way. So, they followed the tracks of the caravan deeper into the desert.

For several days, they hadn't seen anyone up close. Tonight, they saw a few lights behind them. "Looks like another caravan. Should we stop and let them pass?" Allenthal asked, peering into the dim light.

"They aren't very close yet," Kylith said. "We can keep going for a while."

They hurried on in the moonlight, only to see their path blocked by a group of men in the ragged clothes of bandits. "Well, I don't know about you," Kylith growled, glancing over at

Allenthal, "but, this time, I won't wait and see what they do. If they attack me, I'm going to fight back. Finding myself tied to a rock and left to bake in the sun is not an experience I want to repeat."

Allenthal didn't hesitate before answering. "Agreed."

They didn't try to run. The men had already seen them, and there wasn't any place to go at the moment. They walked slowly up to face them.

"What do you want?" Kylith growled, in his best imitation of a desert dweller.

The leader of the bandits looked him up and down, assessing Kylith's height and size. He was tall himself, and while not heavily built, he moved with a fluid grace that hinted he might be a talented fighter. "There's a toll to pass this way. Pay it quickly, and you can be on your way."

They'd had money when they left home but no longer. Zhandar's men had cleaned out the last of their reserves.

"We are traveling in search of work," Kylith said. "We don't have any money."

"Search them," the man ordered.

"Don't," Kylith replied, his tone menacing. The man hesitated.

"Now!" the bandit in charge ordered.

Kylith dropped his pack to the ground, and Allenthal did the same. When the first bandit stepped into his reach, Kylith punched him. The blow landed hard, and the man sank to the ground. Kylith immediately bent to grab the weapons from the fallen man's belt. He drew a scimitar.

Another of the men drew his sword and charged forward. Kylith raised his blade to block the attack. After a short exchange, the bandit was on the ground gripping a wound in his leg. Kylith picked up his fallen sword and tossed it to Allenthal.

For a long moment, they faced the bandits. Kylith stared directly at the leader of the bandits. "If I fight you, man to man, will that pay your toll? Just you and I, in a fair fight. No one interferes. If I win, the rest of you will allow us to pass. If you win, you can do as you like with us."

For a moment silence fell. The bandit leader laughed. He pulled down the cloth covering his face. The moonlight revealed a brutal scar running across his cheek and nose. "Do you know who I am?"

Kylith took a step forward, holding his blade ready. "No idea."

The bandit laughed. "I thought not. No one who knew who I was would dare to challenge me. I am Hakkir. Do you still want to fight me?"

Kylith didn't move a muscle. "I've never heard of you."

The bandit drew his own blade and advanced. His men stepped back to allow them to fight. Allenthal did the same. Hopefully Kylith knew what he was doing. For a moment, all was still except for the hiss of the night wind against the sand.

Hakkir stood confidently, his blade held ready, waiting for Kylith to make the first move. Slowly, they circled each other, each watching his opponent, learning his movements. Kylith moved forward in a sudden attack, and their blades crashed together, the sound ringing out in the quiet night. Hakkir followed with his own attack, and the battle became a deadly dance, back and forth. Kylith moved with practiced grace, his every movement calculated and precise.

The white moonlight glinted on their blades as they attacked and parried. Hakkir cut through his opponent's defenses, and his blade sliced into Kylith's arm. Kylith made no outcry. Instead, he took full advantage of the moment when his opponent was over-extended. His blade cut into Hakkir's leg.

The bandit shouted in fury. The battle went on. Both men were breathing hard now, and sweat glistened on their faces. Kylith increased the pace of his blows, and Hakkir was forced to match him, his steps slowing after the injury to his leg.

Kylith smiled, his teeth white in the dim light. "Someone should have challenged you a long time ago."

His voice remained cool and even, not betraying a trace of emotion. Hakkir had less control of his temper. He shouted in rage, attacking ferociously.

Kylith had trained for years, and he knew better than to let anger interfere with a fight. His movements remained tightly controlled, while Hakkir's motions had lost much of the grace he had begun with. He stared at Kylith.

"I'll kill you," he snarled. "No one insults me. You're going to die. Or maybe I won't quite kill you. I'll leave you alive for the azarim to finish."

His words didn't appear to affect Kylith. They battled on. Hakkir grew angrier and more desperate. Kylith broke through his defenses to cut him three more times. The bandit screamed in rage and lunged toward his foe.

Kylith was ready. With a quick stroke, he knocked Hakkir's weapon from his hand and plunged his blade into the bandit's heart.

"No! No one beats me." Hakkir's voice faded quickly. A trail of blood ran from his mouth. Slowly, he crumpled. Kylith jerked the blade free of his body and held it ready, facing the rest of the bandits.

They didn't honor their leader's agreement to let Allenthal and Kylith pass. Yelling, they attacked in a rush. Allenthal leapt forward to stand with his friend. Metal clashed against metal, the moonlight glinting on steel. Allenthal and Kylith stood back-to-back, defending themselves as the bandits rushed them. For several moments, all was noise, motion, and confusion. Their attackers were poorly trained, none of them matching their leader's skill with a blade. Several of them went down quickly.

All at once, the survivors fled, disappearing into the night.

A sudden flash of lantern light illuminated them and several bandits lying on the ground. The large caravan had come up behind them.

"What happened?" a man on a camel asked.

"Bandits," Kylith explained. "They attacked us."

The man surveyed the scene, taking in the groaning men on the ground. "All those men attacked the two of you?"

Kylith shrugged, nodding out toward the dark desert. "The rest of them ran."

The man's eyebrows shot up. "From the two of you?" He dismounted, walking through the fallen bandits and looking down at them. He came to their leader, staring in surprise at his blank eyes. "It's Hakkir."

Another man rode forward. He had a wide, friendly face and a gray beard. "I am Raz Abbas, Chieftain of Crimson Sands. We are journeying to Saarin. Who are you?"

Kylith turned to face him. "Just two weary travelers looking for work."

Raz Abbas looked them up and down and smiled. He directed his camel to sit, slid out of the saddle and walked over to stand by his friend who still stared down at the dead bandit leader.

"Is it true?" He bent to one knee to examine the fallen bandit more closely. "By Karineth's beard!" His eyes widened. "It *is* Hakkir. He's been robbing and killing all over this desert for twenty years, and no one ever managed to beat him. Which one of you did this?"

Kylith stepped forward, the scimitar still in his hand. "I did."

Raz Abbas got to his feet and went to face Kylith. The short, round man barely came up to Kylith's chin, but he grinned, ignoring the sword, and clasped Kylith's arm. "I wish I could have seen it. Was it a good fight?"

Finally convinced that the new arrivals weren't going to attack, Kylith lowered his weapon. "Good for me. Not for him."

Raz Abbas laughed heartily. "So I see. You have my admiration, friend. You said you're looking for work? I need two more guards, if you're interested?"

Allenthal looked at Kylith. Traveling with a caravan would be a much better way to reach their destination, as long as no one asked too many questions. "We'll take it," Kylith said.

"Good!" Raz Abbas exclaimed. "Your names?"

"I'm Al," Allenthal said.

"Kylith."

"Please, join us. When we halt in the morning, there will be plenty of time to discuss the details."

Kylith bent beside the bandit whose sword he had taken, unbuckling the scabbard and transferring it to his own waist. The injured robbers did not object as Allenthal did the same. They shouldered their packs and joined the caravan, leaving the fallen bandits where they lay. It would be up to their companions to return for them or not.

They marched on through the cool darkness. Raz Abbas had several guards with his caravan already, and that fact alone was enough to deter all but the boldest of thieves. No one else disturbed them that night. As the sun rose and the heat grew in the sky, they stopped to rest.

Camels were unloaded, tents pitched, people and animals given food and drink. Now off his camel, Raz Abbas came to talk with them. Despite a long night's journey, his round face remained jovial.

He offered each of them a warm handshake. "Welcome!" He grinned. "I'm pleased we had the chance to meet you last night.

We must have been behind you on the road. From a distance, we saw the two of you walking, when the bandits set upon you. By the time we caught up, you two had finished the fight. You're very skilled to survive an attack from so many."

"Thank you." Kylith nodded in acknowledgement. "We're grateful to you for offering us work."

"Of course," Raz Abbas said. He beckoned over another man, who was of medium height but strongly built. They recognized him as the man who had spoken to them last night. "This is Barik. He'll explain your duties. I will be giving each man his pay when we arrive at Saarin. I'll give the two of you one share, since you weren't working the entire way."

"Fair enough," Kylith agreed.

"Good!" He clapped his hand on Kylith's shoulder. "I'll check in with you later. We all need some rest."

Barik looked them both over carefully. "My chieftain has chosen to trust you. Whether I agree or not, the choice is his. He is a friendly man, but also a very dangerous enemy. I warn you not to betray his trust."

"No, of course not," Kylith said. "We are grateful for his generosity."

After meeting their eyes for a long moment, Barik turned away. "Follow me."

They made their way through the people setting up camp. Barik introduced several of the other guards. He paused at one of the packs, took out two red tunics like all the other guards wore, and handed them to Kylith. Pausing at another bundle, he retrieved some pieces of clean cloth and a small jar of something. "For your cut," he nodded toward Kylith's arm. "We don't have anyone with us who might stitch it, but we could find someone when we reach Saarin."

Kylith shook his head. "No need, it's not deep."

Barik nodded, and they moved through the camp until they came to a low tent. "You can rest here for the day. Be ready to move again before sunset."

It had no floor except the sand, but inside, it was blessedly shady. They took off their packs. "Let me see your arm." Allenthal took out his waterskin.

Kylith didn't protest, but moved to sit beside him where he could reach the cut. When Allenthal examined the injury, he saw that Kylith had been right, the cut wasn't deep. He cleaned it, and Kylith handed him the supplies Barik had given them.

"How long has it been since you let someone cut you in a fight like that?" Allenthal asked.

"A long time," Kylith admitted. "He was good. A large part of his reputation must have been earned. I gave him the chance to cut me because I knew he would take it and it would leave him open. I'm sure it's been a long time since anyone even tried to fight him. Without making him angry, it would have been much harder to win."

Somehow, Allenthal wasn't surprised that Kylith had done it intentionally. "Were you sure you could beat him?"

One side of Kylith's mouth lifted. "Nothing is ever sure. When you pick up a blade to fight, any number of things might go wrong." He paused. "But yes, I was fairly sure I could take him."

Fairly sure. Allenthal drew in a long breath. "You saved our lives. Even if we could have handled the rest of them, we wouldn't have been able to take him and the others at the same time." He finished wrapping the cut and stowed the supplies in his pack.

He took out the jar Kyjia had given him. The burns from their time on the rock were still healing. He spread a little more of the salve over his skin and then offered the jar to Kylith. When they finished, he put the ointment away and stretched out to rest with his head pillowed on his pack.

Though he was exhausted, Allenthal's thoughts drifted to Kyjia. With the spicy scent of the salve in his nostrils, he recalled feeling the soft touch of her fingers against his skin. She'd risked herself to save them. Without her, they would have ended up fried on top of a rock for some lizard's supper.

His memory brought up the way her thick dark lashes had brushed against her cheeks, the soft pink of her lips and the way she had looked at him. The way her slender hand had felt in his. He wanted to see her again, but apparently, she didn't feel the same. She'd told him to leave the desert as fast as he could and never come back. Had she wanted to get rid of him so badly?

Where was she now? Kyjia had gone with Lord Zhandar, the one who had decided to execute them. It had been one of his men who had murdered Ashkan. There was no way Kyjia and her family were safe with them. The man who searched for the tablet hadn't gotten what he wanted from Ashkan, and he would come after the others sooner or later. She must have known that.

Why had she agreed to go with him? It made no sense. Whatever decisions she made now were leading her toward that moment in the cave, toward trouble and pain. Kyjia had mentioned a cave Northeast of Saarin, but she hadn't known exactly. He needed to know where the place was.

"Kylith?"

"Mmm?" His friend sounded more than half asleep already.

"We need to find out exactly where that cave is. I'll bet these people know. If we know that, we know where Kyjia is going."

Allenthal and Kylith settled into the rhythm of travel. The caravan moved steadily across the sand, resting during the heat of the day

and traveling during the cool hours. The other guards appeared to accept them. Kylith had done well picking up the accent of Tyar. He could converse without instantly announcing that he'd come from somewhere else. Allenthal tried to do the same, but he wasn't as adept at it. He spoke as little as possible while he learned.

When the sun rose higher, they stopped to make camp. It took only a short time for them to set up, and the guards all sat together for a morning meal before they rested. The story of how Kylith had fought Hakkir had already spread through the entire caravan, and everyone was impressed.

"Kylith, come and sit with us," the other guards invited, making a space in the circle for them. They sat down cross-legged on the sand. The circle was full of laughter and talk, and they passed around food and drink.

One of the guards looked at Kylith, folding his arms across his chest indicating doubt. "You're sure it was Hakkir you fought with?"

Before Kylith had a chance to answer, another man spoke up. "He's sure! Raz Abbas took a good look and saw the scar on his face and everything. It was Hakkir. Was he as good as everyone says?"

Kylith shrugged. "We haven't heard as much about him as the rest of you. We've never been so far north before. We've come from the south looking for work." He gave them the story they had decided upon. They couldn't let Zhandar hear that two rivermen were still in Tyar.

"If you don't choose to continue working for Raz Abbas, you should be able to find something in Saarin," a guard assured him. "Especially if everyone knows you're the man who killed Hakkir. Word of something like that gets around quickly. Lord Zhandar's been trying to catch him for years."

Kylith exchanged a brief glance with Allenthal. "And does Lord Zhandar have a lot of power in Saarin?" Kylith asked.

They all nodded. "He has a lot of power everywhere in Tyar. Working for Raz Abbas is the only way not to bow to Zhandar."

Kylith grinned. "Then we're in the right place."

They all laughed.

"We want to know this part of the desert better," Kylith suggested causally. "Someone told us there is a great cave beyond Saarin."

"Yes," one guard answered. "Izana Cave. My father explored it once, many years ago. From his tale, the place is something to see. He told me there were plants growing inside. A hidden garden beneath the surface of the earth."

Exclamations of surprise and disbelief ran around the circle.

"A garden, in the desert?" Kylith asked dubiously. "It's too hot for that."

"No, it's true!" the guard protested. "There's water in the center of the caves. The whole place is huge, shaped something like the web of a giant spider, with caverns and passageways going in all directions. The center of the cave is a deep well with plants growing around it."

"If it's true, I'd like to see that," Kylith said.

"Maybe it would be worth it, if you didn't get lost inside. The entrance is several days northeast of Saarin. It's not the entrance that's hard to find, it's the way out, once you're inside. I've heard many tales of people getting lost and wandering inside until they lie down and die in there."

Kylith shivered visibly. "Maybe it wouldn't be such a good idea. I don't want to explore the cave only to run across what's left of the others who didn't get out."

"Don't worry about that," another guard said, with a grim laugh. "There are azarim inside. They make sure anything that dies inside doesn't lie there for long."

Kylith gave an exaggerated shudder at that suggestion. "I hate azarim."

The circle laughed, but sympathy was written on all their faces.

"You're not alone. None of the desert people love them," the first guard said. "Who wants to lie there watching, not even fighting back, while being eaten?" He shuddered.

CHAPTER 16

Kyjia

Two weeks after they left the abandoned city behind, Zhandar's caravan arrived in Saarin. In contrast to the quiet of the empty desert, the city appeared full of life and motion. Most of the permanent buildings were built of clay bricks the same faded color as the hard ground. Tents of all kinds had been set up anywhere there was space. At the center of everything, a clear spring bubbled up out of the ground creating a pool of water, and a stream flowed out of it for a short distance before the rocky ground swallowed it again.

Tall, beautiful date palms grew around the water, surrounded by other plants with actual green leaves. The spring was busy with people coming to take fresh water. There was even room for all the animals to drink.

Kyjia had never been here before. Used to the open space of the desert, she felt overwhelmed by so many people everywhere: so many voices talking all at once, and the sounds and scents of animals on every side.

Caravans arrived or prepared to depart, carrying all sorts of goods in every direction. Many of the armed men wore the white tunics identifying them as members of Zhandar's Sunfire Clan.

Kyjia also saw soldiers dressed in other kinds of uniforms, red, blue, or green.

Crowds of merchants displayed their wares, all sorts of clothing, jewelry, beautifully woven rugs, fruits, vegetables, and food. The sights and smells were dazzling. Kyjia would have loved to stop and look at all of them. She spotted a few wood carvers, but none with talent to rival her father. He'd been very skilled at his craft, though it had been difficult for him to find wood. There weren't many trees in Tyar. He'd often purchased the wood from Niaz at the edge of the desert.

Saarin had an open central square, beside the water. Zhandar's house stood on one edge of the space. For here in the city, he had an actual house, more like a compound. When he led them through the gates, they saw living quarters, servants' quarters, and stables. He showed them a set of two small rooms. "This place was used before by a healer." He looked at her mother. "Will it work for you?"

She looked around the space and nodded. "Yes."

"I'm sorry it's not in better order," Zhandar apologized. "It's been some time since it was used. Still, there are a few supplies here." He pointed to the nearly empty shelves. "When you've had some time to settle in, you can make a list of what you need, and I'll send one of the servants to the market to get them for you."

She nodded. "Thank you, Lord Zhandar."

"You can prepare meals here if you wish, or you can go to the kitchen and eat. Please let me know if there is anything you need." He bowed and left them with their packs.

Kyjia quickly explored their new quarters. The front room appeared to have served as an area to tend to those who were sick, while a second room was furnished with four cots. A back door led to a little washroom. The place was comfortable, especially compared to the cave they had lived in before.

They took their packs into the back room and sat side by side on one of the cots. "Being here isn't what any of us expected," her mother said, looking from Kyjia to Terjan. "We thought we'd have your father with us—" Her voice broke, and Kyjia put an arm around her, but she went on. "But we are here, and we have shelter, water, and food for the time being. Our focus must be on finding out the reason behind what happened to your father. It would be dangerous if anyone found out who we are. We cannot afford to become too connected with Zhandar. He is very close to Jaro. So, for now, we do what we can to get along and not draw attention."

Kyjia nodded. She hadn't told her mother about her and Terjan's midnight trip into the abandoned city and what they'd observed there. They already knew Jaro was dangerous. The strange events they'd witnessed proved it even more.

Her mother got to her feet. "Now, let's bring water. I can't even remember the last time we had all the water we wanted. We can take as much as we wish from the spring. All of us need to wash, and Terjan, it's time to take out those stitches."

The next several days settled into a routine. They had cleaned their rooms thoroughly. Her mother had stocked the shelves with supplies and medicinal herbs. People began to stop by when they were ill or injured. Soldiers under Zhandar's command, or servants, or even other people from Saarin were patients. Only a few came at first, but she did a good job, and word spread rapidly. Kyjia and Terjan assisted her.

One night, Kyjia opened the door to see a young man standing outside, pale and shaking. "Come in," she invited. "What's wrong, are you ill?"

He shook his head. "Not me. I came to find the healer. I serve Sinjar, Chieftain of the Oasis Clan. We traveled here from our home in the south to trade. My master is injured and ill. Can you come? I don't know where else to go for help."

Her mother gathered several of her supplies into a bag, which she handed to Terjan. "We will go together. I may need assistance." Kyjia added a few more items to her own bag, and they lit a lantern to follow the boy out into the city.

Night had fallen over Saarin. Even this late, people moved around, lighting their way with lanterns or torches. Their own small pool of light helped them find their way. They passed through the town to the very edge of the dunes where several groups had set up camp.

The young man led them into an encampment hung with the blue banners of Oasis Clan, where they passed between the tents to the largest one in the middle. Inside, several lanterns hung from the tent poles. A man lay on a pallet on one side of the tent. Three other people surrounded him.

At a glance, it was obvious the man wasn't well. A sheen of sweat covered his face, and he shifted restlessly on his bed. He was a big man, broad through the shoulders and chest. His features were strong, with a bold nose and a short beard over a strong jaw.

"What happened?" her mother asked, kneeling beside the man.

A woman sitting beside him answered. "This morning, he was entirely normal. He was strong and healthy. We only arrived in Saarin yesterday. When he returned this afternoon, he wasn't well. I don't know what happened to him."

"Where was he today?"

"Our people have fought many times with the Sunfire Clan. We hoped by meeting with Lord Zhandar, we could make an agreement for peace. There are few tribes left that haven't fallen under his rule. We have survived all these years without joining him and want to be free. My husband," she nodded down at the man on the pallet, "went to tell Lord Zhandar so."

They went to work. Her mother sent everyone away except the man's wife and Kyjia. Terjan guarded the doorway. Other servants gathered beside him, waiting anxiously in case they should be needed. Kyjia stayed beside her mother as she examined the man.

Placing her fingers on his wrist, she counted his heartbeats. Gently, she pulled aside his tunic to reveal the skin of his torso. Several shallow wounds formed strange symbols across his belly. They weren't deep, but the surrounding skin was black, almost as if it had been burned.

The woman gasped, horrified, her hand going to her mouth as she saw it. "What could have done this?"

"Send one of the servants for clean water."

She nodded to one of the boys at the tent door, and he hurried off. Only a few moments later, he brought a large bowl of water and set it beside them. The man stirred and opened his eyes.

"Mya?" His voice was hoarse.

Mya took his hand. "I'm here, Sinjar. Just stay still, we brought the healer. You're going to be all right."

"Where are you?" his eyes searched vainly for her, though she was very near.

"I'm here," she repeated.

"Why is it so dark in here? Can't someone bring a light?"

Kyjia shivered. The man couldn't see.

Shocked by his words, Mya waved her hand directly in front of his open eyes. He didn't even blink. Realization crossed her face, and she began to cry, clinging to his hand.

Her mother did what she could for the wounds, treating them as she might a serious burn. Her kir leaf ointment appeared to help, for he quieted after she applied it. He burned with fever, and she gave him a tea brewed with several herbs.

Finally, she drew back. "I've done everything I can," she admitted. "I wish there were more. There's some kind of poison in the wound. I've never seen anything like it before. Watch him tonight, and I will return in the morning."

Mya nodded. "Thank you for coming to help us."

They left her, still bent over her husband, holding his hand.

When they returned in the morning, Sinjar was worse. His fever had risen. They gave him more of the medicine in an attempt to bring it down, but nothing helped more than using a damp cloth to cool his burning skin.

They checked on the Oasis chieftain several times during the day, but nothing they tried helped. It was past midnight when they finally returned home. Kyjia picked up a note that had been left under the door. With the parchment still in her hand, she followed her family into the back room where they sat side by side.

"You both provided excellent help today," her mother said. "I've never seen a poison like that one before. If nothing changes, he won't last much longer. I wish there was more we could do."

"Do you think Zhandar knows what it is?" Kyjia asked, turning the message over in her hand. It had her name on it, written in a firm script. The woman had told them that Sinjar had been to visit Zhandar. "We could ask him if he spoke to the man, maybe he knows what happened to him after that."

Zhandar had to realize that a sick person might come to the healer for aid, but what if Jaro had something to do with it? If the mystic knew the cause, it could be dangerous to ask Zhandar about it. Maybe by tomorrow, the poisoned chieftain would begin to recover.

Sliding one finger under the seal, Kyjia opened the note.

Lady Kyjia, I would be pleased if you would dine with me tomorrow evening. -Zhandar

"It's from Zhandar, asking me to eat with him tomorrow night."

When they had all settled to rest, Kyjia sank into sleep on her cot with questions running through her mind.

By the next evening, there had been no noticeable change in Sinjar's condition, despite their efforts to help, and she couldn't wait any longer to ask Zhandar about it. Kyjia washed herself and brushed and braided her hair. Her clothes were clean now, but she couldn't do anything about them being old and worn. From her rooms, she crossed the wide courtyard to the door of Zhandar's living quarters.

Two guards stood on either side of the door. One of them bowed and opened it for her. "Please, follow me."

Inside, the room was spacious and elegantly decorated with beautiful rugs, polished wood furniture and graceful artifacts. Kyjia had never seen any place so luxurious.

The guard led her down a hall into a room with a large table surrounded by comfortable chairs. No one else was in the room. She took a seat that the guard held for her and stared at the opulence of the room. Her eyes ran over the polished wood of the tabletop. It had been made out of a single giant slab of wood.

She tried to imagine a tree that large. She'd never seen one that size. During their journey, she'd felt small and shabby in Zhandar's tent. Now, the feeling was magnified in this beautiful dining room. Zhandar had everything: wealth, power, the respect of his people.

She had nothing besides her family and a faint hope that the god of the desert would someday break His long silence and offer help to His people.

Heavy footsteps outside in the corridor announced Zhandar's arrival. Kyjia got to her feet and turned toward the doorway.

Zhandar wore a rich tunic and a large gemstone hung from a gold chain around his neck. A smile lit his face when he saw her. "Lady Kyjia, it's been too long since we were together. Is your family settling in well?" His hand was warm as he took hers and bent to kiss it.

"Yes, thank you, Lord Zhandar."

He brought her fingers to his lips again. "Please, in private, you never have to say that. I hope we know each other well enough that you may call me Zhandar."

She smiled. "Thank you, Zhandar." Her mind flashed back to the injured man's suffering. She needed to find out what he knew about it.

"Please, sit." He helped her into her chair and took the one beside it.

Several servants entered the room bearing dishes and trays of food. Kyjia had never seen so much food prepared at one time before. She had thought the meal in his tent had been lavish, but it didn't compare with this. Was he expecting more people to join them? It appeared to be enough to feed a dozen, at least.

He offered dishes to her, and they filled their plates. The smell of rich spices was intoxicating.

"I'm glad you're here." He smiled more deeply, his eyes lingering on hers.

Thank you," she replied. All his actions indicated that he cared about her. Was she ready to allow him closer? Not yet. She needed to learn the truth about what had happened to her father first.

If things had been different, if she'd been able to trust him, she could have cared about him. At least until... Her mind rushed back to her time with Allenthal, to the warmth she'd felt when he gazed up at her and told her she was beautiful. In that moment, he'd been entirely unguarded. As he'd gradually become aware of his surroundings and felt the brush of her fingers against his skin, his gaze had focused on hers, the heat in his eyes revealing that he savored her touch.

But Allenthal was gone. He'd probably already reached Niaz and left Tyar for good.

Kyjia turned her gaze back to Zhandar, and they ate together. Laughing, she tasted foods she'd never even seen before. Most of them were excellent. Eagerly, he tried to get her to taste every item until she couldn't eat another bite, and she held up her hand to beg him to stop. "I can't eat anything else," she protested.

"But you haven't tried everything." His dark eyes met hers. "Perhaps you would consider dining with me again tomorrow?"

What could she say? "I would be honored."

"How is your mother doing with her work?" he asked.

"She's doing well. We've been able to help many people already. Yesterday, we were called to attend to a man with a most unusual illness. Perhaps you remember? His family told us he intended to meet with you. Sinjar, the chieftain of Oasis Clan?"

"Of course," Zhandar nodded. "We met. It didn't go exactly the way I hoped, but we agreed to speak again. What's wrong with him?"

"Something must have happened to him after he met with you. Perhaps someone attacked him? We don't know who it might have been, but it appears that his wounds are poisoned. My mother hasn't been able to find anything to cure it. Sinjar was not doing well when we left him."

Zhandar's brows drew together. His concern appeared genuine.

"That's terrible news. Sinjar has been a stalwart leader for his tribe for many years. We must help him recover. They need him."

"Do you have any idea what might have caused it?"

He rubbed his chin for a moment considering. "Nothing comes to mind at the moment, but I will consult with Jaro. He is very knowledgeable. It's possible he will be aware of something I have not thought of. I will speak to him in a short while."

A shiver passed through Kyjia. If her fears were accurate, Jaro would have more information about the poison, and he would soon find out that she'd asked about it.

The next morning, when Kyjia went with her mother to check on Sinjar, they found him sitting up on his pallet, thick pillows stacked behind him. Mya invited them inside, ushering them over to where he sat. "Sinjar, this is Tillian and her children. She's been here, helping to care for you while you were so sick."

A gasp almost escaped Kyjia's lips as she saw the man who had been blind look up, meet Tillian's eyes, and smile.

"I'm very grateful to you." His voice was much stronger than the day before.

Her mother returned his smile. "I'm so pleased to see you feeling better. What brought about this wonderful change?"

Mya smiled. "The mystic, Zhandar's loyal friend, visited us last night. He brought a small glass vial of medicine with him. I don't know what it was, but it helped my husband immediately. We're so grateful. The whole thing made me think that perhaps we've misjudged Lord Zhandar. He didn't have to help us in our hour of need, and yet, he did."

"Yes," Sinjar added. "I have decided to meet with him again and reconsider our alliance. Our tribes should be more closely aligned. The cost of conflict is too high."

Sinjar appeared to be moving quickly toward recovery. When she'd asked Zhandar about it, he had brought help to this man, someone who had been a rival or even an enemy before. He must truly care about his people.

But Jaro? The mystic had helped this man as well. Had her fears about him been misplaced?

CHAPTER 17

CROWN PRINCE ALLENTHAL

THE CARAVAN OF RAZ Abbas traveled for several days before it reached Saarin. When the city came into view, Allenthal was surprised at the size of it. In the midst of the barren land surrounding it was an actual city, bustling with people. There was a pool of actual water, with real trees growing around it. Amazing. Allenthal fought a powerful urge to take his boots and shirt off and jump into the clear water. That idea wouldn't go over well. No one was *in* the water; instead, people gathered reverently around the pool, dipping the precious liquid up carefully and carrying it away. No one put their feet in it, and the animals were led to another area to drink.

Now was not the time to make a scene. Even though they'd just arrived, he'd already seen plenty of Zhandar's guards in their white tunics. If they discovered who they were, it wouldn't be good. He and Kylith needed to keep their heads down and blend in. The red uniforms were a big help. No one looked twice at them as they became simply two more members of the caravan guard.

Once the caravan had arrived in the courtyard of his house and unpacking began, Raz Abbas came to speak to them. Grinning, he dropped a small but heavy pouch of money into Kylith's hand. "Your pay, as I promised."

"Thank you, Lord Abbas," Kylith said. "It was kind of you to take us on, strangers in the desert."

Raz Abbas returned his gaze. "Perhaps it was," he said finally, "but you have given me no reason to regret my choice. Do you wish to stay on in my service?"

"I wish we could," Kylith said, "but we need to find some of our friends. We have reason to believe they're in trouble, and we must make sure they're safe."

"And you believe they're here in Saarin?"

Kylith nodded. "Yes."

Raz Abbas nodded. "Then you may stay here with the other guards for as long as you need until you find them."

"Thanks," Kylith said. "Your offer is very kind."

"And don't forget, the man who killed Hakkir is always welcome here. You two can have your jobs back any time you want." Raz Abbas grinned at them and hurried off to supervise the unloading of his goods.

The guards were housed in a long room with rows of cots. It was simple but comfortable enough. Allenthal and Kylith got a night's sleep, a hot breakfast, and then went out to see what they could find. They wore their cloaks and wrapped their scarves to cover their faces. They moved quietly through the city, observing, not speaking to anyone or drawing any attention to themselves.

It didn't take long to find Zhandar's compound. It was the biggest in the entire city and near the central square. Idly leaning against a doorway on the other side of the street, they watched the entrance. They'd been observing for a while when three familiar people came down the street: Tillian, Kyjia and Terjan. They carried small bags as if they had been performing some task, but not big enough for them to be traveling. They entered Zhandar's compound and didn't reappear.

At length, Kylith and Allenthal moved from their place and wandered through the rest of the city. Zhandar's guards were obvious everywhere. Near the edges of town, men with other caravans wore different uniforms, but from here, it was clear who was in control of this place.

CHAPTER 18

KYJIA

THAT EVENING, KYJIA SAT beside Zhandar to eat a magnificent dinner. "I enjoy spending time with you," he said when they had finished. "I feel we've gotten to know each other a little, and I wish to know you even better. Kyjia, do you realize what your presence is beginning to mean to me?"

It was hard not to notice when he looked at her like that. She met his gaze. "But I'm only a girl from a poor family. You know we have nothing. We might not have even made it to Saarin alive without your aid."

He drew in a slow breath. "All that is true, but I've always believed you have a great deal to offer. And you care deeply about the fate of our people. I still believe we could do much for them if we work together."

She looked up at him, but, inside, questions spun through her mind. Even knowing her family's situation, he had not changed his mind about wanting more from her.

"I'm planning a banquet," Zhandar said. "Would you go with me? I wish to introduce you to everyone."

Her eyes widened. "Why? Who would want to meet me?"

He smiled and reached out to take her hand. "I believed you when you said you wanted to help our people. They need to know who you are. And," he brought her fingers to his mouth and kissed them, "day by day, you become more important to me."

"When is this banquet?"

"Tomorrow night."

She drew in a deep breath and shook her head. "I don't have anything appropriate to wear."

He waved off her concern. "Don't worry about that for a moment. With your permission, I will send one of the servants to the market. She can find something and then alter it as necessary to make sure it fits you. Oh," he looked down at her worn boots, "perhaps you'd better go with her and select some shoes to match."

Heat rushed to her cheeks at his scrutiny. Maybe she should have refused, but instead, she bowed. "Thank you."

The next morning, when someone knocked at their door, Kyjia opened it to see a girl outside, two guards flanking her. She bowed, her expression serious. "My name is Hafila. Lord Zhandar sent me to accompany you to the market."

"Very well," Kyjia said. "Thank you, Hafila." She'd explained this outing to her mother last night. She hadn't been pleased at the idea, but she had agreed.

Kyjia walked beside the girl toward the vast collection of stalls, tents, and booths that formed the market. The two guards in their white tunics said nothing but dutifully followed behind them. Kyjia had never seen so many items for sale or so many people everywhere. The whole scene was instantly overwhelming, but

Hafila had obviously been here many times. She appeared totally unconcerned as they began to make their way through the crowd.

"Lord Zhandar's orders were to purchase a dress and make sure it fits you. All we need today are shoes to go with it," Hafila explained. "I didn't know what you preferred, so I chose a blue dress. I think the color will work well on you, and, with a few touches, it should fit. There are several merchants down this way who sell shoes."

"Thank you for helping me," Kyjia said.

The girl nodded, her serious expression relaxing into a smile. They found a merchant displaying a whole stall full of beautiful slippers. They looked soft and pretty, sparkling with beads, gems, and bright embroidery. Kyjia had never owned anything so beautiful. In fact, she'd never even picked out a pair of new shoes. She'd always worn boots, much more practical in the desert. Those delicate slippers wouldn't last a day in the rocks, and they wouldn't keep out the sand.

But they were lovely.

CHAPTER 19

CROWN PRINCE ALLENTHAL

THE NEXT DAY, ALLENTHAL and Kylith returned to their place watching Zhandar's door. They hadn't been there long when two girls appeared. He immediately recognized Kyjia, while the other he'd never seen before. Two well-armed guards with stern faces marched right behind them.

Were they taking Kyjia somewhere against her will?

Allenthal moved to follow a little distance behind them. They walked purposefully through the city until they reached the market. If something was wrong, Allenthal saw no sign of it. They appeared to be shopping. Kyjia still wore her frayed tunic, trousers, and boots. In such a crowd, Allenthal hoped they wouldn't be noticed following the girls. With so many people around, how could anyone tell?

They moved slowly through the crowd, keeping sight of Kyjia. Allenthal saw her eyes widen in wonder as they stopped in front of a booth of shoes. She stared at them with such amazement that he felt a flood of guilt for the luxury of his own upbringing. He'd never lacked for anything, never been poor, never gone without. He'd completely taken for granted things like new boots and clothes.

Here in the desert, she'd had to live on nothing. He'd seen the cave her family had called home for years. When they'd left it, everything they'd owned had fit into a backpack.

He and Kylith moved closer, pretending to admire a display of hand-woven rugs. From the corner of his eye, he watched her, stealing brief glances. She pulled off one boot, and the merchant measured her foot. He brought out several pairs of delicate slippers, beautifully beaded and embroidered. Allenthal loved the expression on her face, a mixture of wonder and disbelief, as the man brought out a stool, seated her on it, and helped her try them on.

Inside Allenthal welled up an urge to give her everything she needed, all the necessities of life that were so hard to come by in the desert. He wanted to give her whatever it took to bring that smile back to her face. She looked happy, and the light in her expression only made her more beautiful.

No one would purchase shoes like that without a purpose. Where was she going?

He couldn't tear his eyes away from her as she tried on pair after pair of shoes, eventually selecting a lovely silver pair. The merchant wrapped them carefully and handed them to her. She smiled and thanked him. The girl beside her discreetly paid the man. They wandered through the market for a while after that before returning the way they had come.

CHAPTER 20

KYJIA

HER MOTHER AND BROTHER would attend Zhandar's banquet as well, but since Kyjia had agreed to go with Zhandar, she went to his house, where his servants would help her get ready. When she knocked, Hafila opened the door. "Please come in, Lady Kyjia."

Hafila led her into a room, and when Kyjia saw the dress hanging ready, her stomach quivered with nervousness. She couldn't wear *that*. At the sight of it, she almost lost her nerve and left.

The dress was heavily embroidered with silver thread and was the most ornate garment she'd ever seen. It went beyond what someone rich might wear. It might have belonged to a queen. Why would Zhandar do this? The pool of unease rose higher in her middle, along with a sudden urge to grab her pack and her family and slip away into the silent desert night.

She couldn't do that now. She needed to know what their plans were, and she needed to know the truth about what had happened to her father.

After Hafila helped her into the dress, Kyjia took out the carefully wrapped shoes they had purchased this afternoon. She slid them onto her feet. They fit well, so light and soft they barely felt like anything on her feet.

Hafila hung an ornate gold necklace around her neck and wove gold chains and gemstones into Kyjia's hair. When she finished and offered a mirror, Kyjia didn't recognize the girl who looked back at her. Zhandar shouldn't have done all this. He obviously intended their relationship to become much more serious, and she wasn't ready. She needed to be clearer with him before he grew to expect more from her than she wanted to give.

When all was ready, Hafila led her to a door. Outside, she heard Zhandar's powerful voice speaking to a crowd. How many people were out there? The door opened, and Hafila pulled her forward.

"...and now I want to introduce someone very important to me." Zhandar turned and held out a hand to her.

Drawing in a deep breath, Kyjia walked slowly out into the lights to stand beside him. He turned to smile at her before continuing with his address.

"We want to restore the nation of Tyar to what it once was, powerful and prosperous, and she has agreed to help me. My people, this is Kyjia, daughter of Ashkan and Tillian. She is the heir of the lost royal family of Tyar, born to lead and care for our people as Princess of Tyar."

The crowd cheered enthusiastically, but the noise couldn't drown out the ringing in Kyjia's ears. Zhandar knew who she was. He knew who her family was, and now he'd shared their precious secret with everyone. All these years, her parents had hidden the truth about their lineage. Now the entire city knew.

"Tyar has no king," her father had said. "Not anymore. But we will keep the tablet safe in the hope that someday it will be different."

But they had never told anyone else. *Never*. How had Zhandar discovered who they were?

Kyjia stood frozen in shock, under the glare of bright lantern light, looking out into a sea of faces, all staring at her. Surprise, speculation, disbelief. What in the world was she supposed to do now?

She caught her mother's eyes, down in the crowd, a look of horror frozen on her face.

How could Zhandar have done this? And why?

Kyjia turned back to the crowd, putting on a smile appropriate for a princess. She lifted her hand in a wave. Zhandar took her other hand, lifted it to his lips, and kissed it ardently, while the crowd applauded. She nodded to him graciously, turned on her heel, and left the square.

CHAPTER 21

CROWN PRINCE ALLENTHAL

TONIGHT, THE WHOLE TOWN gathered, packing into the brightly lit central square. Standing at the edge of the crowd, Allenthal's eyes were drawn immediately to the head of the square, where a familiar loud voice addressed the people. Zhandar. His imposing figure and rich clothing were distinctive. Every eye rested on him.

"...and now I want to introduce someone very important to me." Zhandar held out his hand and Kyjia walked gracefully into view to take it.

Allenthal felt his jaw fall open. When he had seen Kyjia in a threadbare tunic and desert boots, she had been breathtaking. Now, she wore a stunning gown. Her thick dark hair glittered with gold and gems. Below her hem, he could just see the lovely shoes from the market. Her face remained impassive as she looked out at the crowd.

"We want to restore the Tyar that once was, powerful and prosperous." Zhandar's voice rang out over the assembled people. "She has agreed to help me. This is Kyjia, daughter of Ashkan and Tillian. She is the heir of the lost royal family of Tyar, born to lead and care for our people as Princess of Tyar."

Even from this distance, Allenthal saw her expression tighten. She had warned him never to speak of her rank or the tablet again. How could Zhandar not have known that she hid her lineage? Kyjia couldn't have realized that he planned to reveal her secret to the entire city. If she had known his plans, she wouldn't have been there.

Under the gaze of so many people, Kyjia gave no obvious signs of distress. She smiled serenely and waved at the crowd. A moment later, she disappeared back through the doorway. This situation would mean nothing but serious trouble for her. He needed to find a way to talk to her.

CHAPTER 22

KYJIA

⁂

WHEN THE DOOR CLOSED behind Kyjia, shutting out the crowd, she leaned against it, breathing hard, her knees trembling beneath the gorgeous gown. She looked for Hafila, but for the moment, no one else was in sight.

Kyjia headed for the room where she had left her old clothes. Before she reached it, the door behind her opened and closed again, and heavy footfalls crossed the room. Zhandar came around the corner and spotted her. His expression appeared calm and happy. "Why did you leave so soon, my dear? Come back, please. There are so many people who want to meet you."

She whirled to face him, anger boiling inside her. "Why did you do that?"

His brow wrinkled in confusion. "Do what?"

"Why did you tell everyone that I'm the Princess of Tyar?"

He raised his eyebrows. "I thought you would be happy to finally have the respect that should be yours by birthright."

Happy? Her eyes widened. He thought she would be happy? "There is no Princess of Tyar! There's no such person!"

He smiled slightly. "But, of course, there is. Who else would be the perfect person to help me restore our nation? We talked about this. We agreed to work together to rebuild our nation."

Her voice rose. "We did *not* discuss you claiming a title on my behalf!"

He looked abashed. "Well, I am sorry about that. I couldn't imagine you'd be anything but pleased to have your title and office restored."

She stared at him in disbelief. "Nothing has been restored. Our people are still wanderers, eking out a scant living in the desert. Our royal palace is nothing but a ruin, and I'm not a princess. Our kingdom is nothing but sand."

He took a step nearer and took her hand. She wanted to jerk it away, but his face was earnest. "How long do you intend to hide your true identity? You're meant to be a queen. You have the power to help our people. Through your royal lineage, your family can connect with Karineth, and He will speak to you. It is time for the prophecy to be fulfilled. Karineth will awaken. With His help, we can restore our nation."

She bowed her head. "Karineth doesn't speak to me," she confessed. "He's never spoken to me."

His dark eyes met hers. "But He must! You have the tablet."

Kyjia's stomach clenched. She'd been a naïve fool to think Zhandar cared anything about her. He only wanted to use her title and find the tablet.

His gaze didn't release hers. "He's been asleep all these years, and only the heir to the royal family can wake Him. Now is the time to reveal the tablet. When we show it to the people, we won't need to wait for Karineth anymore. All of them will swear loyalty to us. They will come from far and near to join us. All of Tyar will be united."

Zhandar bent to one knee, still gazing up at her. "You want what's best for your people. I know you do. You must do this to help them. Please Kyjia, by now you must realize how I feel. I love you. I want to marry you. Please say yes. We will work together to rebuild Tyar."

Shock stole her powers of speech for a moment. There was a long pause as he looked up at her.

"Zhandar, I—"

"Please Kyjia, don't turn me down. I've waited, moved slowly, given you time. You must know how badly I want you." Moving nearer, he stood too close, towering over her. He pulled her even nearer, cupping her face with one hand. Then his mouth was on hers, his lips moving over hers, hot and hungry.

For a fleeting moment, she succumbed to the warmth of his kiss. She felt the power in his arms, the solid strength of his body. She felt his passion, and some part of her wished she could share it. But mixed with wanting her was his desire for control, for dominion. Ruling Tyar together, for him, meant ruling her as well.

She had lived in isolation for years. Except for the unwanted advances of a bandit, no man had ever kissed her before. But she couldn't give in to Zhandar. She tore her mouth free of his, twisting from his grasp, driving her foot down onto his, and her fist into his belly.

"No!"

He seized her wrist, his large hand encompassing her slender arm. He stared into her eyes, his gaze hot and his breathing ragged. "You don't mean that. We've talked about this many times. I know you want us to work together. That's what you said. All we need now is the tablet. There is no reason to hide it any longer. I know you've kept it secret out of fear, but I have the power to protect you. Give it to me and we will rule together. Without my help, you would have been nothing. You'll go back to starving in the desert without me. If you won't think of the rest of Tyar, think of your family."

She twisted, wrenching her arm free of his grip, and ran. Her blood pounded in her ears so loud that she wasn't sure if he pursued. She reached the door, entered the dressing room, scooped up her old clothes, and escaped into the cool, quiet night, running toward their quarters.

A moment later, she burst through the door. Her mother and Terjan waited there, already dressed in traveling clothes, packs already on their backs. Kyjia threw off the ridiculous gown, dragged on her old clothes, and tugged on her boots.

Only a moment later, they slipped away. They barely made it out into the streets before a company of Zhandar's guards pursued them. They ran toward the edge of town. Behind them, others raised the alarm. They were almost to the market when a hand seized Kyjia's arm in a strong grip. She twisted, trying to free herself. When she couldn't, she brought her knee up hard into the man's crotch. A gasp of pain escaped him, and she tore herself free of his grip.

Beside her, Terjan drove his fist into the face of the guard holding him. The man cursed. A moment later, he was free. They ran into the maze of stalls and tents, winding their way through the narrow aisles. Her mother was just ahead of them. They reached the edge of the market and slipped away into the desert night, running hard.

In the empty darkness outside Saarin, her mother led them northeast. For the moment, Kyjia didn't question where they were going. They ran as long as they could, pausing to walk and catch their breath, then running again. Zhandar had hundreds of men and horses in his service. They didn't have much chance of escaping mounted men unless they hid. Before dawn lit the horizon, they stopped. Kyjia and Terjan lay flat between the rocks and sand, while their mother partially covered them with sand, making it look as if it had drifted there in the wind.

"Stay still," she warned.

As the light brightened, Kyjia lay flat, exhausted from the exertion of the night. She could just see between the rocks out into the open.

She'd been such a fool. Zhandar had appeared caring and concerned, only wanting to help her family in their hour of need. In the end, all he'd wanted was power. He had declared her a princess. What he really hoped for was to use her name and legacy to hold the tablet in his hand and become the King of Tyar. He never cared about her. Making her a princess and marrying her would legitimize his pursuit of power.

Still and silent in her hiding spot, the sun grew high, heating up the sand covering her, but she couldn't move now. Before long, the distant sound of horse hooves pounded against the dry earth. Was her mother hidden too? Kyjia wanted to look around to be sure, but she remained still.

Kyjia held her breath as a large group of riders passed by them. When they moved on, she allowed herself to breathe again. They were soon back, separating into smaller groups, combing the land, examining each little rock and hollow.

Several of them passed by only a few feet from her hiding place, but they moved on without discovering her.

As the search went on, they stayed where they were all day. The hunt continued, sometimes further away, sometimes nearer, but it was late in the day before the last rider disappeared back in the direction of Saarin. In this heat, they must care for the horses and give them water and rest.

When full dark had fallen, their mother appeared. "You did well, both of you," she praised them. "We need to go on now."

"Where are we going?" Kyjia asked, stretching muscles stiff from holding still for so long.

"There's only one place out here where we might have a chance of hiding from them and surviving, the caverns of Izana. There's water inside, and with the food we carry, we might survive until the search dies down a little. The caverns are vast and intricate. I don't think Zhandar will try to search all of them. If we hurry, we can get there in three more days."

They traveled as far and fast as they could all night, hiding again before dawn came. The second day, the search came even closer to them, but they refused to break cover, and the horsemen passed them by.

Exhaustion grew worse each day, but they kept going. They were nearly to the caves. The searchers grew closer than ever. Kyjia held completely still, convinced at any moment that they'd be discovered. One of them rode directly toward her. Kyjia held her breath.

A shout from another direction caused him to look away, and he turned his horse and rode away. Kyjia heard shouts and voices, and then the group of horsemen rode by to meet several men on foot. She caught a glimpse of Zhandar's tall figure, dragging another person with him. Her mother. "Tell me where they are!" he demanded.

"I left them days ago," she lied. "I think they went west, but I don't know where they are now. They couldn't agree on a direction, and they split up."

Kyjia almost cried out when he saw Zhandar lift his hand and strike her. "Where is she? Tell me the truth. Why would Kyjia refuse my offer? I would have given her anything she wanted. Did you tell her to refuse?"

"She's gone," her mother repeated. She mopped a trickle of blood from her mouth with one hand.

"Take her back to Saarin and lock her up," Zhandar ordered. "The rest of you keep searching."

When darkness fell, the silence was deeper than it had been before. Their mother was gone. She'd led the search away from them to give them the chance to escape.

Tears burned Kyjia's eyes as she ran.

They reached the entrance to the caverns, and before daylight lit the landscape, they hid inside. Their mother had given them two packets of powders that, when mixed together in a bowl, gave off an acrid scent and faint glow. They had used the substance many times back in their cave. It was difficult to find fuel in the desert to make a fire. The dim glow was enough to find their way.

The passageways spread out like an enormous web surrounding the hidden well. Terjan had a piece of parchment and a bit of charcoal. Each time they came to an intersection, he used it to carefully map their progress and their path.

After two full days, they were near the middle. Their glowing bowl of light lasted nearly the whole way. When its light grew too faint to guide them, they mixed a little more of the powder. Near the center of the cave, they found an underground stream. The water was cool and fresh, a welcome change from the supply they carried with them. They drank their fill, refilled their waterskins and washed. Finding a cavern a little way from the water, they sat close together in the dark to rest.

"Do you think mother's all right?" Terjan asked.

The memory of Zhandar striking her returned vividly to Kyjia's mind, and tears welled in her eyes. "I hope so." She shook her head. "I was such a fool. I thought Zhandar actually wanted to help, but all he really wanted was power."

"So, he thinks if he marries you and gets the tablet, he will be the king?" Terjan asked.

"That's his plan. I can't believe I thought he cared about me as a person." How could she have thought that the first man who had paid attention to her actually cared?

"I'm sorry, Kyjia." Terjan gripped her shoulder. "He doesn't deserve you."

Her brother's kindness made her smile. "Thank you."

"Did father give the tablet to you?"

"Yes." She knew Terjan must have guessed, but they had never discussed it specifically before. "I hid it before we left the canyon."

"You know if they catch us, they'll try to make us tell them where it is."

She heard the fear in his voice, and she found his hand in the dark and gripped it. "Don't worry. I'm the only one who knows where it is. I can't let them find out, no matter what. Father trusted me to keep it safe."

"Have you ever talked to Him? To Karineth?"

She didn't want to share her own doubts with her younger brother, but she answered honestly. "I have prayed many times, but I have not heard His voice yet. I guess He's still sleeping."

"Why wouldn't He answer us, if we really are the royal family? Where is He? We're supposed to be able to wake Him up. It's what we need more than anything. Our people need it. Why would He leave us to wander the desert with no help?"

"I don't know, Terjan. I don't know how to wake Him. Maybe I'm not the right person after all. Maybe someone else would hear His voice if they held the tablet. Not Zhandar, but someone else belonging to the ancient king's family."

"I'm scared, Kyjia," he admitted. "What are we going to do if they find us? If they don't, what are we going to do when we leave this cave?"

Kyjia put her arm around him. "We'll do our best to solve one problem at a time. For now, try to get some rest."

When Kyjia woke, several sets of glowing eyes faced her across the cavern. She started up, waking Terjan. They stumbled to their feet. Kyjia held up the glowing bowl. In its light, she saw a pack of azarim creeping forward. The foremost one hissed at her. Terjan picked up a rock and threw it at the lizard. It hissed and backed up as the stone glanced off it. They shouted and threw more stones until, finally, the azarim disappeared into the dark.

Trying not to think about what had almost happened, Kyjia took a deep breath of relief and found she was shaking. "M-maybe we should take turns sleeping from now on."

After their close call, they slept in turns, one resting, one guarding. Having no other weapons besides small knives, they began collecting a pile of stones before they slept, in case they needed to drive the azarim back.

Day by day, passage by passage, they explored the cave. Though Kyjia's eyes grew used to the dark, what she needed was air. There never seemed to be quite enough in here.

She imagined the night sky, with the vast dome of shining stars, imagined space all around her. When she opened her eyes, the immensity of the rock ceiling weighed her down. The air was still and close, and there were miles of stone between her and the open air.

As they sat sharing a meager meal, Kyjia heard the distant whisper of voices. She clutched Terjan beside her. It must be Zhandar and his men. Maybe after failing to find them outside, they had guessed they would seek refuge in the cave. Kyjia and Terjan put on their packs and crept away in the dim glow of light.

The caverns seemed to go on forever, passages, galleries, rooms. They found a narrow passageway with a hidden nook. They climbed up into the small space and sat there, side by side, covering their glowing bowl to leave themselves in complete darkness.

They waited in silence for hours. From time to time, they heard voices or saw distant flickers of torchlight. They remained still and silent, hardly daring to breathe.

CHAPTER 23

KYJIA

AFTER SEVERAL DAYS INSIDE the Cave of Izana, some of the passages became familiar, and they knew their way around somewhat. How long could they stay here? Even with the strictest rationing, their food stores were already growing seriously low. They had water, but they couldn't stay in the cave indefinitely without supplies.

"We're going to have to leave soon and find food." Terjan voiced what they had both been thinking.

Kyjia nodded in the dim glow. They couldn't afford to wait too long either, because there was no place to get food anywhere near the entrance of the cave.

One day, they found the very center of the cave. Kyjia's jaw fell open in wonder at the sight. Light came in through a few vents in the ceiling, and the water welled up into a beautiful pool, wide, clear, and endlessly deep. Even there, underground, there was enough light that plants managed to grow, even a few trees. The narrow path around the edge of the pool led them to a thicket of Rala trees. Kyjia laughed in wonder at the sight. Soon, their pockets were filled with nuts, and Terjan had found two fallen branches, fairly straight, that were certain to be useful.

They went back to the cavern they had used as sleeping quarters the night before. It wasn't far from the center, and it also contained a vent in the ceiling that allowed a sliver of light in. They used stones to crack the nuts. Some had gone bad, but most were firm and tasted good.

Terjan sharpened the ends of the two sticks until they became crude weapons. He took a glowing bowl and one of the spears and returned sometime later with the body of one of the azarim impaled on it. In the dim light, he cut thin strips of meat from the carcass. They had no way to make a fire, so they ate the meat as it was.

Two or three meals finished off the animal, and Terjan took the remains far away and left it to be cleaned up by its fellows.

They had long lost any real sense of time or of day and night. As they rested, they both tensed immediately when they heard the voices of Zhandar's men. They were close. Kyjia gripped her brother's arm, motioning for him to follow her into the passageways.

"They're coming," she gasped.

No matter where they went, lights and voices followed them. No turn they took managed to leave them behind. "They're going to find us!" Kyjia whispered. "What can we do?"

Terjan got to his feet and met her eyes bravely. "There's only one thing we can do. I'm going to lead them away from you. Once they are further away, hide."

"No! You can't." She couldn't let him do it. The memory of watching their mother be captured to give them a chance to escape came back sharply. She couldn't let her brother do the same.

Terjan hadn't changed his mind. "It's the only way," he said calmly. "I know my way around enough by now. I'll lead them toward the other side of the caverns, and then I'll come back here and find you. Keep moving this way and stay out of sight."

She wanted to stop him. She was older. It should be her who risked getting closer to the men to lead them away. But Terjan had already gone. He was faster than her. Maybe it would work. It had to work. She uttered a silent prayer that he would be safe. The sound of his retreating footsteps faded quickly.

Kyjia was alone.

She'd hated the silence before, now she prayed for its return. Silence meant safety. A voice echoed down the passageway, near and loud, and she crept away. The chase went on for hours. They came closer. She crept away, waiting quietly until they grew too near again. It was a tiresome game with no end in sight. For hours, she evaded them, until, in one dim passageway, hard hands seized her, dragging her against a man's body and holding her securely. She was caught. Kyjia drove her elbow into his gut. He grunted in pain. She twisted wildly, trying to free her arms. "Hold still," he growled, tightening his grip.

She couldn't just give up. She needed to get away. When she continued to fight, he twisted her arm until she groaned in pain. Gasping, she quit struggling, but the pain in her arm increased, and she cried out.

"Stop!"

She recognized Zhandar's voice coming out of the dark passageway. At his command, the man holding her loosened his grip. Zhandar stepped between them, putting his arm protectively around her. "Do *not* hurt her," he ordered the man.

Kyjia stood, her heart pounding, rubbing her arm. Several more men closed in around them. This room had only one exit, and they had it well guarded.

"Are you all right?" Zhandar's brows drew down in concern. "Kyjia, I've been so worried. It's dangerous in here, and I've been searching for you for weeks."

She took a step back. "Where is my mother? I saw you strike her."

He shook his head. "I'm sorry. I shouldn't have hit her, but she refused to tell me where you were, and I was worried beyond enduring. I had to find you. Don't you realize how dangerous it is?"

His tone reminded her of a reprimand to a wayward child.

"We need to get you out of this cave." He attempted to take her arm.

She threw off his hand.

"Kyjia, just a few moments ago we drove off a pack of azarim. Do you know how frightened I was thinking of you in here? We need to get you somewhere safe."

She looked up at him, meeting his gaze. "I can't go with you."

His eyes widened in surprise. "You can't mean that. I only want to help. Please, tell me what you need, water or food?"

She shook her head. "I need you to go. Leave me behind and forget you ever met me."

He didn't go. "Why would you say that? I believe in your heart you know we need to cooperate. It's the only way to save our nation. They need us. They need us together. We can help them. Please, I only want to help our people. I meant what I said back in Saarin. I want you to be my wife."

She lifted her chin and stood up a little straighter. "How could you and I ever work together when you listen to Jaro? He's a murderer. I won't put our people in his power. He doesn't want to help anyone but himself. He is a servant of evil."

Zhandar's eyes widened in surprise and his heavy brows lifted. "Why would you think that? He's been by my side all my life. There's nothing he wants more than to help."

"No," she protested. "He killed my father. All he wants is power and control for himself."

A shorter figure stepped out from behind Zhandar. She hadn't seen Jaro there. His thin face gave away no emotion. "Why would you say I killed your father? I only tried to help him. The two strangers—"

"No!" she broke in, "it was you. My father tore away a piece of fabric from your hem. He had it in his hand when he died. The piece he took exactly matched your tunic."

Jaro's eyes darted back and forth uneasily, but his voice remained smooth. "I'm sure there's been some mistake. We executed the men who murdered your father. You need to come with us now. We only want to help you, but you need to cooperate."

For a long moment, no one spoke, and Jaro met her gaze, waiting for her to submit. Kyjia stood still. She would not change her mind. Finally, he spoke again. "You need to give us the tablet."

Her eyes darted between the two men and her fingers tightened into fists. She didn't answer.

"Our people need you," Zhandar pleaded. "They need your leadership and guidance. That tablet is a symbol of our connection with deity. Our people need it, and we need you with us. Please, Kyjia. You must see that it's the right thing to do!"

She shook her head. "My family is sworn to protect the tablet. I cannot give its power into your hands. I won't."

"Yes, you *will*," Jaro hissed. "You must. I know it will happen. With my powers as a mystic, I have foreseen the very moment when I take the golden Tablet of Karineth from your hand. And my sacred foresight *never* lies. Don't try to fight against us. I promise you'll regret it. Zhandar, search her. She might have it with her." One of the others pulled her pack from her back and began to rummage through it.

Zhandar stepped closer. When she backed away, one of the others grabbed her from behind and gripped her wrists tightly. She stared into Zhandar's dark eyes. "You said you cared about me."

"I do," he protested, "but I also have a duty to all my people. And we must have the tablet."

"I don't have it!"

Jaro laughed, shaking his head. "Forgive me for not simply taking your word for it." He nodded toward Zhandar.

She tried to twist away from the man holding her, but more of them seized her, holding her immobile. His hands were gentle as they skimmed over her body. He found and removed the small knife in her boot but nothing else.

"Nothing," Zhandar said.

"I suspected she'd hidden it somewhere." Jaro nodded, stepping forward to face her. "You have one last chance. Zhandar will ask you nicely. If you still won't tell us where it is, we will make you talk."

Kyjia's stomach clenched. What would they do to her? She would undoubtedly find out, because she couldn't tell them where it was. They wouldn't believe her if she said she didn't know. Had Jaro really foreseen himself taking the tablet from her? How was that possible? It must be a lie. She wasn't going to give it to him.

Zhandar stepped nearer to face her. He reached for her wrists, replacing the hands of the man who had held her with his own grip. She wrenched herself from his gentler grip and tried to run. He seized her from behind, pulling her back against him. His strong arms pinned her, one across her arms, the other around her waist.

The guards moved to block the exit. Kyjia didn't have any real way out, only the powerful instinct to run. She felt the solid power of his body behind her. "Please help us," he whispered. "Please!"

For a long moment, they were still. She sensed that he didn't want to hurt her, but he would not give up his goal or Jaro's. He would not allow her to escape. She put her hand over his, gently. "Zhandar, please don't let them hurt me?"

He turned her to face him. His eyes appeared tortured as he looked down at her. "But we must have the tablet. It's the only way we can save our people."

"I don't know where it is," she lied, hoping to convince him. "Please. Don't let Jaro hurt me."

His confining grip grew softer until he held her gently in his arms. "Kyjia, I need you to do this, for our people."

She refused to believe giving him or Jaro the tablet was best for anyone else. She had promised her father she would keep it safe. "I can't."

"She won't say anything unless you force her," Jaro snarled. "You're a fool to think she would do anything for you."

At his words, Zhandar's jaw tightened, but he looked down and met her eyes. "Please?"

But she couldn't do it. Jaro stood behind her now. He unfastened her cloak, pulled it away and, while Zhandar gripped her wrists, he cut through the fabric of her tunic, pulling it aside to expose the skin of her back. From the corner of her eye, she saw a strange green glow.

Zhandar's eyes widened at the sight of it. "No! You can't—"

Jaro's voice was as cold and hard as stone. "This is the *only* way she will tell us."

"You promised not to hurt her," Zhandar protested, his voice tight.

"There will be pain for a little while," Jaro admitted. "But as soon as she tells us what we need to know, we'll give her the cure, and she'll be completely fine." He came up close behind Kyjia. "You've already seen what the rhan stone can do," Jaro hissed. "You helped your mother treat chieftain Sinjar."

Kyjia drew in a sharp breath. It had been obvious that something poisoned the man.

"What happened to Sinjar was only the beginning. If I drove the stone into your flesh, you would die within hours. But if the stone only pierces your skin, the poison will kill you very slowly. The pain will last for weeks. Now, I'll ask you one more time. *Where* is the tablet? If you refuse to tell me, I will use the stone to curse you. It will poison your blood, blind you, and there is no escape from death except the cure in my possession."

She struggled against Zhandar. "How will you find the tablet if I'm dead?"

She turned her head to see Jaro's hand holding a small vial, its contents glowing a pearly white. "I'm trusting you'll come to me for this before that happens. It will stop the pain and save your life. You're not ready to die, Kyjia. I know that by how hard you've already tried to survive. As soon as you're ready to tell us, you can have the cure. We'll be camped at the cave entrance, waiting for you."

Zhandar's jaw was clenched, his eyes looked over her shoulder toward Jaro, pleading. His voice came out choked. "I can't..." For a moment, his grip on her loosened.

Jaro's voice didn't soften. "You must. We plan to save our people, and we must have the tablet to do it. She has no choice but to tell us. This is the only way. I know this is difficult for you, but you must be strong, for our people. Can you, Zhandar? Everything depends on this."

"Zhandar, no!" Kyjia pleaded.

His dark eyes glanced down at her, before they looked back to Jaro. He nodded, tightening his grip on her.

Jaro's voice, suddenly powerful, reverberated against the walls of the cavern.

Kyjia's breath came hard and fast in panic. She struggled against Zhandar's hands where they circled her wrists like iron bands. A strange green light lit the cavern. A prickle of cold ran up her spine to the back of her neck. A glow of green appeared as the sliver of icy chill circled her neck.

She struggled harder, her breath coming in gasps. "Please don't." She looked up into his face as the green light slid up over her ear and across her face, shining in her eyes until she couldn't see anything but the light.

Jaro's voice grew louder, speaking a strange, guttural language. A sharp pain bit into her back along her spine. Her jaw clenched, all her muscles tightening. The burning pain grew, spreading from its starting point over her shoulder blade and down her back, nearly to her waist.

She screamed.

Kyjia woke to cold, unyielding stone against her face. She opened her eyes to see nothing but the eternal dark of the caverns. There was no light, not a speck or glimmer anywhere. She felt weak, and the parts of her skin not chilled by the stone burned with fever. When she moved, hot pain raced from her back through her whole body.

The cavern was silent around her. Zhandar and Jaro had gone. They'd left her alone to endure the pain of the curse until she gave up and yielded to their wishes. She couldn't think about them right now, not with the flesh of her back on fire. She desperately needed a way to cool it. In the pitch black, she crawled, finding the cavern door by feel, and inching her way through the passageway toward the center of the cave where the water flowed.

Moving inch by inch, the journey took hours. She drifted in and out of consciousness along the way. At last, she heard running water. She made her slow way to the edge of the flowing stream and rolled over to allow the cool water to run over her damaged skin. The water eased the pain, and she slept.

Kyjia screamed as pain in her arm dragged her back from unconsciousness. Something hissed angrily right in her face. She smelled the fetid breath of a carrion eater. Azarim. In the complete dark, she heard it back up when she moved and cried out, but it had already bitten her. The bite wasn't deep, maybe not bad enough to paralyze her completely, but she couldn't remain lying here, or it would soon be back to finish what it had begun.

Warm blood ran down the torn flesh of her arm. Cradling the injury against her body, she dragged herself to her feet. All her limbs shook. The dark remained impenetrable, but if she wanted to survive this, she needed to move. Placing her hand on the wall, she took a few halting steps. She heard another vicious hiss before sharp teeth ripped deeply into her leg. She stumbled forward, kicking at it with her other foot, trying to get away.

More hissing advanced behind her. There was never just one azarim. Now, the whole pack had come. "No," she gasped.

It was so dark, she couldn't see exactly how many, or where they were. She no longer had anything with her to make a light. Bending to the floor, she felt for a rock with her uninjured arm. Finding a loose stone, she threw it toward the hissing sound. The rock clattered against stone. A miss. She found another and threw it. This time, it landed with the softer sound of stone striking scaly flesh. Perhaps one of them backed off, but the others came closer.

Stumbling in the dark, she moved away. She couldn't be sure exactly where she was. A breath of air brushed against her face. She must not be too far from the central chamber. The sound of water grew louder as she struggled forward.

An azarim pushed against her legs. Its claws sharp digging into her skin, its teeth biting into the leather of her boots. The second attack came higher. Teeth ripped into the flesh of her leg. She was out of time. If she didn't escape now, there would be no second chance. Already, paralysis spread through her body, making it difficult to move her limbs. Her feet barely obeyed her desperate desire to flee.

Her foot came down on air, and she toppled forward into empty space.

A cold surface ended her fall. Not rock, she sank through it. Water. The deep pool in the central room. Kyjia had never felt the sensation of water entirely surrounding her body. She slipped deeper. Her struggles grew feeble as the venom took over, binding her muscles and nerves so she couldn't move her limbs. There was no way out. She couldn't breathe. Fighting against the paralysis, she tried to reach the surface, but in the black dark, she was no longer sure which direction to go.

Her limbs felt as though they were weighted with lead. She could barely move, and it grew worse every moment. She had no way to escape the water. Perhaps it would be better to drown than to be eaten alive by the azarim. Losing all ability to struggle, she drifted, her lungs burning.

CHAPTER 24

KYJIA

TRAPPED BENEATH THE SURFACE of the water, something seized Kyjia, pressing hard against her belly. Something dragged her through the water. Was she moving back toward the top of the pool? She needed air, desperately. Everything was beginning to fade.

Her head broke the surface, and she could hear again. Water splashed around her. She dragged in a panicked breath. The water pooled, cold all around her, she felt nothing but the liquid, and... something holding her head above the water.

"Kyjia!" the voice called her name from just behind her.

Another person was in the water with her. Someone had pulled her back from the black depths. How was that possible? How could anyone have found her in this impenetrable darkness? The venom bound her muscles, leaving a great weight on her chest. She could barely breathe, let alone speak.

The voice called her name again. "Kyjia?"

Who called her? It wasn't Terjan. It definitely wasn't Zhandar. One of his men? She had thought they were all long gone. What reason could any of them have to help her? Perhaps they had been watching her. After all, if she died at the bottom of the pool, they would never find their precious tablet.

An arm held her head above the surface. They moved through the water. After a few moments, she felt solid rock brush against her shoulder. Her instinct urged her to cling to the solidness of it, but her limbs refused to obey her wishes. Hands gripped her under her arms and lifted her out of the water. Her legs slid limply against the edge of the pool until she rested flat on the rocks.

Relief flooded through her at being back on solid ground. Her body lay completely still. A hand touched her shoulder. In the dark, she couldn't see who it was, and she couldn't make her jaw move to form the words to ask. Another person climbed up over the edge, out of the water. There was more splashing, and then someone bent over her and touched her face.

"Kyjia?" The voice sounded tight with panic.

"Is she alive?" another voice asked.

"I don't know." Hands touched her face. A weight settled on her chest, someone listening for a heartbeat.

"Her heart is beating." The voice exclaimed in relief. "She's breathing, barely. Look at this."

He lifted her arm where the azarim had bitten her. Did they see the bite? It felt like they did, but how could they see anything in the dark?

"There are more, here on her leg. The azarim must have bitten her. She won't be able to move for hours."

Usually, that allowed plenty of time for the reptiles to finish their supper. Had she escaped the azarim only to fall back into Jaro's hands? Who were the men beside her? If they were loyal to Jaro, they would take her directly to him. She never wanted to see him again.

They had called her by name, so they knew who she was. The more she listened, the more she realized that she did recognize their voices. They had the strange accent of outlanders, but she'd told them to leave Tyar weeks ago.

Relief flooded through her. They were friends, and they would help. Obviously, they hadn't obeyed her and left, but she couldn't express how glad she was to see them now. "Al!" she gasped.

"Kyjia! Can you hear me?"

She managed a tiny nod, though it would do little good in the dark. Pain raced through her body. The torn flesh on her arms and legs hurt, but it was nothing next to the raging fire in her back. It was already burning again, and lying on it like this was quickly making it worse. She groaned.

As if he already knew her back was injured, he helped her roll onto her side, lying with her head rested against something. She felt leather against her cheek and guessed he must be sitting cross-legged, her head against his leg. Gently, his fingers pulled aside the torn remnants of her tunic.

She heard his sharp intake of breath. "What in the name of the goddess did that?"

He had to be seeing the marks of the curse, but how? It was too dark.

"It looks like a burn."

She recognized Kylith's voice. What they said must be true; her back felt like it was on fire.

"I still have the jar of ointment she gave us." She heard him shuffling through his pack and the tiny sound of him setting the lid on the rocks.

"I'm going to try some of this," Al said. His fingers brushed against her skin, easing the pain a little.

"Helps," she gasped. It still felt difficult to breathe.

Moving slowly and methodically, he applied the cream to the entire area. She sighed in relief. "Better."

"Is there anything we can do for the azarim bites?" he asked.

She twitched one shoulder in the barest of shrugs. She'd never heard of a remedy. Usually, by the time they were chewing on you, it was too late. They had arrived barely in time.

"We're going to move a little further from the edge of the water," Al murmured. "We'll try not to hurt you." He lifted her shoulders, while Kylith must have lifted her feet. They moved her to a place that felt drier.

Gentle hands cleaned the torn flesh on her arm and bandaged it. Al's voice sounded heavy with sorrow. "I tried to get here in time to stop them."

She wasn't sure if he meant the azarim or Zhandar and his friends. Maybe both. When he finished with her arm, he moved to her leg, cleansing and wrapping. In her wet clothes, the cave felt chilly, and she shivered. Someone wrapped a cloak around her, and she drifted into unconsciousness.

Kyjia must have slept for a long time because it was still completely dark when she opened her eyes. What time of day was it? From here, she couldn't see the vents in the ceiling. That was strange. She could usually see at least a couple of stars through them.

As she stirred slightly, a gasp escaped her lips as pain radiated from her back through her whole body. A comforting hand touched her shoulder.

"I'm here." It was Al, she knew his voice, even in the dark.

She stayed still, waiting for the pain to ease to a bearable level. Slowly she took a deep breath and was relieved to discover that she could. Carefully, she moved her arms and legs a little. She felt horribly weak, but she could move again. The azarim bites hurt, but her back was the worst. Every bit of motion sent pain shooting through her. She took in another breath. "I can move again," she murmured.

"You're still in a lot of pain," Al observed. "Is there anything more I can do?" His large, warm hand took hers.

"You've already done so much. Thank you for coming to find me." Her eyes welled with tears of gratitude and relief. "I needed help."

"Where are your mother and brother?"

More tears filled her eyes at that question. "Terjan is here somewhere inside the caves. He tried to lead Zhandar and his men away so they wouldn't find me, but I don't know where he is. I don't know if they found him. They captured my mother before we got into the cave."

"Did they hurt her?" Al asked.

"I saw Zhandar strike her, but then they took her away, and I don't know. She allowed them to find her so we could escape." She tried to stop crying, but she couldn't. When she tried to push herself up from the ground, she sank back with a gasp of pain.

He lifted her gently, helping her sit up.

"I have to help them," she gasped. The warmth of his shoulder beside her provided a safe spot to rest her head.

"It will be all right," he promised. "We'll find them." His arm felt warm and comforting around her. "We'll look for Terjan first."

She drew in a ragged breath. "I'm sorry," she said, rubbing her sleeve across her face. "You're right. We should focus on one problem at a time. There are some vents in the large cavern that let in a little light. When morning comes, we can find the supplies we need and start looking for Terjan."

Al's voice was suddenly tight. "It's morning now."

What was he talking about? If it were already morning, they'd be able to see the light, even a tiny scrap of the sky from this room. "It can't be."

"Kyjia?" His voice was directly in front of her. "Can you see me?"

"No. It's too dark in here. Later when there is more light..."

His arms tightened around her. "Kyjia."

"No!" She didn't want to hear his gentle explanation.

Jaro's words came back to her as he explained the curse. "It will poison your blood, blind you, and kill you." It would blind her. There *was* light in the cavern. *She* just couldn't see it.

"No!" she cried out again. She couldn't stop the tears that came. Allenthal's arms came around her as she sobbed.

"I'm sorry," he murmured. "I'm so sorry for what they did to you. It was Zhandar and Jaro, wasn't it?"

Wordlessly, she nodded.

"They wanted you to give them the tablet?"

"Yes."

"You were very brave, Kyjia."

She didn't feel brave. She was terrified. At least now she wasn't alone. With the endless dark surrounding her, she clung to him.

When her crying gradually stilled, he drew back, and she felt the weight of a waterskin in her hands. "Have a drink of water and something to eat. I'll stay, and we'll rest here while Kylith goes to find your brother."

"All right," she agreed. "If you go back down that passageway, the fourth opening on the left is the cavern where I left my pack. If it's still there, we have a way to make light to help you find him."

"I'll go and get it," Kylith offered.

She heard his footsteps retreating down the passageway. Allenthal placed a handful of nuts into her hand.

"Eat," he ordered.

She couldn't even remember how long it had been since she ate, and the last few meals had been raw azarim meat. She put the kernels in her mouth one by one, savoring them.

When Kylith returned with her pack, she sorted through it by feel, finding the packets of powder. "Mix a little of each of these in the bowl," she instructed. The familiar acrid scent rose up, only now, she couldn't see the glow.

"It works," Kylith exclaimed in amazement. "Light. How long does it last?"

"It shines for a long time," she said. "Nearly two days before it begins to fade."

She felt his hand on her shoulder. "I'm going to look for your brother. Just stay right here until I come back. We could all wander in here for months and never find each other."

"We won't move," Al replied.

His footsteps went away down the corridor, and silence returned.

Kyjia drew up her knees and rested her aching head on them. She was still so tired, her body alternating between sweltering heat and chill.

A hand touched her cheek. "You're burning with fever." Al's voice was tight with concern.

Jaro's poison was working.

"Here," he helped her lie down on what felt like a cloak. It was more comfortable to lie on her stomach. Her burning back cooled as he spread a damp cloth over the wounds.

"Thank you." She drifted off. She was blind, but it was a blessing not to be alone.

Kyjia reached out in the dark and felt Al's leg as he sat beside her. His body felt rigid, not moving at all except for a slight tremor that ran through him. "Are you all right?" she asked, her own pain forgotten for the moment.

He didn't respond.

Slowly, she pulled herself into a sitting position, resting her shoulder against the cavern wall. By feel, she found his shoulder and shook him. "What's wrong? The azarim haven't been here, have they? Did they bite you?"

He drew in a sharp breath, as if she had woken him from a nightmare. "N-no. No."

She ran her fingers from his shoulder along his arm to find his hand, taking it in both of hers. He clung to her hand, his own fingers trembling.

"I'm sorry," he murmured. "I didn't mean to doze off. It was a dream. Only a dream."

It couldn't have been simply an ordinary dream, his reaction to it had been too strong. "You dreamed of something specific," she guessed. "Some painful event?"

"Yes."

"Will you tell me?" She wanted to comfort him, to ease the hurt that he must be carrying inside where no one could see it.

"I can't." His voice was tight with pain. "I've never spoken of it to anyone, at least, not all of it."

She brought his hand to her lips and kissed it. "You will carry it all alone?"

"I have for many years already."

"Must you?" she asked. "You helped me when I most needed it. Now, if I can help you, I will. You're a good person, Allenthal. I have never known you to harm anyone else, except in defense. I have seen you protect and help others even when it caused you great harm."

"You wouldn't say that if you knew. Someone I cared about died because of me."

Tears welled in her eyes at his words. "I'm so sorry."

"I don't deserve your comfort." His voice was rough with emotion. "No matter what I do, how hard I try, I fail to protect others when they need it. I came here to help you, but I failed again, and now you are suffering because of it. I saw... you."

What was he talking about?

He took a deep breath and went on. "It was months ago, before I left my home. It was a dream, and yet not like any dream I've ever had. I saw you. They held you so you couldn't move and demanded you tell them where the tablet was. I saw how brave you were. They meant to force you to tell them, and when you wouldn't, they cut the marks into your skin. That's why I left my home. Everything I've done was because I wanted to stop that moment from happening. I came to Tyar because of you, and I failed."

Kyjia's mind spun. No one had ever told her such a tale. "That's how you knew who I was, on the day we met?" At the time, she'd been afraid and offended that he knew her name.

"Yes. The Goddess told me your name."

"Why would you travel so far and put yourself in such danger for a stranger?" Kyjia had never known anyone so caring.

"From the moment I saw you, I had to come. And the Goddess asked me to help you. She told me the words of the prophecy and that your family kept the tablet. My whole goal was to find my way to this cave, and to find you *before* they harmed you. I failed."

She put her hand on his cheek and felt his head hang in despair. With her fingertips, she brushed away his tears. He held more inside him. She sensed it. "Was there someone else you feel that you failed?"

She felt the motion as he nodded.

"My brother." His voice sounded broken. "All my life, I looked up to him, followed him around. I wanted to be just like him. If not for me, he would still be alive."

His muscles tensed under her hands, as if the memory had turned him to stone. "But you didn't harm him yourself, did you." It wasn't a question. He cared deeply about others. The fact that he carried the weight of guilt proved that he would never intentionally harm his brother.

"No," he admitted. He sat silently for a long moment before he went on. "We were riding along a narrow trail in the mountains. A rockslide came down from the cliffs above us. It would have hit me. Instead, he pushed me out of the way, and the falling rocks took him over the edge."

Her heart hurt for him. It must have been a terrible moment, heartbreaking. But it hadn't been Allenthal's fault. His brother had chosen to save him.

Kyjia didn't speak. He had more to say, and she didn't want to stop him.

"He fell down into the rocks. His leg was broken, but he wasn't dead. We climbed down to him as quickly as we could. It took hours to get him out. It got dark and started to rain. It was so cold. I remember him shivering as I tried to keep him warm. I wrapped my cloak around him, but the wind was so cold, and he was badly hurt. By morning, he was dead."

Kyjia wrapped her arms around him. What words could she say that would ease the pain inside him?

"It should have been me." His voice was choked with tears. "Now he's gone, and I am still here. Why did he do it?"

She hoped he would take a little comfort from her presence and her embrace. "Was he wrong to sacrifice himself for you? He loved you. Was it not his choice to make?" she asked gently.

"I didn't want him to do it!" he cried.

"No," she agreed. "But he did. You must live your life in a way that will reward him for his sacrifice."

"It was my fault," he protested.

She brushed her fingers against his cheek, feeling the rough stubble of his unshaven jaw. "Was it really your fault?"

He drew in a long breath and then another. "Maybe not. But I can't bear that he made that choice for me."

"He loved you," Kyjia said firmly. "You must respect his decision. Your brother has my gratitude as well. If he hadn't saved your life, you wouldn't have been able to save mine. And you did save me, Allenthal. I don't know how you managed to find me at all, but you did. Who's to say you'd have been able to stop them if you'd gotten there earlier? It's more likely that they would have killed you or cursed you too. And if they had, we'd both be dead. Forgive yourself for your failures, Allenthal. Accept that you don't have the power to save everyone."

"Thank you, Kyjia," he murmured. "You're very wise." He brushed a hand across her cheek. "You're still feverish; you should rest again."

He offered her water, and she drank. The cuts on her back stung too badly for her to sleep. Somehow, he could tell. She heard him digging through his pack. "I'll apply more of the ointment, if you'd like."

"Yes, thank you." She lay down on her side with her knees curled up to her chest. His touch was feather light against her damaged skin as he applied the medicine to her back, allowing her to sink back into sleep.

For days, she drifted. The fever came and went. It was always night to her now, and she lost track of time. But Allenthal was still there. She woke to hear his breathing fast and shallow. "Al?"

"I'm all right," he replied. "It's just that... I feel the weight of all that rock above us. I'm sorry. It's better if I don't think about it too much. I need to see the sky. I can't stand small spaces. There's enough room in here that I've been able to get by, but I need more air."

She smiled. "I feel the same. I understand why it's difficult for you to be here, but I'm so grateful not to be alone. Without being able to see, I would never find my way out. I'd be left to wander until the azarim found me again."

His arm tightened around her. "I won't let that happen. We will escape from this cave, I promise you."

"I've been thinking about everything you told me, and I understand that you feel you must pay back the debt you owe your brother. You traveled all this way into the desert, endured hardship, pain, and great danger. You've done all these things to help me and my people. Can you allow this to pay the debt?"

"Can it be paid?"

"I believe you've already more than paid it. From where he rests in the eternal world, your brother would agree."

His breathing sounded slower now, calmer.

She leaned against him. "There is room here. There's air. There's enough space."

He repeated her words like a chant. "Room. Air. Space."

In the darkness, she found his hand and held it. "There is room for you in this world, Allenthal. You belong here. We need you. So many people need you. Please don't feel that you shouldn't be here."

CHAPTER 25

KYJIA

AL'S HAND TIGHTENED ON Kyjia's shoulder. "Can you get up?" His whisper was urgent.

A moment later, she realized why. Voices. Her stomach tightened in fear, and she clutched at him.

"Don't worry," he murmured. "It will be all right. But we need to move."

He pulled her to her feet, but her legs felt weak and shaky.

With his arm around her waist, he helped her along. Silently, they moved through the corridors. For a time, she could no longer hear anyone behind them. Al led her into another room where she sank gratefully down to rest.

It didn't last. Soon, they had to move again. He helped her back to her feet. Without her sight, she couldn't tell exactly where they were, but it felt like they followed several passages before they paused.

He helped her down. "Stay still. Don't move, and they won't find you in here." The rough edges of rock surrounded her, closing in as his footsteps moved away. Kyjia tried to calm her breath, tried to stay still while straining to hear where he had gone.

"Who are you?" an unfamiliar man's voice asked.

"Just a lost guard," Al replied, a little distance away. His tone sounded casual. "I work for Chieftain Abbas. Can you tell me how to get back to the entrance?"

"No one from Crimson Sands is anywhere near here," the other voice protested.

"I'm lost," Al repeated.

The long pause convinced her that their pursuers didn't believe him. While he wasn't who they expected to find on their hunt for Kyjia and Terjan, the fact that he was here at all made them suspicious.

"You can tell your story to Lord Zhandar. Come with us," the man demanded.

The footsteps and voices of several men drew near. Al could try to fight, but were there too many? Would they take him away, leaving her alone in the dark? Icy fear twisted in her belly.

"I'm not one of his people, and I'm not going to Zhandar," Al said firmly.

Derisive laughter echoed through the taverns. "Yes, you are. It won't bother us if you visit him in pieces."

Another man spoke suddenly. "Look behind him, someone is there."

They'd seen her. Her hands tightened into fists. How many of them were there? If Al tried to fight them, he'd be hurt or even killed. She couldn't let that happen. By the time she had struggled to her feet, the sound of blades crashing together filled the chamber.

Standing beside the wall, she felt the rock against her side. There had to be something she could do to help him, but what?

The fighting drew closer to her. She heard someone coming near, and when rough hands seized her, she knew it wasn't Al. She struggled against the man holding her, but the fever had seriously weakened her. She groaned in pain as he gripped her hard, holding her injured back against his body.

"Leave her alone." Al's voice came from somewhere in the middle of the fight. At least when he spoke, she knew he was alive.

The sounds of fighting were terrifying when she couldn't see what was happening. Any cry or groan of pain could be him, injured or dead. She had to find some way to stop them.

The man gripping her tightened his hold. "Stop fighting or I'll kill her."

Kyjia felt the pressure of a keen blade against her throat.

The sounds of the fight gradually stilled. "You've already hurt her enough," Al protested. "Do what you must to me but leave her alone."

They laughed. "You're both going back to Lord Zhandar."

She heard him struggling and the sound of blows. They were hurting him. All her muscles tightened at the sound. He had only been protecting her. Tears ran down her cheeks. In this condition, she was worse than useless. She had no way to help him, and she'd caused him to get caught.

The man holding her dragged her forward, and she heard the sounds of them forcing Al along ahead of her. "No!" She couldn't let them take him too. "Take me to Zhandar. This man has nothing to do with any of this. If you release him, I'll go with you without fighting."

"No." Al's voice sounded choked.

Sudden sounds of fighting broke out all around her. Kyjia felt the knife against her neck suddenly pulled away. When the hands gripping her released, leaving her off balance, she sank to her knees on the rocky floor.

"Kyjia!"

She heard a very familiar voice beside her. "Terjan!"

Her brother embraced her, his scent and the feel of his arms familiar.

"Stay right here," he instructed.

More weapons clashed. She found the rocky wall and huddled against it. Several moments of chaotic noise echoed off the passage walls. Her heart pounded in panic, and her breath was shallow and fast.

"That's all of them."

Kyjia recognized Kylith's voice. A moment later, she felt a hand on her shoulder.

"Are you all right?" Terjan asked.

She wasn't, not even close, but her brother was here. She hugged him tightly. "You're alive."

He returned her embrace, holding her carefully. "I shouldn't have gone," he murmured brokenly. "Look what they did to you."

"There's nothing you could have done to stop them," she assured him. "Are you hurt?"

"Nothing serious."

She heard Kylith again. "We need to move."

"Kyjia?" She recognized Al's hand as it took hers. "Can you walk?"

She nodded, accepting his help to rise. They walked for hours. Exhaustion dragged at her limbs, and she leaned more and more on Al.

"Rest," he whispered, lifting her into his arms.

Eventually, the motion of him walking ceased. He set her gently down and covered her with a cloak. She slept.

As the sun rose over the distant hills, Kyjia stood on the rocks, looking down into the narrow sandstone canyon they had called home for years. At the sound of footsteps behind her, she turned to see her father approaching.

He smiled, coming forward to embrace her warmly.

"Father?" Kyjia's voice was choked with emotion. How could her father be here? She never expected to see him again.

"I've missed you," he said. "You've done what I asked, kept the tablet safe. Thank you. I am so proud of you." He looked into her eyes. "When Jaro demanded the tablet, you wouldn't bend to him. Maybe not the wisest, but very brave."

Kyjia shook her head. "I'm not brave," she admitted. "I was terrified. And I didn't win. I completely failed. If help hadn't reached me, I would be dead right now."

His gaze remained steady. "If there was no danger of failure, choosing to act would not require courage."

Kyjia reached out to hold her father close. The solid strength of his body was reassuring and familiar. "Why did you leave us?"

He sighed. "I don't know the reasons for everything. I never did. I only lived the best life I could, working hard, loving and protecting my family. Our bloodline is meant for a larger destiny. You've heard the prophecy. It's time for it to be fulfilled. My time has passed. Now, I cannot wake Karineth. I need you to speak to Him in my place. Will you?"

Kyjia gasped. "How?" She looked into her father's eyes. "I don't know how to do it, I can't—" Her stomach twisted with fear.

He smiled. "You can. With the power of God on your side, who can stand against you?"

"But I don't know how to wake Him!" Kyjia protested.

"Go and reclaim the tablet now. Move forward with courage, and everything you need will come to you." He embraced her, smiling again. "Move forward in faith, my daughter." With a final embrace, he turned and strode away into the gathering night.

"Wait!" For a few steps, Kyjia tried to follow him, but the figure of her father had vanished, his gray cloak blending into the twilight.

CHAPTER 26

KYJIA

I N THE BLANK DARKNESS, Kyjia heard the others talking. It didn't take long to realize they were discussing her.

"We have to get the medicine from Zhandar, somehow," Terjan protested.

"I agree," Al said. "There has to be a way to find the cure."

"No," Kyjia protested, breaking into their conversation. "He will only give it to us in exchange for the tablet, and I can't do that."

For a long moment, they were all silent.

Finally, Al spoke. "Then we need to decide what our next move is. First, we need to get out of this cave."

Kyjia agreed completely, even though for her, the rest of the world would now be just as dark as this place. The dream of her father still filled her mind. "We need to get to the tablet. It's time to awaken Karineth. That's the only thing we can do that will truly help."

"Did you learn something new? Do you know how to do it?" Terjan asked eagerly.

"Not exactly," Kyjia admitted. "I dreamed about Father. It was so clear, I felt like he was really there. I told him I didn't know how to awaken Karineth, but he promised we would receive the information before we got there."

"Your prophecy already tells you what to do, doesn't it?" Al asked. "Just hold up the tablet, say his name three times—"

A moment of shocked silence fell. Kyjia turned toward him, amazed. He was a stranger in this land and talked about the cryptic prophecy as if it should be obvious what it meant. "What did you say?"

"The instructions were part of the prophecy, weren't they?" Al's voice sounded confused.

"Our father repeated it to us many times," Terjan said. "*While I sleep, my land is buried in sand. The people of Tyar must rise again. A new ruler shall rise in the desert and my power shall be in their hands and a river shall flow out of the sand.*"

She heard the slight sounds as he got to his feet, and his voice moved as he paced the room, reviewing the words. "No, I'm very sure that was all. The line you just said was nowhere in the version I learned. Those were my father's exact words. He made us memorize it years ago."

"That's the way I remember it too," Kyjia agreed. She reached out, looking for Al's hand, and he placed it in hers. "Are you saying the prophecy you heard is different?"

"Much of it is exactly the same," Al said. "But not everything. This is how I received it: *While I sleep, my land is buried in sand. The people of Tyar must rise again. Hold the tablet aloft, and speak my name three times, and I shall hear and answer. A new ruler shall rise in the desert and a light in the night sky from the ancient city of kings shall proclaim their coming. My power shall be in their hands and a river shall flow out of the sand.*"

Terjan gave a shout of triumph that echoed around the cave. "Are you telling me that's all it is? Speak my name three times and I shall hear and answer? It's so simple."

"Where did you hear those words?" Kyjia asked.

"In the Seven Rivers, we serve the Goddess Namradill, and She communicates with our family. She gave me the prophecy."

Joy and relief welled up inside Kyjia. "That's it! That's the key." Her father had been right. The information she desperately needed would come to her. They had to get back to the tablet. The first step was escaping the cave. They couldn't exactly stroll out the main entrance if they intended to remain free.

"Zhandar said he would wait at the cave entrance. If we go that way, we'll walk right into his hands, and he'll have a lot of men with him."

"Couldn't we sneak into his camp to find the cure?" Al's hand tightened around hers.

"No," Kyjia protested. "It's too closely guarded. And there are so many of them. We aren't ready to fight them all."

"We came in the main entrance," Kylith said, "but as we explored, we found a side passageway that we might be able to get through. We could see through it, but it's a little tight. Maybe we can use it to escape. I don't think Zhandar's men would be able to see it from where they camped."

"Will they try to follow us?" Terjan asked.

"We'll leave in the dark," Kylith said. "I think if we're careful, we can be out of their sight before dawn. It will give us a head start at least."

They needed to get moving. Kyjia sat up slowly. Her head and body ached from the fever, but the pain from her injuries had improved a little. Somehow, she needed to find the strength to walk.

"Breakfast." Al placed food in her hand, and she ate. Around her, she heard the others doing the same. Where was her pack? The thought of wearing a backpack now was horrible. Maybe she could carry it in one hand?

But Al had already thought of that. "I'll carry your pack."

"Thank you." He had been so kind to care for her.

"I think that's all," Kylith said when they finished. "Ready?"

Using the wall for support, she got to her feet. Now standing, weakness permeated her whole body, but they needed to go. She would have to find the energy somehow. "Ready."

Kyjia felt a steady hand find hers, offering support. Before she'd been injured, good health had been something she took for granted. She belonged to the desert people. They were tough, and so was she. But now she needed Allenthal to help her.

She clung to his arm, feeling her way forward. They walked for hours. She went on as long as she could, before her feet refused to go any further, and she sank to her knees.

"Don't worry," Al murmured beside her. "Just rest for a while." He lifted her into his arms.

Gratefully, she curled against him, feeling the warmth and solid strength of him, and let exhaustion claim her. She slept restlessly, a dream following her. She wandered alone in the caverns, fleeing blindly from the azarim who snapped at her. Her limbs grew weaker, and she sank down to the floor. Teeth tore into her flesh.

In a panic, she started awake, expecting to feel sharp teeth sinking into her body. Instead, protective arms tightened around her. "It's all right, Kyjia."

Her breathing was ragged with panic, and she tried to slow her racing heart.

His voice was low and soothing. "It's all right. Nothing will harm you."

"S-sorry," she gasped. "It was the azarim. I felt them attacking me."

"I will make sure they don't." Allenthal's voice was calm, his arms around her.

Her fear faded.

They made their way steadily back toward the outside world. Several times, they hid to avoid parties of men passing them, apparently on their way to search deeper in the cave. Zhandar meant to find Kyjia again. As another small group passed, they rested in a hidden nook in the rocks, Terjan beside her. It appeared that Zhandar had waited as long as he could to force her to cooperate. They expected to find her. After all, without her sight, how would she find her own way out?

"Where did the others go?" she murmured, not hearing anyone else.

"Kylith said he needed to restock his supplies," Terjan replied.

Eventually, she heard footsteps returning.

"They're not fools." Kylith's voice sounded satisfied. "Every one of them carried food and water. There's enough to get back to Saarin with this."

He must have gathered a significant stock of supplies. Kyjia didn't say it aloud, but they had to get out first, past Zhandar's camp. If his soldiers pursued them out into the desert, how would they escape?

They were approaching the main entrance now, and Kylith led them toward what they hoped would be another way out.

"Are you ready to climb, Terjan?" Kylith asked.

"Ready," her brother replied.

"I'll stay with you, Kyjia," Al promised, putting his arm around her.

Quietly, she expelled a sigh of relief. She didn't want to admit how badly she feared being alone. Without her sight, she couldn't tell where she was, couldn't avoid any danger or trouble. Al seemed to understand this.

"We'll be out soon," he promised.

By feel, she found his hand, and took it. "Can we get out without getting caught?"

He squeezed her hand reassuringly. "I think we can. We'll make sure they don't see us."

His presence felt comforting, solid, and dependable beside her. She leaned against him. "I would be dead without you."

In reply, he lifted her hand to his mouth and kissed it. For a moment, she felt the warmth of his breath against her skin, the prickle of his short beard.

"What will you do when all this is finished?" she asked.

"I will have to return to my homeland," he admitted. "I have duties there that I cannot ignore."

She had been afraid that would be his answer. Their time in the cave had forced her to realize that she desperately wanted him to stay. But why should he? He was such a kind person, but now she was blind and ill. No one would want to be with someone in that condition. If she didn't get the cure, she'd die. Al would be better off forgetting her and going home. "Your land must be beautiful," she whispered, instead of sharing the soul-wrenching pain brought on by the thought of being without him.

A smile was plain in his voice. "Well, it's not so hot."

"And you have lots of water? Many wells?"

"Not wells, rivers and lakes, springs of water. It's very green. Plants grow everywhere, trees and forests."

She'd never imagined a land with growing things everywhere. Perhaps it would be like an oasis but much larger. "What is a forest like?"

He took in a long, slow breath. "You saw the plants growing in the center of the cavern? It's like that except the trees are taller. It's cool and shady beneath them. Many birds and animals live there. It's beautiful. You'd love it. You should see a real forest someday."

Her stomach clenched. The lovely description he'd just given might be as close as she would ever get.

He appeared to realize what he'd said. "Sorry," he muttered.

The others soon returned. "It's there," Terjan said excitedly. "I went all the way through the passage. It will be dark outside in a few hours. We'll get through the passageway and get all our things to the entrance, then we can slip away when it gets dark. We'll have to climb a little to get there, Kyjia."

How could she climb when she couldn't see? Fear tightened her muscles. "I don't think I can," she admitted.

"You can," Terjan insisted. "You're a strong climber. I've seen you do it a hundred times. We'll help you."

Now, the fever had left her limbs weak and shaking. She wouldn't be able to see where she was going. "How high is it?"

"We're going up about twenty feet," Terjan said. "After that, there's a ledge. I've been up to it already. There are plenty of good holds. You can do this."

The men spent some time repacking. They moved the supplies they had stolen into their own packs, and Kylith went back toward the main entrance to leave the empty bags behind so they wouldn't point to their escape route.

Allenthal helped Kyjia to her feet and led her to follow the others. "The rock face is right in front of you," he murmured.

She reached out to touch the wall, cool and smooth under her palms.

"I'll tell you where to put your hands and feet," Terjan promised.

Her stomach tightened. She drew in a breath. The others were beside her to help. She didn't have to do this alone. With their guidance, she could climb.

"I'll be right below you. If anything goes wrong, I'll catch you," Allenthal said.

He was optimistic to assume he could catch her if she fell. More likely, she'd knock him off the wall with her. But, if she was careful, only moving one hold at a time, she should be able to stay on the wall.

"We're going straight up until we reach the ledge," Terjan said. "We'll be up in only a few minutes."

She drew in a deep breath. Twenty feet. She had climbed many rocks, and she could do this. Sliding her hand up the rock face, she found a hand hold.

"Are you ready?" Terjan asked.

"Yes." She didn't feel ready, but they had to go on.

Terjan's voice came from one side of her. "I'll stay beside you the whole way. There are plenty of good holds. Lift your left leg about a foot off the ground."

Keeping the hold above her head, she obeyed. For better or worse, she was off the ground now. It was disorienting. She was aware of nothing around her except the points where her hands and feet met the rock. A small point of panic rose, but she shoved it down, concentrating on her brother's voice.

"There's another hand hold on the same ledge as your left hand." Terjan's words sounded calm and steady. "Move your right hand there."

She moved. A comforting hand reached to touch the uninjured side of her back. "You can do this," Allenthal said. "I'm right here."

Obeying Terjan's instructions without question, she moved slowly up the cliff. Her hands and forearms burned with the effort, and pain radiated from the partially healed bites on her arm and leg. Once, her foot slipped from its hold, but she kept her grip with both hands, and Al reached from below to support her. Terjan helped her find a new foothold. At last, she felt the sheer face give way to a flat ledge, and Terjan helped her scramble onto it, relief flooding through her.

She lay on the stone gasping for breath, her arms and legs shaking.

"You did it!" Terjan exclaimed, squeezing her shoulder. "You're amazing."

Still trying to catch her breath, she couldn't answer him. A moment later, Allenthal climbed over the ledge behind her. She heard his breath, and the tiny sounds of his hands and feet against the rock.

"I'll go back for the last of the packs," Kylith said.

Kyjia lay on the flat, stable ground, breathing, trying to calm her racing heart. They had to go on. When her breath had a chance to slow, she sat up. Only a few moments later, Kylith had returned, and they continued their climb.

They made it up two shorter rock faces. At the top of the last one, Kyjia felt the others standing nearby as all of them gathered in a narrow passageway.

"Now," Kylith said, "this is the hard part. We have to get ourselves and our packs through that crack."

She couldn't see the way forward, but if Terjan had already climbed through, the rest of them should be able to make it.

"I'll go first. Give me two of the packs," Terjan said. "I already know I can fit through."

A few moments later, Kyjia heard his voice coming from a short distance away.

"I'm through. Send Kylith next. If he can't fit, we'll have to go back and start a fight with Zhandar's guards."

That didn't sound like a good plan at all. They needed to make it through this passage.

For several moments, she heard the scraping of a person against rock. "Pull," Kylith ordered in a strained voice.

"I *am* pulling," Terjan's reply. "It's too tight."

"Keep pulling!" Kylith urged.

She heard the sounds of struggle. At last, a groan and then a breath of relief drifted to her. Kylith had made it.

"Take these." Al must have been handing the packs through. A moment later, he was beside her. "You're next." From behind her, he guided her forward. Rock closed in on both sides of her. "You need to slide about five feet forward. They will help you from the other side as soon as they can reach you. I'm coming behind."

Feeling the walls surrounding her, Kyjia pushed her way forward. The further she went, the tighter the space became. The ceiling above grew lower until it pressed down on her. The stone chafed the raw skin of her back, sending pain through her body. This was impossible. She couldn't do it. She would go back. There had to be another way. Panic welled up, and her breath came in gasps.

"You can do this," Al said. His voice sounded strained, compressed. She took a deep breath. This could work. She imagined the men fitting through here. They were bigger than she was. They had fit themselves through, somehow. She reached behind her and felt Al's hand take hers.

She pushed forward, despite the hot pain in her back, sliding forward, an inch at a time.

"Almost there," Terjan promised.

CHAPTER 27

CROWN PRINCE ALLENTHAL

HE HELD KYJIA'S HAND tightly, his only point of human contact. Rock surrounded Allenthal, pinning him from both sides, its unyielding surface hard against his body. He couldn't move, and his heart pounded in his ears, his breathing fast and shallow. There wasn't enough space here. He had gone in as far as he could, and the ceiling lowered until he couldn't raise his head. He pushed still farther forward.

Panic struck him at the moment he realized he was trapped. His head spun, and he saw bright spots before his eyes. He couldn't move in either direction. Hard rock pressed against his chest, stealing his breath. There was no way out.

"We'll get out," he gasped. "Don't worry. Don't worry, Alvaren, we'll find a way to get you out."

On the day of the accident five years ago, they had rushed to the place where his brother had fallen. Alvaren had tumbled from the trail over a series of boulders and cliffs, coming to rest in a narrow crack between two granite faces.

Allenthal had climbed down to reach Alvaren, finding him pinned between two boulders. His eyes were wide with panic. "Can't breathe, can't..." He couldn't speak any more after that.

From above, they tried to pull him out. They had managed to lift him a little, enough to provide room for him to breathe. When they pulled harder, Alvaren screamed. His leg was broken. They kept trying to free him, for hours.

"Alvaren," Allenthal gasped. "Please hold on. We'll get you out. We need help."

A hand tightened on his. It was the only thing he noticed other than the rock trapping him, and the memory of terror in his brother's eyes. "We can't get out."

"Allenthal!"

The voice penetrated his panic. Alvaren wasn't here. That terrible day had been long ago. The voice belonged to Kyjia. He clung to her hand. "Kyjia? Please help. We can't get out. We can't—"

"We'll get out," she assured him. "We'll be all right."

He couldn't speak. He didn't have enough air to talk. His breath came in tiny, short gasps, and his vision grew dark.

"Allenthal," she repeated.

Her voice sounded calm. She was here with him. She would help.

"We can't get out! We can't get Alvaren out. He's going to die and I can't help him! Please, there has to be a way to help him."

Her fingers laced between his. His hand was the only part of his body free to move.

"Allenthal," she said, her voice soothing. He concentrated on it. "Alvaren loved you. He wanted you to live and be happy. He's safe now, resting. It's time for you to let him go."

"No!" He couldn't do it.

"You must," Kyjia said, sternly. "You loved him, and he saved your life. Send your love to him, wherever he is now, and release him to be at peace."

"I can't! If not for me—"

Her hand still held his. "He had the right to make a choice," she said. "It was his decision, not yours. Accept his choice. Accept what he did for you and let him rest now."

"No!" He was pleading now, not protesting. She was right, and in his heart, he knew it.

"Let him rest."

Allenthal closed his eyes and drew in as much breath as he could. His body shook, his hand trembled. The memory of his beloved brother, injured and trapped in the rocks, haunted him. It had taken hours, but they had finally gotten him out. They'd carried him to a makeshift camp in the rocks. The freezing mountain night had settled around them. Icy wind blew down from the frozen peaks. In his arms, Alvaren shivered. Allenthal took off his cloak and wrapped it around his brother.

"Thanks," Alvaren murmured, looking up at him. His brown eyes weren't afraid anymore. He smiled slightly. "I couldn't ask for a better brother."

Kyjia's voice broke into the memory. "It's time for him to rest."

Allenthal had spoken the same word to his brother. "Rest." He tightened the cloak closer around Alvaren's shivering body. "It will be all right. Rest."

His brother hadn't spoken again. Before dawn, he had slipped away. Alvaren was resting now.

Allenthal raised his eyes to see Kyjia. She had turned her head toward him, even though she couldn't see him. "Goodbye, Alvaren," he whispered. He had to go on.

"That's right," she said. "You can do this. We'll make it through together."

"Together," he gasped. Letting all the air from his lungs, he pushed himself closer to her.

"That's right." Gripping his hand, she pulled as hard as she could.

The ceiling hung lower here. His tall frame had no more room. The rocks gouged into his scalp. Blood ran down his forehead. Kyjia hooked her ankle around his and pulled his foot and leg forward. Changing the angle of his body gave his head slightly more room. Inch by inch, they moved forward.

"Almost there," Terjan said from outside.

Suddenly, Kyjia's hand pulled free of his, and panic welled up in him again. A moment later, Terjan grabbed him, pulling hard. Freedom was only a few feet away. Allenthal attempted to calm his mind and release the breath he fought so hard to take in. It came out in a gasp as Terjan dragged him a little further.

They were moving, slowly. Much too slowly, but with help, Allenthal moved toward the opening. A few moments later, Terjan bent to grab his foot, and Kylith reached in to grasp his hand.

"Ready?" Kylith asked.

Allenthal nodded desperately.

"Exhale. Now!"

At the moment the breath burst from his lungs, Kylith pulled hard on his arm, and Terjan on his leg. His hand was out in the open air now. So close.

One more effort freed Allenthal, and he collapsed to the ground, gasping. Kylith knelt beside him, putting a comforting hand on his shoulder. He gripped the hand in relief and gratitude. They were alive. They were out.

"You made it." Kylith grabbed a piece of cloth and wiped the blood from his forehead, examining the cut. "It's not deep," he said. "Was it really necessary to grow those extra two inches so you're taller than everyone?"

Allenthal felt the urge to laugh and to punch Kylith. He didn't have the energy for either one. They let him rest. Several moments passed before he could breathe properly again. Turning his head to the side, he saw Kyjia resting against the rocks. She had gotten him through. Without her, he'd still be back in the crack between the rocks, trying to breathe.

She sat with her arms wrapped around her knees. Fresh blood soaked through the torn remnants of her tunic. They should have thought about her before they tried this plan. Now, she was in even more pain than she had been.

When he could move again, he dragged himself up and across the rock to sit beside her. "Kyjia?"

She turned toward the sound of his voice, and a sudden smile lit her beautiful face. "You did it, Al."

He took her hand and kissed it. "You rescued me."

They rested, hidden in the rocks, while the sun sank slowly into the west. Allenthal sat with his legs stretched out, resting his back against the stone. Kyjia curled up beside him, her head resting against his shoulder. He looked out into the distance. It felt so good to breathe the free air. He hoped he never saw the inside of a cave again.

Night fell, and the clear dome of the sky arched above them. He watched as, one by one, the glittering stars appeared. He wanted to shout in relief at being free again, but in the distance, he saw the lights of Zhandar's camp near the main entrance. They would not be truly free until they got the cure.

The night deepened. It was time for them to get away, and quickly. The opening they had come through had left them part way up a steep rocky ridge. They needed to climb down. Gathering up their things, Allenthal tossed his pack to Kylith.

He reached out to take Kyjia's hand. "We need to climb down through the rocks," he explained. "It will be easier if you hold on to my back, and I'll climb."

After everything else she'd been through, she didn't question his plan. Using his arm as a guide, she moved to stand behind him.

"Ready?" she asked.

"Yes." He bent down to allow her to clasp her arms tightly around his shoulders. She used her legs to grip his hips. Slowly, he stood.

"All right?" Her breath tickled his ear. "Can you climb like this?"

He could. Already he had begun to recover from the panic of earlier. "I won't let you fall," he promised.

He tried to make his movements as smooth as possible. It must be terrifying to feel the motion, and know they might fall, but not be able to see anything. Clinging to him tightly, she left his arms free to guide them between the rocks. She trusted him to get them safely down, and he couldn't fail her.

They descended to the plain below. With any luck, Zhandar would remain searching the caves for a long time before he gave up or realized they'd escaped.

"We're down," Allenthal said when his boots were firmly on the sand. Kyjia slid to the ground. He shouldered his pack and took her hand, and they slipped away into the darkness.

Before dawn lit the desert, they found a hiding place between the rocks. They were all tired, but Kyjia was far beyond exhaustion. The poison had sapped her strength.

"May I?" he asked, touching her shoulder.

She turned so he could see her back. Using a little of their precious water to clean it, he applied more of the ointment. The wounds looked worse than ever after sliding against the rock.

The cure. They had to find it. Maybe they should be headed back for Zhandar's camp, but he had a strong force of men, and he wouldn't give them the cure unless Kyjia bent to his will, which she wouldn't do even if it meant saving her life. So, for now, they would do as she and Terjan chose.

He looked down at her. She had fallen asleep, curled up with her head pillowed on one of the packs. Her face was drawn with weariness, illness, and pain, but she was still so beautiful. The night-dark softness of her hair framed the pale clear skin of her face. Her long dark lashes brushed her cheeks. She was strong, and she'd held on bravely through the most difficult of circumstances.

Allenthal found a place to watch while the others rested. Quiet covered the barren landscape, the only motion was the heat waves shimmering. Hours later, when Kylith came to relieve him, he slept, tucked into the shade of the stones but still feeling the blazing heat. At least it had been cool underground.

By nightfall, they prepared to go on. Kyjia still slept, and when he attempted to rouse her, it took a long time for her to wake up.

"Can you go on?" he asked.

"I'm fine," she mumbled.

They continued their journey, but she leaned on him more and more as the night passed. By the time they stopped at dawn, she was barely walking. He had to coax her to eat and drink before she collapsed into sleep.

"She isn't doing well," Kylith said. "Maybe we should be going the opposite direction, trying to fight our way to that cure."

"Zhandar has too many men," Terjan protested. "We can't defeat them alone."

"We need allies," Kylith said. He looked at Allenthal. "Raz Abbas doesn't like him much."

"True, but that's very different from openly starting an armed conflict with him," Allenthal pointed out. "Raz Abbas and his men won't take on Zhandar directly."

"Karineth will help us," Terjan said stubbornly. "He's the only one who really can."

How could Allenthal argue with that? He believed Namradill would help him. Why should he try to tell the boy that his God wasn't going to act?

Slowly and painfully, they made their way back to Saarin. By keeping careful watch and traveling at night, they had reached their destination unobserved. Once inside the city, they needed to keep away from anyone loyal to Zhandar. After a quick discussion, Kylith went to Raz Abbas's house. He was grinning when he returned. He tossed Allenthal a red tunic. "He's leaving with another caravan tomorrow."

Allenthal looked at Terjan. "That only leaves us tonight to find your mother."

Kylith took Kyjia to gather with the caravan, while Allenthal and Terjan moved quietly through the dark streets toward Zhandar's house.

The place was emptier than it would be if Zhandar were here, but there were still many people around. Terjan stole the tunic of a stable hand and slipped inside to look around. He returned to Allenthal. "She's locked in a room beside the stables. I need you to distract the guard so I can get the keys."

Allenthal sneaked through the gates. Once inside, he sauntered across the courtyard to the guard's quarters, where a man sat in his chair looking bored. "Get up!" Allenthal barked. "Lord Zhandar is just outside the city, he'll be here in three minutes."

The man cursed and jumped up, running for the door. He was several paces outside when he turned to look at Allenthal. "Who are you? You shouldn't be here."

Terjan still needed more time, so Allenthal hit the man in the face. The guard cursed and came up swinging. A moment later, several other guards joined the fight. Allenthal grunted as a fist landed in his belly. He retaliated with a solid blow to the man's chin that knocked him down. Someone grabbed him from behind, pinning his arms to his sides. Another man struck his face, sending pain radiating from around his eye. The man drew back to strike again, and Allenthal lunged forward suddenly, causing the blow to miss him and strike the man gripping him. He twisted away, escaping the hold.

From the corner of his eye, he saw Terjan and Tillian slipping out the gates.

Allenthal dodged and swung. More men were drawing weapons and running toward the fray. Throwing back the nearest of his opponents, Allenthal knocked down another of them and bolted for the gates. He struck another of the guards on his way out and then dashed into the maze of the city. They chased him, right on his heels for a long way, through the winding streets. Near the edge of town, he slipped into a tent, hiding between stacks of crates. He stayed still while his pursuers passed by, and, gradually, everything got quiet.

Though his face throbbed from the beating, he didn't think any of the injuries were serious. He waited in hiding until he was sure it was safe. Around him, the night grew old. It wouldn't be long until dawn.

By the time he reached Raz Abbas's house, Allenthal found the caravan already loaded and ready to depart. He put on the red uniform, buckling on a sword belt. Terjan had done the same and now stood with the other guards. Allenthal made sure their packs were loaded. Kylith nodded toward a supply wagon hitched to four camels.

Allenthal looked inside. Between the stacks of goods, he saw Tillian, her arms around Kyjia. Tillian had a few cuts and bruises but appeared mostly unharmed. She held her daughter gently, brushing the hair back from Kyjia's face. Her dark eyes glittered with fury, but her expression softened when she saw him.

"Thank you for what you did last night," she said. Her eyes paused on his battered face. "Come in here and let me take care of that."

He jumped into the back of the wagon, unbuckled his sword belt, and sat down.

"Al?" Kyjia turned toward the sound. "Is that you? What happened? Are you hurt?"

"I'm fine," he protested.

"Stop talking," Tillian ordered, moving away from Kyjia to find her pack. "Your eye is already beginning to swell."

"Al?" Kyjia exclaimed in dismay.

"It was only a little fight."

Very slowly, the caravan began to move, and the wagon rolled forward.

Tillian dug in the pack, pulling out several items. While he sat as still as possible in the moving wagon, she applied a strong-smelling mixture around his eye. It stung like fire when it reached the place where his skin had split over his eyebrow.

He hissed in pain. "What is that stuff?"

"No more questions. It will help." She applied more of it to his split lip.

He gritted his teeth until the sting eased.

"Are you hurt anywhere else?"

"No," he said hastily. "I'd better get back to work." Picking up his sword, he jumped back out of the wagon to resume his post. The caravan wound its way out of Saarin. No one noticed them among Raz Abbas's guards, and no one followed them.

The caravan headed southwest out of Saarin, bound for Niaz with a load of goods to trade. They traveled slowly, moving during the cool night hours and resting through the heat of the day. They tended Kyjia carefully, but no matter what they did, her fever came and went. From the caravan's stores of medicinal herbs and her own meager supplies, Tillian compounded mixtures to use on the burns, but they provided only temporary relief.

One evening, Tillian came to walk beside Allenthal as they marched. For a long time, they were silent.

"You saved my daughter's life and helped me escape from Zhandar," she finally said. "I'm very grateful."

"I wish I could have done more for her."

"She cares about you," Tillian said.

He waited for her to go on. Did she feel that her daughter must never care for a foreigner, or did she simply want Kyjia to be happy? Tillian didn't elaborate.

As the silence lengthened, he said, "She's the bravest person I've ever known."

CHAPTER 28

KYJIA

L OST IN THE BUSTLE of the caravan, Kyjia wanted nothing more than a few moments of solitude. Her mother had walked with her a short way from camp into the shade of a large boulder, and then left her to herself. She'd heard the crunch of sand beneath her boots as she walked away, and then nothing more than blessed silence.

Around her, the day was hot and still. The heat of the bright sun burned against her eyelids. But whether sunlight shone or night fell made no difference; she saw nothing. She sighed and rested her head against the rock, allowing herself a moment of self-pity.

Sometime later, she heard footsteps, a heavier tread than her mother's. The steps paused in front of her.

"May I join you?"

Recognizing Allenthal's voice, she smiled slightly. "Yes." What was he doing out here? Wouldn't he rather be resting?

He sat close enough that their shoulders touched.

"How are you feeling today?"

She shrugged. "I'm all right."

For a time neither of them said anything. He sighed, settling back against the rock. His hand found hers, and she liked the touch of his calloused fingers. She had seen his hands, back when she could see, big and capable. She traced the lines of the tendons on the back of his hand with her fingertips.

"Kyjia," he whispered.

Her skin tingled under the soft brush of his fingers smoothing back a stray lock of her hair.

His voice was quiet. "It won't always be this hard. We'll find a way to make things better."

It was a sweet thing to say, and tears welled in her eyes. "Better..." she murmured.

"It will be better," he promised.

He was very close. She felt the brush of his breath against her skin when he spoke. Would he kiss her? Did he want to? Without being able to see, how could she evaluate the expression on his face?

With a quiver of anticipation, she realized that she wanted him to kiss her. She had little experience. Neither of the previous times had been her idea. Of course, the bandit hadn't been. And Zhandar? Though he had done many good things, and if everything had been different, she might have grown to care for him, she had not wanted his kiss when he'd given it. He'd betrayed her. The very last thing she'd been able to see was his hand gripping her wrist so she couldn't escape.

Allenthal was different in every way. He'd treated her with kindness and respect, never tried to force his will on her. They had been close together many times. Though he had only been caring for her when she was sick and injured, she hadn't been able to completely ignore the pull of attraction to him. He must feel it too. She sensed that he wanted to kiss her. Could he tell that she felt the same?

She reached out, tentatively, to touch the side of his face, the stubble of beard on his chin. She allowed her hand to follow the strong line of his jaw, sliding around the back of his neck and into his hair.

His hand touched her waist, pulling her closer. "Allenthal," she whispered.

Softly, his lips brushed across her cheek.

The sharp crunch of boots on the gravel interrupted the moment, and Al dropped his hand. His voice sounded casual. "Terjan? What is it?"

How much had her brother seen?

"Mother sent me to ask if Kyjia is ready to come back to camp," Terjan said.

"Thanks," Kyjia replied. "I'll be back in a few moments. You can tell her that Al will walk back with me."

"I'll tell her." Terjan sounded embarrassed. His footsteps departed swiftly.

The moment had passed, and Kyjia couldn't see if Allenthal was disappointed or relieved.

CHAPTER 29

CROWN PRINCE ALLENTHAL

THE NEXT EVENING, AS the caravan began to move, Allenthal placed himself near the supply wagon. Tillian walked a little ahead of them, taking the time to stretch her legs, leaving Kyjia alone. No one else was paying him any attention. He climbed up into the wagon. Kyjia turned to look toward the sound of his boots on the wagon bed.

"It's me," he said.

At the sound of his voice, she relaxed in obvious relief. "Al."

"Would you like some company?"

"I'm glad you're here." A smile lit her features.

He unbuckled his sword belt and sat down beside her, his back propped against the side of the crate. Moving closer, she leaned against him, laying her head against his shoulder while he put his arm around her. She rested one hand against his chest. The contact sent heat racing through him. Even through the fabric of his shirt, he felt every tiny motion of her fingertips.

He drew in a breath and covered her slender hand with his. "Kyjia," he whispered.

She nestled a little closer, sliding her hand around his neck and reaching up to brush a light kiss on his cheek.

"Thank you for coming to spend time with me," she murmured. "I would go out and find you if I could."

He smiled at her words, warmth growing inside him. "Would you?"

"Yes," she replied. "I wanted to be with you again." Her lips brushed lightly against his jaw. Her mouth was soft and smooth, and he couldn't think of anything else with her so near.

Abruptly, she pulled back. "But maybe you don't... You're a very kind person. Don't think that you have to... that you... I mean, I understand if you don't feel the same." She turned her face away from his, but not before he'd seen her cheeks color.

In response, he slid his fingers along her jaw, gently turning her back toward him and pulling her nearer until his mouth found hers. Her lips were soft and sweet, and she answered his kiss. She tangled her fingers through his hair, pulling him closer still.

Her kiss sent heat racing through him, and he tightened his arms around her. She felt warm and willing against him.

Finally, she pulled back, and he saw tears welling in her beautiful dark eyes.

"Kyjia, what is it?"

"How can you still want me after this?" She pointed to her eyes. "If I don't get the cure, I'll die of it."

"I'll do everything I can to stop that from happening," he said. "You think I don't want you because of the curse?"

"Why would you, if I can't see?" She blinked back tears and wiped her eyes. "I want to do everything by myself, but I can't."

She didn't seem to realize how enchanting she was, whether she could see or not. "You are brave, caring, and beautiful. How can I keep from wanting you? The curse has nothing to do with it, except that if I could take your pain on myself, I would."

More tears ran down her cheeks. "I believe you would, but none of this is your responsibility. There are too many problems in Tyar. You should go home to the river country and forget me."

He caressed her cheek with his fingertips, brushing away the droplets. "Impossible. I will never forget you. Not if I lived a hundred years without you."

He pulled her close again, his mouth moving against hers, allowing the heat and tenderness of his kiss to explain what she meant to him more completely than words could. He could never get enough of her. Knowing that he might lose her to the curse only made him want her more.

They had been with the caravan for nearly three weeks. The hot sun rose higher in the sky, and everyone halted to rest in the shade. Tonight, they would approach the point where they would need to turn aside to reach the tiny canyon where Ashkan had lived with his family. Kylith and Al went to find Raz Abbas. They found the chieftain comfortably seated in his tent, sipping from a goblet.

"Come in," he invited them. "Sit down, be comfortable. Have something to drink. What can I do for you?" He filled two more cups, handing one to each of them as they sat down opposite him.

"You have already done great service in allowing us to travel with you," Kylith said, taking a sip of his drink.

Raz waved a hand in dismissal. "That is nothing. Even the bandits and scorpions living in the rocks have heard of you by now. If they know you're still with my guards, none of them will dare to attack me. And that is a service you have done for me."

Kylith grinned at the chieftain. "I'm sure you had nothing to do with making sure that story got around."

Raz mopped beads of sweat from his forehead with a handkerchief. "I'd be a fool if I didn't. Maybe the tale even grew a little as I passed it on. I've lost a huge amount of profit to bandits over the years. With you around, they'll never dare to bother me again."

"I hate to disappoint you," Kylith said. "But we have an urgent errand."

"Here? In the middle of the desert?" Raz gestured at the desert outside the tent. "There isn't a good well for many days travel in any direction. How can you have an errand here?"

"But we do," Kylith said firmly.

The merchant's eyes turned to Allenthal. "Would this have something to do with the young lady you have taken such meticulous care of during our journey?"

"It might," Allenthal admitted.

Raz looked at them both in turn without saying anything. Finally, he rubbed his chin thoughtfully. "I see. These are momentous times for Tyar. If the old tales are to be believed, the fortunes of our nation are fated to improve. Perhaps this family has something to do with that."

Raz was a shrewd man, and his guesses were very close to the truth.

"Perhaps," Allenthal said.

"And the two of you, rivermen, come to visit the desert. I've never heard of that happening before. You must have a part to play in the fate of Tyar." He glanced from one to the other. "Can you tell me anything more?"

Kylith shook his head and took another sip from his goblet.

"They are not our secrets to disclose, Lord Abbas," Al said, hoping their employer would not interpret this as disrespect.

"Well," Raz looked thoughtful again, "so, you must turn aside on your errand. When?"

"Tonight," Kylith said. "And we must not be seen leaving. We hope to slip away during the dark hours."

"I will do what I can to hide your departure." Raz grinned at them, raising his glass. "I wish you luck, long life, riches, and many children. But perhaps I have a part to play in these events too. If so, we will meet again."

When the caravan moved again in the evening, Allenthal and Kylith made sure their packs were ready and waiting together in the wagon with Kyjia. They took up positions guarding the rear of the column.

As the long line moved slowly along, darkness fell around them. They slipped their packs from the wagon and put them on. Last of all, Allenthal lifted Kyjia out and set her on her feet, offering his arm to guide her. When no one was looking, they moved quietly away.

They crept through the rocks, staying out of sight. A long night's journey brought them back into the canyon where Ashkan and his family had lived.

After such a long march, Kyjia was barely on her feet. Allenthal walked with his arm around her to support her. She lifted her head as they entered the narrow sandstone canyon. "I feel my father's presence here," she said. "This place feels so familiar, I can almost see it."

"Why don't you rest for a while, and we'll have a look around," Allenthal suggested. He helped her into the sheltering shade of the cavern that had once been her home.

"Thank you." She sank to the ground in relief. Her eyes closed.

CHAPTER 30

KYJIA

As she rested in the shade, Kyjia felt her mother applying something to her back. It helped. Slowly and methodically, she cleaned and re-wrapped the injuries, passing the bandages around Kyjia's body to hold them in place.

"I'll be back in a moment," she said as she finished.

Kyjia heard the sound of her footsteps walking away. Moments passed, and her mother didn't return. Somewhere outside the cavern, soft footsteps whispered against the dry earth. Something was wrong. She sensed a change in the feeling of this place. Enemies.

Had they already attacked her mother? Where was Terjan? Where were Al and Kylith? They intended to look for danger. Had they seen this attack coming?

Feeling around herself, Kyjia located her own small pack. With trembling hands, she searched through the contents until she found her knife. Slowly, she stood, the weapon gripped in her hand. Moving slowly, feeling the stone beneath her feet, she made her way toward the entrance.

This place was so familiar. How many times had she found her way in the dark? She knew every stone. She paused in the entrance, the solid rock of one wall against her shoulder. No sound came from outside. She waited in silence.

There were more than one of them. At least two, no three? The tiny sounds of their boots against the earth gave them away. They came nearer, one of them ahead of the others. She caught the scent of weapons, rust and oil, leather, and the sour tang of sweat.

She held her blade ready.

The attack came with no warning. Hard hands seized her arm. She struck with the knife and heard a hiss of pain. He twisted the knife from her hand, and it fell to the ground. She struggled and fought. It felt like more than one person attacking her. They knocked her to the ground, and one of them straddled her, pinning her down.

A cry of pain escaped her, as her weight landed on her injured back.

"Tell me where you hid the tablet!" an unfamiliar man's voice demanded. "We know one of you has it. Maybe you'd like to decide who else dies first? Your mother or your brother?"

"No!" she pleaded, "don't hurt them. Please!"

A blow struck her face. Her head snapped to one side, pain blossoming from her cheek and jaw.

"Tell me where it is!" he demanded.

The pain in her back burned through her whole body, and she clenched her teeth to stop a moan.

"Bring the boy," the man snarled.

Feet shuffled and someone struggled. Did they have Terjan?

"Say something, so she knows you're there," another man ordered.

Now came the sound of a hard fist against flesh.

Terjan groaned. "We won't help you."

"You don't have to help," the man snarled. "Just scream. She'll tell us what we want to know."

"She won't," Terjan protested. "We don't know where it is."

Tears welled in Kyjia's eyes. How could Terjan expect her to remain silent while they tortured him? No tablet was worth that. Nothing in the world was. She couldn't do it.

Another gasp of pain escaped her brother. Her body shook all over. She couldn't do this. "Stop," she begged. "Please! Don't hurt him anymore."

"Tell us what we want to know," the man above her demanded.

Kyjia hesitated.

From her brother came a strangled groan of pain.

"No!" Kyjia cried. "You can't do this. Leave him alone. I'll tell you."

"You can't, Kyjia, no. Not because of me," Terjan gasped.

For the moment, he was still alive and able to speak. A little relief washed over her.

"Don't worry about me—" The sound of a blow cut off his words.

The man pinning her got up and dragged her to her feet. She barely managed to stand, shaking with pain. "Lead us to where you hid it. It's not far away, is it?"

She couldn't get her legs to move properly and took a single, halting step forward.

"Do it now," the man screamed, "or I'll make sure your brother pays."

He struck her again. The blow would have knocked her down if he wasn't holding her up with a painful grip on her upper arm.

She took another step.

Sound and movement exploded all around her. Feet on sand, weapons clashing together, and something that could only be the sound of a body falling limply to the ground.

"Terjan!" she gasped, terrified.

Her brother didn't reply.

The man grasping her lurched to the side, dragging her with him. When his hand released her, she tumbled to the ground. The sound of violence seemed to come from every direction. Metal struck metal, someone groaned. There was no way to know which direction to go or how to identify or avoid the threat.

Abruptly, the sounds of fighting stopped. Silence fell, except for the heavy breathing after a strenuous exertion. Who fought? Who won?

When a hand touched her arm, she started violently.

"Kyjia?" It was Al's voice.

She burst into tears of sheer relief. His hands were gentle as he helped her back to her feet. Her body shook, but his arms wrapped around her and held her close, taking care to avoid her injuries.

"It's all right," he murmured. "You're safe now."

"Terjan?" she gasped.

"He's all right. Your mother is here now too; she'll take care of him. It's not too bad. He'll recover."

She wanted to stop crying. She tried, but in that moment, the weight of everything was too much. At the threat of her brother's safety, she'd agreed to give up the tablet. Zhandar's men would have killed them, undoubtedly, as soon as they had what they wanted.

For the moment, she didn't try to do anything. She let Allenthal hold her, allowing herself to take comfort from his strength. His fingers brushed her tangled hair back from her face.

"It will be all right now," he promised. "Kylith is checking to make sure there aren't more of them."

He guided her back to the cave, where she heard her mother attending to Terjan. They were alive, both of them. Gratitude filled her heart. Al was safe beside her. He helped her to a seat.

"I need to make sure Kylith didn't find anyone else."

She rested her head against the stone wall beside her and concentrated on breathing, wishing for his warmth to be beside her once more.

A short while later, she started into alertness, terrified at the sound of boots walking nearer.

"It's Al and Kylith," her mother's voice assured her.

Letting out a deep breath, she relaxed again.

"We didn't see anyone else," Kylith reported. "From up above, we saw these four and we came back as fast as we could. They're Zhandar's men, I'm sure, and there might be more of them. Even if they didn't follow us here, he might send soldiers to search this place. We need to leave as soon as we can."

Even sightless, Kyjia felt all of them looking at her.

She nodded. "We need to find the tablet now."

It had to be done. They needed to take the tablet and leave this place as quickly as they could. Still, at the moment, she wanted nothing more than a drink of water, a bite of food, and to sleep for a week. That would have to wait.

Gathering her determination, she struggled back to her feet. Al stepped close to help her, and she stood, leaning on his arm.

"We'll all go together," she said.

Moving slowly, feeling her way between the familiar rocks, Allenthal helped her up the path behind the cave. The others followed.

"There's a small opening in the rocks to the right," she said, sliding her hands over the rocks. "Help me find it."

In a few more steps, Al paused beside her. "Is this it?"

She explored the shape with her hands. Too small. She shook her head. "We need to go a little further."

They made their way upward. Kyjia moved very slowly, stumbling frequently, leaning on Al to keep herself upright. He paused again, and she felt the shape of the place, mapping it with her hands.

"Yes. This way." Not far now.

They climbed. By feel, she made her way up the narrow notch in the rocks until they emerged into a small, flat place.

"Tell me what you see," she said. "There should be a small, round, flat place with a rock that I like to sit on."

Beside her, Al answered. "I think this must be it."

She turned her head slowly from side to side. "The tablet is close, but I never thought I wouldn't be able to see when I came back to get it."

"Look," Kylith said, his tone urgent. "Out there."

Al made sure she was steady and quickly left her side. A twist of fear gripped her when she couldn't make out their low whisperings.

"There's a group of men coming," Kylith said louder. "Out in the desert but moving this way. It won't take them long to reach this place. I can't tell how many are coming, but there are several. Is there another way out of this canyon?"

There was. A small, secret path led through the rocks to another exit. Terjan knew it too.

"I know the way." Terjan's voice sounded confident.

"Good," Kylith said. "You, Tillian, and I will go back to get the packs. Kyjia and Al will stay here and find what we're looking for. Before those men get here, we need to be long gone." His footsteps retreated back the way they had come.

Kyjia took a deep breath, forming a detailed mental image of this familiar place. She remembered hiding the tablet. From her favorite rock, she walked a little way... she took a few steps and stumbled. Al caught her before she could fall. With his help, she moved a little further into the rocks, sinking to her knees, exploring the stones with her fingertips.

Allenthal knelt beside her. "What are we looking for?"

"A small, square stone." She shook her head. "I'm afraid it looked just like all the others, but one of them is loose."

Together, they searched, pushing and pulling at the rocks, looking for the exact one she described.

The others were soon back, carrying their water, supplies, and gear. "We left nothing of ours down there," her mother said, "only the men who attacked us. We have no way to hide them or bury them before the others reach us. They will know someone was here, and they will follow."

"Have you found it? We're out of time," Kylith's voice sounded tense.

Kyjia continued her desperate search. At last, she heard Allenthal give a cry of triumph.

"This one is loose."

Kyjia felt him guide her hands to the opening. She reached inside to withdraw a familiar shape wrapped in a bundle of cloth. She unwrapped it to feel the smooth gold of the precious tablet. Letting out a sigh of relief, she held it reverently close to her heart.

"We need to leave quickly," Al said. "Unless we want another fight."

None of them wanted that. Kyjia replaced the cloth around the tablet, placing it carefully into the pouch at her belt. With Al's arm guiding her, they moved away.

The day grew hot as they traveled, moving as fast as they could, despite the heat. Even with her companions carrying her share of the supplies, bone deep exhaustion weighed on Kyjia. Sweat beaded on her face, and her mouth felt dry. They needed a cool place to rest. Now that they had moved down from the ridge, they would no longer have a view behind them, and the others couldn't see if anyone followed.

They kept going all day. Kyjia walked as long as she could. When she stumbled to a halt, her breath coming in gasps, too tired to go on, Al carried her. More hours passed in a blur of hot sun, rocks, sand, and the steady motion of his footsteps. Eventually, the motion ceased. In the stillness, she slept deeply.

CHAPTER 31

CROWN PRINCE ALLENTHAL

AFTER RESTING FOR A few hours during the night, they'd gone on before the day had a chance to heat too much. When he looked behind them, Allenthal saw nothing but sand and a few scattered rock formations. A tall sand dune blocked the view ahead. He shook his head. The desert seemed to go on forever. Nowhere within his sight was any sign of water or plant life. If they couldn't find water, they would die out here.

Beside him, Kyjia struggled forward. She didn't complain, though he knew she must be in pain and desperate for rest. A little way up the dune, he stopped beside a boulder partially buried in drifting sand. It offered a tiny scrap of shade.

He guided her to sit near the rock. "Rest for a moment."

Kyjia sank down gratefully. Though she couldn't see it, she found the shade by feel.

He gripped her hand for a moment and then released it. "The others are climbing the dune. I'm going to take a look at the view from the top. I'll be back in a moment."

She didn't speak, but nodded wearily, leaning her head to rest against the stone.

It made no sense to use what remained of her energy to climb this dune if there was an easier way around. He followed the others upward. The loose sand felt hot around his boots, and with each step, he slid back almost as much as he moved forward.

When he finally reached the top, just behind his companions, a gust of hot wind drove sand into his face. Squinting, he looked out. The dune was tall enough that he could see for some distance around them. The only unique feature nearby was a tall column of rock standing alone in the sand. The wind blew harder. Beside him, Tillian cursed.

A moment later, he realized what she saw. A wall of sand and wind bore down on them. Sandstorm.

"Get to that rock!" Tillian yelled above the rising wind, pointing toward the formation.

"Go!" Allenthal yelled. "I'm going back for Kyjia." Tillian nodded. He turned to Kylith. "I'll meet you there."

Allenthal's stomach clenched as he saw how quickly the storm raced toward them, swallowing everything in its path. Turning back the way he'd come, he stumbled through the loose sand, heading for the small rock where Kyjia sheltered. It seemed so much further away than it had been. Already, he heard the roar of the rising wind.

A moment later, the storm swallowed him, the wild wind dragging at him. The dust blinded him, and he coughed, trying to breathe. He'd never seen anything like this in his life. He took the cloth from his head, attempting to re-wrap it. The wind nearly tore it from his grasp. Pulling it back, he wrapped it tightly around his face, covering his mouth and nose.

He still couldn't see properly, but at least now he wasn't choking so badly on the dust. He had to find Kyjia. The wind felt like it came at him from all directions, making it difficult to walk in a straight line. He went downhill. Where was that rock?

It didn't take long to realize that he'd gone too far. He should have reached it by now. All around, he saw nothing but sand and wind. The flying sand stung his eyes. Beneath his feet, the sand flattened out. He'd passed her. The rock she sheltered beside had been part way up the slope.

He turned, the wind tearing at him even harder. He pushed back up the slope, wandering from side to side in an attempt to spot the rock. He had to find her. The wind grew stronger as he searched. Where was Kyjia?

CHAPTER 32

KYJIA

KYJIA LEANED HER SHOULDER against the rock, allowing it to support her. Exhaustion dragged at all her limbs. She needed rest and water. With the others gone, silence surrounded her. A breath of wind caused the loose sand to whisper over the dune.

She heard the wind growing stronger, not a good sign in the desert. The weather must be changing. Where were the others?

For a moment, she heard a distant voice. She thought it was Al, but she couldn't be sure. A growing sense of unease twisted through her. She got to her feet, facing in the direction she'd heard his voice.

The wind and sand struck her in a sudden unexpected blast, stinging her face and throwing her off balance. She stumbled on the slope, falling and sliding down the dune. When she raised her head, blowing dust surrounded her, and she pulled her head cloth tightly over her face to filter the air so she could breathe.

Bracing against the wind, she struggled back to her feet. Feeling a fleeting touch in the wind, she knew something had brushed against her fingertips. The end of a cloak?

She stepped toward it, trying to find the fabric again. Her outstretched hand caught something and held on tightly. A moment later, hands gripped her shoulders.

"Kyjia!"

Allenthal. He had found her. She clung to him in relief. She couldn't speak. They could barely hear each other above the howling wind. Holding onto her arm, he led her a little way back up the slope. The wind diminished slightly as they reached the shelter of the rocky outcropping where she had rested. He pulled her down into the shelter of the stone. The fabric of his cloak covered them both, shutting out the worst of the storm.

His arms encircled her protectively. "Are you all right?"

She coughed before she could get the word out. "Yes."

He drew her closer. "I was afraid I'd never find you."

The fear in his voice reminded her how much he cared for her. "Thank you for coming for me. Where are the others?"

"We saw a tall rock formation a little way ahead. They hoped to find shelter near it. I told them we would meet them there."

He wasn't from Tyar. He'd likely never seen a storm like this before. "It may be impossible to find them until the wind dies."

"What do we do?"

She smiled slightly. "You've never seen a sandstorm before?"

"No!"

"We stay out of the wind and work on staying alive while we wait for it to pass."

"You don't think we should try to reach a better shelter?" he asked.

She shook her head. "We might never find it."

"Very well."

She felt him moving around, sliding himself into a better position. As he moved, the wind blasted through, driving dust and sand against them. The storm surrounded them. Allenthal pulled her closer into his arms, and the wind stopped. For several moments, they coughed and tried to catch their breath.

"Sorry," Al muttered. "I was trying to take my pack off and move us closer to the rock."

"It's all right," she said. "You have nothing to apologize for. You came back to help when I needed you."

For a few moments, she'd felt completely lost, entirely at the mercy of the weather. She might not have survived the storm without his help.

She barely had the strength to move. Her body ached with fever, her head pounded, and the injuries on her back throbbed. No, she wouldn't have lived long on her own.

She leaned against him, her head resting against his chest.

"Drink a little," he murmured.

She felt him holding the waterskin to her mouth, and she gratefully took a swallow. The water soothed her dry mouth and throat.

"Take more," he urged.

She shook her head.

"You must be thirsty."

"Yes," she admitted. "But we don't know when we'll find water again. We have to be careful."

"Just one more swallow."

Her body cried out for water, and finally, she agreed and took another mouthful. "Thank you." She sighed and allowed her eyes to close.

As the wind and sand raged around them, she drifted. Allenthal was there. He would guard her.

Outside their meager shelter, the storm still howled. Kyjia's empty stomach pinched. In the small space, she heard Allenthal breathing. Under her ear, his heart beat steadily, and his chest rose and fell in sleep.

Tentatively, she rested her hand against him. She'd never known anyone who gave so much of himself to others. This journey to Tyar had put him in terrible danger, but he'd come anyway. She'd grown to really know him over the last few weeks. How could she not love him?

Even though she couldn't see him now, she remembered the earnest expression in his beautiful brown eyes. She'd seen the strong contours of his muscular body. Even without her sight, she felt the shape of him beneath her fingertips. It seemed a miracle that he still wanted her, even after the curse. He hadn't changed the way he treated her, even though she was injured and weak.

How could anyone really know him and not want to keep him? She never wanted to let him go. Her fingers softly glided over him, reaching up to trace the strong shape of his neck, and the ends of his hair.

The rhythm of his breathing quickened as he woke to feel her touch. He didn't move yet, allowing her to brush the short beard along his jaw. When her hand reached his chin, he kissed her fingers.

"You're awake," he murmured.

"Yes." Her voice came out as a gasp as she felt his warm breath against her skin, his lips against her hand. She turned her face toward his, tangling her fingers in his hair to pull him closer.

In the endless dark that now surrounded her, the touch of his mouth on hers burned like bright fire. They moved together as if they had waited their whole lives for exactly that moment. She never wanted to be separated from him again.

When he finally pulled away, their breath was ragged.

"You can wake me up any time." He chuckled. "I don't want to stop, but you need another drink of water and something to eat."

He was right.

Moving slowly and carefully in the small space, he offered her another swallow of water and a little food.

The storm went on as if it would never stop, but Allenthal cared for her patiently, and she savored the time to be near him.

CHAPTER 33

KYJIA

WHEN THE WIND FINALLY died, they left their refuge, shaking the sand from their clothes. Exhaustion dragged at Kyjia. After walking only a short way, she couldn't continue. Half awake, she felt the gentle motion of Allenthal carrying her. They moved for some time before she heard other voices.

"Is she all right?" her mother asked.

"Yes," Al answered.

Her voice sounded concerned. "I was so afraid you'd both be lost in the storm. Thank you for keeping her safe."

Kyjia felt the coolness of shade and the sand beneath her as Allenthal set her gently down. He lifted her head and placed something soft beneath it. Kyjia woke to hear Terjan's voice.

"It's time to speak to Karineth."

Forcing herself to wake fully, Kyjia nodded, with difficulty, pushing herself into a sitting position. Terjan was right. They needed guidance. At the moment, they didn't even know where they were going. They had no plan beyond trying to escape their enemies.

She swallowed the fear rising in her belly that when they took out the tablet and made the attempt, nothing would happen. She repeated Al's words in her mind.

While I sleep, my land is buried in sand. The people of Tyar must rise again. Hold the tablet aloft, and speak my name three times, and I shall hear and answer. A new ruler shall rise in the desert and a light in the night sky from the ancient city of kings shall proclaim their coming. My power shall be in their hands and a river shall flow out of the sand.

Beside her, Al said, "She can't climb that."

"She can if we help her," Terjan assured them.

She heard Terjan kneel beside her. "It's time, Kyjia. Are you ready?"

At the moment, she didn't exactly feel ready for anything, but they had to do this. Her father had entrusted the tablet to her, and it was her responsibility to help her people. She extended her hand. His fingers closed around hers, pulling her to her feet. She touched the pouch at her belt to feel the solid shape of the tablet. Beside her, she felt Al's hand steadying her.

"There's a tall column of rock," Allenthal murmured in her ear. "We're going to climb. I'll hold on to you. Just go carefully."

She should never have agreed to climb anything in her condition, but with their help, she kept moving. It felt high. Without her sight, she had no idea how high. Her grip on Allenthal's hand tightened. She moved slowly, allowing the others to support her, until the rock flattened beneath her feet, and they stopped.

Allenthal let out a breath. "You can see everything from up there." His voice was filled with wonder. "The desert spreads out in all directions around us. The sun is just rising over the hills."

Kyjia imagined the rosy light of dawn glowing all around them. She turned her face toward the warmth of the new day.

She felt Allenthal turn. "What is that?" he asked.

Her mother's voice answered grimly. "Another storm is coming. We need to get down, fast."

"Wait!" Kyjia protested. They had already climbed up here, and they couldn't leave until they made their attempt. She took out the tablet, gripping it in one hand and raising her arm high above her head. "Terjan?"

His hand joined hers where it gripped the tablet.

Together, they spoke slowly and clearly. "Karineth. Karineth. Karineth."

For a long moment, nothing happened. The gold grew warm against her skin as she held it tightly. The voice was barely audible at first, nothing more than a distant whisper. Kyjia sank to her knees, and still holding the tablet together, Terjan moved with her.

As still as stone, they waited.

"We don't have much time," Kylith said. He was right. This tall rock was no place to attempt to survive a sandstorm.

Kyjia couldn't give up yet. She bowed her head, waiting.

I am Karineth.

The voice grew nearer and louder.

I am Karineth. All the land of Tyar is under my keeping. Kyjia and Terjan, children of Ashkan, I hear your voices.

"We need your help, Divine Karineth. All of Tyar has become a burning desert. Our people struggle to survive," Kyjia said.

Where have all my rivers gone? The fields and orchards? Now, I see barren sand in every direction. Have I been asleep for so long?

"It has been generations, Lord. The rivers dried up long ago. Our people are scattered and divided."

There is nothing left here but wind and sand. I must use what power I have left to tame the desert. Our people need a leader. The time has come for a new ruler in Tyar. Kyjia and Terjan, children of Ashkan, you are descended from many kings. One of you must lead our people.

"But there are others who hold more power," Kyjia protested.

It will be my power that matters. Either of you shall have my blessing to rule Tyar.

Kyjia gripped her brother's hand. Terjan must be able to hear the words, just as she could.

Kyjia took a deep breath. "We will do as you command, Lord Karineth, but we are few. Zhandar commands thousands of men. How can we stand against him? How can we defeat Jaro and the dark magic he wields?"

Jaro was a mystic once, given to teaching and serving the people. Perhaps the blame is mine for not hearing him when he called to me. Instead, he turned to the powers of darkness. Now, he is a servant of evil. He must be stopped.

"How?" Terjan asked. "He cursed Kyjia because he was trying to force her to give him the tablet. She needs help. He has the cure."

Your pain grieves me, Kyjia, my brave daughter. I'm afraid even I cannot completely undo the harm that has been done to you. Go to Kallah, the holy city, to my temple, and there I will give you my blessing. On the altar of my temple rests the Sword of Kings. In my name, you shall wield it in defense of Tyar. Your enemies shall not have the power to overthrow you.

Kyjia waited, but she heard nothing further. Beside her, Terjan knelt reverently on the rocks. Lifting their hands where they held the tablet, he raised them high above their heads. "We will do as you command, Divine Karineth."

Silence fell over the top of the rock. Nothing else had changed. The rising wind still rushed around them. Yet, everything had changed. Eternal Karineth had spoken once more. He had committed to help them save their land.

"Look!" their mother cried.

Kyjia's stomach tightened. "What is it?"

Allenthal gripped her hand. "It's all right. She's looking at the storm."

"We need to hurry down?" she asked.

"No." His voice was incredulous. "The storm is stopping."

For a long moment of silence, they remained where they were.

Had Karineth already begun exerting His power over their land? All around them, their air stilled until it was calm. In silence, they climbed down to their camp. No one spoke.

The voice of Divine Karineth rang in Kyjia's mind. The fate of her entire kingdom rested on them. Her father had given her the responsibility of caring for all her people. It had seemed impossible before, but with the divine power Karineth had promised, maybe they could achieve what was needed.

Terjan spoke up. "We're going to Kallah. We will find the Sword of Kings, and, I hope, relief and healing for Kyjia." His voice sounded confident.

"How will we survive there?" their mother asked. "There's no water near Kallah."

Kyjia smiled. "Don't worry. There will be."

CHAPTER 34

CROWN PRINCE ALLENTHAL

As the heat of the day faded and night covered the desert, they set out again. Though the air was cool now, Allenthal felt the feverish heat of Kyjia's body through her clothes as she walked beside him. She never complained, though he could tell she was close to dropping from exhaustion. As ill and tired as she was, she should be resting in bed, not trekking through the desert.

Already practically asleep on her feet, she gave nothing more than a quiet sigh of gratitude as he picked her up. Despite the extra effort of carrying her, he loved having her in his arms.

They kept moving as the night passed, the stars slowly turning above them. Kyjia stirred as they walked, reaching up to slip her arms around his neck.

"Thanks for helping me," she whispered.

"Were you so sure it was me?" he asked. "You were asleep. What if someone else were carrying you?"

He saw her smile in the faint light. "It feels like you. I would know."

They walked for a while before she spoke again. "We did it, Al. We spoke to Karineth. Do you think He will really help us?"

He had never regretted his own faith in Namradill. "Yes. Our Goddess has always helped us when we needed Her."

"And Terjan heard Him too. That's good. He can lead them if I..." her voice trailed off.

It took him several moments to realize that meant he could lead if she succumbed to the poison, that she expected to die.

"No," he protested. "We're getting the cure back from Jaro, and you're going to be fine. Just hold on until we do."

Her arms tightened around his neck. "I'll do my best. I don't want to leave you. Being blind and sick has taught me many things. It's showed me what kind of man you really are. I'm not sure how much time I have and I want to tell you..." she turned her face up toward him. "I love you, Allenthal."

Moisture filled his eyes. She loved him. "Kyjia—"

"You're very kind to help me," she interrupted. "Don't feel obligated. It's all right if you don't feel the same. In fact, it's better if you don't because I don't know what's going to happen to me. But I wanted to tell you while I still could."

"Stubborn girl," he growled. "You are *not* going to die, and if you had let me finish, you would know that I *do* feel the same. I love you with all my heart."

"Truly?"

A smile of such aching joy lit her face that tears pricked his eyes again.

"Truly," he assured her. "So, you have to hold on until we get that cure."

"I'll try," she murmured, her voice fading, the last thing she said barely audible. "I wish you would kiss me again." Her eyes drifted closed.

He bent to brush a gentle kiss across her forehead. Her feverish skin burned against his lips.

As the days of their journey passed, Allenthal watched over Kyjia carefully. Whenever they paused to rest, he set her gently down on the sand and tried to get her to drink and eat. She took a little water, but he couldn't convince her to swallow more than a morsel of food. Sometimes, the fever was so high that she murmured and moved in sleep, not even aware of where she was. Despite their care, she grew no better. Tillian had done all she could.

Terjan watched over her too. "We'll be able to help her when we get to the temple. Divine Karineth promised to bless her." His voice sounded confident. Allenthal hoped he knew what he was talking about. They needed a miracle now. Kyjia wouldn't last much longer without one.

They came over a rocky rise to see a wide valley spread beneath them. It lay still and silent under the light of a full moon. The white light illuminated a stone city at the head of the valley. Kallah, City of Kings. The dry rocky bed of a long-vanished river wound down through the valley.

"We're almost there, Kyjia," Allenthal murmured.

She drew in a breath, shifting in her sleep, but she didn't wake.

They crossed the valley, heading slowly up to the crumbling stone walls.

It was midnight when they reached the ancient walls of the city. Around them, all was silent, with barely a whisper of wind over the sand. They passed the ruined gates and entered. From this vantage point, they could see the city gently rising toward the palace at the top of the hill. The Temple of Karineth lay in the exact center of Kallah, as if the whole place had been planned around it.

Allenthal gazed in wonder at the beautiful buildings now falling into ruins. The wide avenues were empty. He tried to imagine this place as it might have been, full of life, with people filling the streets. They moved on, walking between the empty buildings toward the center of the city.

The temple had been built into a vast, circular structure. Inside the walls, a round courtyard surrounded a smaller building in the center. Most of the inner structure remained intact, except for the roof. They stepped through the broken doors and came out into a room, now roofed only by the night sky. Rubble from the fallen stones filled the space, partially covering a white marble altar placed perfectly in the center.

Kyjia lay pale and motionless in his arms. Worry flooded through him. Was she breathing? He bent his head over her lips and felt a faint whisper of air. She lived, barely.

"Hold on," he murmured, brushing his lips across her feverish cheek.

In the middle of the room, Terjan worked to clear away the fallen stones. Kylith and Tillian moved to help him, and in a few moments, the surface of the altar was a space of clear white stone, bright with moonlight.

As the others stepped back to watch, Terjan stood beside the altar, holding up the tablet. The white beam of moonlight shone down, growing brighter and brighter until they shaded their eyes. A brilliant shaft of light rose from the altar, straight up into the night sky. In the blinding glow, they could barely see Terjan standing so close. Had he become part of the light? Time seemed to stop. They could have been standing there for an hour or a year.

At last, the column of light grew thinner, focusing itself on the altar. It formed itself into the long, slender, deadly shape of a sword. Slowly, the light faded, and Terjan reached forward to take the weapon in his hand. He raised the blade toward the sky and shouted. His voice rang among the ancient buildings.

He held the Sword of Kings.

Terjan lowered the sword and looked at his sister. "Bring her." He gestured toward the altar. "Put her here."

Allenthal obeyed, laying her still form down on the white stone. The moonlight glowed on her translucent pale skin. Except for the midnight waves of her hair, she might have been a statue carved of marble.

He didn't want to let her go. Finally, with an effort, Allenthal released her and stepped back.

Terjan stood beside her, holding up the tablet. The moonlight reflected off its surface, a beam of gold mixed with the silver rays.

The young man spoke in a low voice, but Allenthal couldn't catch the words. Terjan cast his eyes up into the heavens, pausing as if he were listening. One hand held up the tablet, the other was laid on Kyjia's forehead. For a long moment, they remained still.

Finally, Terjan removed his hand and looked at the others. "Even He cannot completely heal her. The darkness is too powerful, and a measure of the poison remains within her. He will return to her what vitality He can. She must rest here for an hour tonight and for six more nights. At the end of that time, Karineth will have done all He can for her."

Terjan stepped back, leaving his sister lying still in the moonlight. They waited. Kylith checked his weapons and went out to look for any sign of danger in the surrounding city.

No one spoke as Allenthal stood with Tillian and Terjan. The profound silence of the night returned. Kyjia looked unearthly, lying there with the moonlight glowing on her skin. Her eyes were closed, her lips slightly parted. One slender arm lay beside her, her hand palm up, the fingers slightly curled. The marks left behind by azarim teeth interrupted the smooth skin.

At length, Kylith returned. "I don't see any signs of people near us," he reported. "Though after what just happened, there will be soon. I drove off a pack of azarim. We should leave someone on watch while we rest."

Allenthal nodded, agreeing with Kylith's assessment. His friend stood in silence, waiting with the others.

When the hour had passed, Terjan returned to the altar, reaching out to touch Kyjia's forehead. "That's all we can do for now," he said.

Allenthal came forward to look down at her. Her breathing was deeper and when he touched her brow, he found the fever reduced. Whatever had happened here tonight, she appeared to have improved. Gently, he gathered her into his arms and stepped back from the altar.

Walking quietly through the city, they searched for a safe place to rest. They set up camp in one of the less-damaged buildings a little way from the temple. Tillian mixed a bowl of her glowing powders. In its light, they explored the room carefully. They had chosen to rest in a place with only one entrance, which would prevent any unwelcome reptilian visitors. They shared a little of their rapidly diminishing supply of water and food.

"We will take Kyjia back to the temple tomorrow night," Terjan said. "She's already a little better."

Tillian hugged him. "Thank you for helping her. You've done well."

CHAPTER 35

KYJIA

KYJIA FOUND HERSELF LYING on a cloak, the ground firm and smooth beneath it. Her thoughts were clearer than they had been for a long time. The fever was lower, the pain less. All was quiet around her, and she lay still, reviewing in her mind everything that had happened.

Her thoughts went back to her father. Missing him remained an ache in her heart. He'd been a good man, a good father. She'd never pictured him as a king, but now that Karineth was awake, there must be a new ruler in Tyar. She was the eldest. The responsibility fell to her, unless the poison took her life first.

Her memory flew back to the ridiculously ornate dress she had worn with Zhandar in Saarin. Would becoming queen mean she'd have to dress like that every day? She had no idea what ruling a nation would be like. Tyar had never seemed like much of a nation before. Perhaps now it would be. Karineth had told them to go to Kallah and find the Sword of Kings. He would give them the power to wield it.

She couldn't see. How could she ever wield a sword? But she couldn't shake off the responsibility that had settled on her. What about Allenthal? The memory of his arms around her sent warmth throughout her body. She hadn't been able to see him as he kissed her, but she would never forget the way it felt. The way his mouth had moved against hers, the feel of his strong arms around her. She would serve her people, but if she became queen, she must remain in Tyar, and sooner or later, he would leave.

She drew in a sharp breath at the pain of that thought.

"Kyjia?"

Allenthal was beside her. Gratitude flooded through her not to be alone. She didn't even know where they were.

"How do you feel?" he asked. His fingers brushed along her forehead. "Your fever is much lower."

She did feel better than she had for several days. "A little better. Where are we?"

"Kallah."

"Did we find the sword?"

His fingers squeezed hers reassuringly. "Yes. Terjan has it."

All her worries came back to swirl in circles in her mind. "I need to talk to him."

"Yes," he agreed. "He'll be back here in a short while. In the meantime, will you have something to eat?"

Helping her sit up, he placed what felt like one of the packs behind her so she could lean against it. He held a water skin so she could drink. After she finished, he placed food in her hand. When she'd eaten, she felt stronger than she had. Maybe there was hope they would succeed.

His hand gripped her shoulder reassuringly. "I'll be back in a little while. Terjan will stay with you."

Putting her hand over his, she clasped it. "Thank you, Allenthal." She held his hand for a moment longer before he slipped away.

"Kyjia!" She heard her brother's footsteps as he approached. "You look better."

She turned toward the sound of his voice. "Yes. Will you come and sit?"

He settled beside her. "What is it? You'll feel better soon. I'll keep the sword for you until you're ready to take it."

The sword. The throne. How could she fulfill her responsibilities to her people if she couldn't see? She bowed her head. "How can I do this blind?"

Terjan took her hand and held it. His voice sounded confident. "You love your people. You are kind and faithful. With Karineth's blessing, you will be Queen of Tyar."

Tears welled in her eyes. Their God had said either of them could rule. She had assumed the responsibility would go to her as the eldest, but would that really be best for her people? How could she rule as she was, blind and ill? Tyar needed a strong ruler. But she must do her duty to her people.

Terjan leaned closer, putting his arm around her. "Kyjia, what's wrong? We have the sword. Everything is going to be fine."

How could she share all her doubts with him?

"He hears you," Terjan said suddenly. "Karineth. He knows everything in your heart." Terjan guided her hand to touch the tablet.

Kyjia slid her fingers around the smooth, heavy gold. "I am your servant, Lord Karineth."

Kyjia, my brave daughter. I feel the sorrow in your heart. After all you have already suffered, I cannot bear your pain. You and your brother are both worthy to rule Tyar, but perhaps you must walk a different path? You love Crown Prince Allenthal, Heir to the throne of Seven Rivers. He is the servant of my sister, the Goddess Namradill. Though he loves you, he cannot stay here in my land with you. I would not bring the sorrow of parting from him on you. Terjan, my son, will you take upon yourself the burden of leading your people and release your sister?

Kyjia's whole body stiffened at the words. Crown Prince Allenthal. Heir. Why hadn't he told her? He said he had a duty back home that he couldn't abandon, but he'd never given her any clue that it might be a throne.

Where was Allenthal? She wanted to demand why he hadn't told her. Instead, she found Terjan's hand and gripped it.

"I thought it had to be me," she admitted. "I felt it was my responsibility. I didn't give you enough credit. You are every bit as able, perhaps far *more* able than I am." Her fingers tightened around his. "I believe you can take care of our people. Will you take the sword and become King of Tyar?"

He drew in a long breath. "I planned to support you as queen."

She held his hand tightly. "I know. I know you would, but if fate doesn't grant me a life here in Tyar, the people would be safe in your hands. You would do everything you could to lead them well, to protect them. Terjan, will you take the throne?"

"Kyjia, are you sure? I always thought it would be you. Once we make the decision, it will be final."

She nodded, a wave of relief rushing through her. This felt right. "I'm sure."

A long moment of silence passed before he answered. "I will."

Together they gripped the tablet again.

My children. I will support the decision you have both made. I have always believed that either of you would make an excellent leader, and I would have supported your choice either way. I will still bless Kyjia as much as I can, but now, I name Terjan, son of Ashkan, King of Tyar.

CHAPTER 36
CROWN PRINCE ALLENTHAL

A S THE AFTERNOON LENGTHENED, a small group of people and camels approached the city. Allenthal kept his weapons close. Kyjia was resting now, and he would not allow anyone to harm her.

Kylith came to stand beside him. Terjan armed himself as well and stood beside them as the small group made their way through the old city. A man in gray desert robes stepped forward. He pulled down the cloth covering his face and bowed deeply to them.

"My name is Onar." He gestured to the people following him. "This is my family. We learned the old legends from our grandmother. She said that in a time of great need, a new ruler would rise in Tyar, and light would shine into the sky from the ancient city of kings. Last night, we saw the sign and have journeyed here in haste to find the new ruler."

Allenthal looked toward Terjan, wondering how the young man would respond. Slowly, he removed the shining sword from its sheath and held it out. Onar and his family gazed at it, their eyes wide in wonder.

Terjan faced them, his back straight, his gaze meeting Onar's directly. He put his sword back in its sheath at his waist and stepped forward.

"I am Terjan, son of Ashkan, King of Tyar."

Onar stepped forward and bent to one knee before him. "I offer you my allegiance, my king."

Terjan placed a hand on Onar's shoulder. "Rise," he said. "I accept your loyalty."

Onar stood and faced him.

Terjan's expression was grave. "Before you join me, you must realize there might be others who will not accept me so easily."

Onar nodded firmly. "I understand that I might be called upon to fight for my king."

"Will you stand with me against Lord Zhandar?" Terjan asked.

Onar's jaw tightened, and the eyes of the woman behind him opened wide, but he responded in a firm voice. "I will."

Terjan smiled at them, the expression making him look more like the ordinary young man he'd been before. "Welcome."

Onar's family came forward to greet him. Within a short while, the newcomers had made space for themselves in another of the empty buildings nearby.

As the sun set, Terjan walked beside Allenthal as he carried Kyjia back to the temple. They entered the circular chamber and repeated their actions from the night before. While Kyjia lay bathed in white moonlight, they stood side by side.

"Divine Karineth told us who you are," Terjan said.

"What?" Allenthal didn't know what he meant.

"He told us you are Crown Prince Allenthal, Heir to the throne of Seven Rivers. Why didn't you tell us?"

Allenthal shifted uncomfortably on his feet. "I haven't told anyone who I am since I left the borders of my own land."

Terjan folded his arms across his chest. "You love Kyjia. Don't you trust her?"

Allenthal drew in a long breath. "I love her," he agreed, "and I do trust her. It just wasn't something we spoke of specifically."

Terjan appeared to consider for a moment. His expression softened. "We would have been happy to have you and Kylith stay in Tyar with us."

Allenthal shook his head. "I appreciate your offer, more than I can say, but I cannot ignore my duty to my own people. I'm sure you understand that."

Terjan nodded. "I do. What I don't understand is why you came here at all. If you are the heir to the throne, why risk yourself in the desert?"

Allenthal put a hand on the young man's shoulder. "My quest was to help the royal family of Tyar."

Terjan turned to him and grinned, his teeth white in the dim light. "You have certainly done that. We couldn't have survived without you and Kylith. You saved all our lives."

"It's not finished yet, not until Jaro and Zhandar are defeated and Kyjia is cured." His eyes went back to where she lay motionless on the altar.

"Will you take her with you when you go?" Terjan asked. "I don't want to lose my sister, but she loves you too. If she stayed behind, her thoughts would always be on you."

Allenthal didn't have an answer. In the end, Kyjia would have to decide.

When the time was finished, Allenthal lifted her from the stone and carried her back to their temporary home. All was silent in the room. Tillian stood at the door, taking her turn to guard their rest. Kylith lay sound asleep, his head pillowed on one of the packs. Terjan paused in the doorway beside his mother.

Al took Kyjia back to her bed, only a couple of cloaks on the floor, and set her down gently. When he started to straighten up, he found her arms still around his neck, holding him in place.

"Don't go," she whispered.

"You need to rest," he protested. She hadn't removed her arms, and unable to get up until she did, he gave up trying and lay down beside her. She curled herself into the hollow of his arm and laid her head on his chest, her arm across his body.

"How do you feel?" he asked.

"A little stronger."

He felt a measure of relief, allowing himself to release a little of his worry for her. "Good. It will keep getting better. Soon, all this trouble will only be a memory." He drew her a little closer.

"I'm so glad you're here." She lifted her hand to his face.

Shivers ran through his body at the sensation of her fingers in his hair and sliding along his jaw. She pulled his head down until his mouth met hers. The kiss began tenderly. He'd been so worried about her. The illness had been serious. Now, she was awake and strong enough to make her wishes known, and she wanted him. He felt it in the way her lips met his eagerly, her hands pulled him even closer, and her body arched against his.

For several long moments, he forgot about everything in the world other than her. Finally, he pulled back. "You might not be able to see her, but your mother is just outside the door," he whispered into her ear.

Tillian wasn't watching them now. He nibbled along her ear, and she drew in a sharp breath. He kissed along the line of her jaw until his mouth found hers again.

He had never felt anything like this. Kyjia knew his secrets and his fears, and she still cared about him. With her mouth moving against his, it became impossible to think about anything else.

Kyjia pulled back. "She can't see us, can she?"

He raised his head to look at the doorway. "I don't think so. If she could, she would be coming in here to kill me."

"No," Kyjia protested. "I'd never let her."

His mouth found hers again, while the darkness and silence surrounded them. Allenthal wanted that stolen moment never to end. They were together now, and who could tell how much time they would have?

He was shaken out of his focus on Kyjia by the sound of someone moving around. He'd forgotten that Kylith lay not far away. He'd appeared soundly asleep when Al had passed him. How much had he heard? Now, Kylith was on his feet, his dark form crossing the room. They heard his voice in the doorway.

"Tillian, I'll take a turn on guard, if you'd like to go inside and get some sleep."

By the time her footsteps crossed the silent room, Al had moved himself a respectable distance from Kyjia and curled up pretending to sleep.

Two days later, a caravan displaying the banner of Crimson Sands approached the city, led by a familiar portly figure. Raz Abbas dismounted and faced the small group of people, bowing respectfully.

"We saw the sign in the sky. Is it true a king has returned to Tyar?" He looked at each of their faces, stopping on Al and Kylith. "It can't be you; neither of you is from Tyar."

Terjan stepped forward. He drew the shining white sword, holding it flat across his palms. Raz's mouth fell open in wonder. "The Sword of Kings. So, it *is* true!"

Terjan nodded. "I am Terjan, son of Ashkan—"

"King of Tyar!" Raz shouted. He raised his arm, cheering, and all his people did the same.

After six nights of lying on the altar, Kyjia had regained nearly her full strength. When she finished her time, Al had helped her up, but she'd walked beside him back to the others. He couldn't find words to express the joy he felt at seeing her able to walk and talk and move, though she still couldn't see. The pain in her back, while not entirely gone, was much reduced.

By dawn, their guards had reported the largest group of new arrivals. Zhandar had come with the might of the Sunfire Clan at his back. Allenthal couldn't see their camp from the city. It lay beyond a large dune near the walls. Only a small group of men entered the city at first light.

Al and Kylith checked their weapons, while several of Raz's guards did the same. They moved to protect their new king as Lord Zhandar, Jaro, and several guards in white tunics walked up the wide street to meet them. A tense silence fell, as Zhandar, standing tall and powerful with Jaro at his side, faced Terjan and the others.

Zhandar offered no gesture of respect. Instead, his tone was derisive. "So, boy, you are attempting to claim the throne after all?"

Terjan stepped forward, displaying the gleaming white sword across his palms. "This sword descended from heaven. Divine

Karineth set it in my hand and ordained me to protect and serve the people. I am King of Tyar."

Watching the confrontation, Allenthal gripped his sword hilt. With an arrogant sneer on his face, Zhandar came to face the young man. Terjan stood, his back straight, showing no sign of fear or doubt.

Zhandar took a step closer. "I have spent my entire life serving our people, working tirelessly to gather them, unite them, and create a new future for them. What have *you* done?"

Terjan held his ground, meeting Zhandar's eyes. "I have only done as Divine Karineth ordered me. Without our God, the people of Tyar have no future."

"You claim to have spoken with Him?" Jaro said, moving to stand beside Zhandar. "Karineth is dead or gone. He cares nothing for Tyar."

The gathered people drew in a collective gasp, shocked to hear those words, especially from a mystic, but Terjan didn't falter.

"That's not true. I have spoken with Divine Karineth. Our God is with us."

"And what about your sister?" Jaro asked coldly. "No power on earth can save her life, aside from the cure I possess. Wouldn't you like her to be able to see again? You care about her, don't you?"

Terjan stared back at them without answering.

"I am prepared to make an agreement with you," Zhandar said. "You will turn the tablet and the Sword of Kings over to me. I already hold power over much of Tyar, and I am the one who should be king. You and your little band of followers will swear loyalty to me. Tyar will be mine. When you've done this, I will give you the cure. Kyjia's sight and health will be restored."

Terjan faced him steadily. "And if not?"

Zhandar's hand strayed to the hilt of his sword. "If not, I will return at dawn with a thousand men and make sure none of you survive."

Kyjia stepped forward, pushing her way by feel through the crowd until she stood alone facing him. "Zhandar? Why are you doing this? You must realize we will never put Tyar in your hands. You have allowed Jaro to control you completely, and he turned to evil a long time ago. We cannot let him rule our people."

Terjan moved forward to stand at her side, putting his arm around her.

Kyjia straightened to her full height. "If I must die to keep our people from being in bondage to you, then I will do it."

Jaro darted toward them, something sharp and green in his hand. Allenthal lunged toward them, along with all the other guards.

Pushing Kyjia safely out of the way, Terjan blocked the poisoned blade with his gleaming sword and shoved Jaro back. The mystic stepped back while their guards closed around them in time to meet the attack of Allenthal, Kylith, and Raz's soldiers. Fighting their way back the way they had come, they retreated out the gates and toward their camp.

Allenthal hurried back to find Kyjia. She still stood with her brother, unable to see what had happened. He pushed his way through the crowd until he stood beside her.

"Are you hurt?" he asked.

At the sound of his voice, she put her arms around him. "No, you?"

He turned toward the young king. "Terjan?"

"I'm all right," Terjan responded.

Allenthal let out a breath of relief. He stood where he was, holding Kyjia. The only way to retrieve the cure now would be to defeat Jaro, Zhandar, and all their men, or to give in to their wishes and sacrifice the hopes of everyone in this group. How could they do it? But they needed a way to save Kyjia.

They had until dawn.

All that day, they gathered and armed as many men as they could. Every man who had come to join them agreed to fight, and from Raz's supplies, they found a store of weapons. By evening, they were as prepared as possible, but how could forty men stand against a thousand?

All the people gathered in the wide space between the ruined buildings. The last rays of the sun lit their faces. None of them knew what the morning would bring. If Zhandar fulfilled his threats, they would all die, the reign of the new king over in only a few days. Everyone stood silently.

The crowd parted to allow Terjan through. He walked to the very middle, turning slowly to take in all of them. His expression remained calm. When he spoke, his voice carried over the hushed crowd.

"Each of us has chosen to place our fate in the hands of God. We choose to side with Him to rebuild the nation of Tyar. In His hands, we will meet the dawn bravely. Our God will fight for us!" Terjan reached beneath his tunic and pulled out the tablet, hanging from a chain around his neck. He took it off and held it high, the sunset shining on the bright gold.

The people bowed their heads reverently.

"Divine Karineth," Terjan said. "We pray for Thy help and protection tomorrow. Our lives are in Thy hands. I pray for Your blessing on these brave and faithful people. Guard them, watch over them, and open a way forward for them."

Quiet fell as Terjan stopped speaking, his head cocked as if he were listening. For several moments, no one moved or spoke.

Terjan lowered the tablet and raised his head. "Our God is with us. He promises that tomorrow will be a new day, a new beginning for Tyar!"

Around him, the people shouted and cheered.

CHAPTER 37

KYJIA

THE STONE OF THE old street felt smooth under her boots. She held Allenthal's arm as he guided her. Terjan's footsteps sounded just ahead. She remembered seeing the ancient temple from a distance when she'd visited the city with Zhandar. She could picture the graceful circular shape of the building. When they arrived at the doorway, Al helped guide her feet between the broken stones. This was to be the final night of healing. Already, Karineth's power had granted her relief from the pain she'd endured, but she understood that He couldn't help her completely. Sooner or later, the curse would take her life. Truly, wasn't one life a small price to pay for helping her nation?

After hearing the way he'd spoken to the people, she knew Terjan would be a great king. It seemed so right that he should be. Though he was still young, he was smart and kind, and he loved Tyar. He had already begun to lead the people well. And what would she do? She didn't want to be separated from Allenthal, but he couldn't stay here, not when he was heir to the throne of his own kingdom. Why would he want to take her with him when he left? In her condition, there were many things she couldn't do on her own. She would be nothing but a burden to him. Yet, if he loved her too, couldn't they find some way to stay together?

"We're here," he said, beside her. Placing his hands on her waist, he lifted her up onto the stone surface of the altar. It felt cool and smooth beneath her. She missed his touch the moment he took his hands away. Finding the edges of the stone by feel, she lay down.

Now, Terjan stood beside her, his quiet voice murmuring words that she couldn't quite catch. He placed something, the tablet, it felt like, on her chest. It rested, smooth and heavy, against her skin. His hand touched her forehead, warm against her brow. She felt a glow of warmth throughout her body.

"Be healed," Terjan whispered. "Open yourself to the power of Divine Karineth. Use it to overcome evil. Take in the healing power."

The warmth grew, moving through all her muscles and bones, comforting, soothing. The sensation was stronger tonight than it had been on previous nights. Perhaps, having regained her strength, she was simply more aware.

She rested, floating in the sensation of being wrapped in warmth and comfort.

The time passed quickly. It felt like only a moment later when Terjan said, "It's finished. Can you get up?"

She could, except that the peaceful feeling had sunk so deep into her body that she couldn't make her eyes open. "I will soon," she muttered. "Sleeping."

Allenthal gave a soft chuckle. "Sleep then," he whispered, gently lifting her.

She obeyed, drifting away with the security of his arms around her.

The peaceful feeling had worked through her body to her very bones, and Kyjia slept for a long time. Since she hadn't been able to see, it had ceased to matter to her if the room was light or dark when she wanted to rest, but this morning was different. Brightness seemed to seep through her eyelids.

Kyjia blinked. Light flooded in. Light. Everything had been dark since that day in the cave. Around her, everything was a blur. She rubbed her eyes and blinked again. Slowly, the world settled into focus, and she stared in wonder. Terjan's healing had restored her sight. Tears of gratitude filled her eyes, and she paused to murmur a fervent prayer of gratitude. She could see.

She lay in a stone room with large openings which now let in the morning light. She sat up. No one else was there. Everyone had already gone. A sudden, terrible weight settled into her belly. They'd gone to meet Zhandar. The battle.

Kyjia got to her feet and went to the door, finding her mother standing there. "Mother!" She threw her arms around her.

She returned the hug fiercely. They drew back and looked at each other. As their eyes met, her mother began to cry. "Is it true?"

Kyjia couldn't keep a smile from lifting her mouth. "Yes. Where are the others? Have they all gone to meet Zhandar?"

Her mother nodded.

Kyjia picked up a sword and buckled the belt around her waist. "We're going after them."

They ran toward the city gates. When they passed through, they saw a small group of men surrounding Terjan, with Allenthal and Kylith beside him, and Raz Abbas and his guards. Onar and his brother stood with them. There weren't nearly enough of them.

With a great shout, Zhandar's army appeared on the crest of the dune above them, a long line of men on horses, the sun glinting on their swords. The white and gold banner of Zhandar's clan waved in the breeze.

At the bottom of the dune, Terjan raised his brilliant sword and shouted in defiance. He swung the sword, striking the sand at his feet. With a roar, a fountain of water exploded out of the sand, shooting into the air. The cascade grew, flowing into a river running out over the thirsty sand.

CHAPTER 38

CROWN PRINCE ALLENTHAL

Allenthal stood beside Kylith, watching in amazement as the new river raged past them. On the other side of the rushing water, their enemies watched them from the top of the dune, an army of mounted men raising their swords.

Gazing up the hill, Allenthal saw Jaro, his predatory gaze fixed on the small group opposing him. He raised his hand and pointed down at them. Despite the distance between them, Jaro's voice came down the hill, clear and powerful.

"Attack! Destroy them!"

At his command, the riders surged forward, thundering down the dune toward the small group of people standing against them.

When Terjan raised his hand, the tablet flashed gold in the sun. A sudden strong gust of wind swirled around them. Sand stung their eyes. Allenthal watched in disbelief as a swirling wall of sand roared across the valley to engulf the oncoming army. The sudden, unnatural storm surged around them, hiding the horsemen from view but leaving a small space of stillness around where he stood beside Terjan and the others.

On the far bank of the strange river, the sandstorm raged around their enemies. A few of the riders, their horses blinded by dust, stumbled into the rushing water and were swept away.

By the time their attackers fought their way through the wind and made their way around the geyser to the other side of the river, their numbers were greatly reduced. Many had been unhorsed or lost in the storm, but more, after seeing the fountain of water appear and the storm rise to block their path, appeared to decide it wasn't wise to fight anymore.

When a rider raised his blade and charged, Allenthal lifted his weapon to meet the attack. Metal clashed against metal. He cut through his enemy's guard, striking his leg and shoving him out of the saddle. Everything turned to noise and confusion around them. Jaro emerged from the storm and passed the water, on foot now, but wielding a sword and holding a glowing green crystal in his hand. He headed straight for Terjan.

The young king raised the shining white sword to meet him. Allenthal moved to guard his back.

They traded several blows, Jaro's sword ringing against the king's shining blade. Terjan moved quickly, striking and parrying. He held his own until Jaro raised his hand. A burst of white light flew from his fingers like an arrow to strike Terjan's body. The young man jerked at the impact, bright blood flowing from the wound, red against the pale fabric of his tunic. His jaw clenched, Terjan kept fighting, never taking his eyes off Jaro. He pushed the mystic back.

Jaro raised his hand again. Now, tendrils of dark mist flowed from his fingers, swirling toward Terjan. The strands of darkness wound around his arms and body and then his throat, binding him, and the young man fell to the ground, still struggling. Jaro raised his blade to finish him off.

Allenthal couldn't let Jaro kill him. Lunging forward, he blocked the blow with his own blade.

At the interruption, Jaro turned his attention to Allenthal, sending a vicious thrust at him. Their blades crashed together as Allenthal blocked it, sending an answering attack. The mystic parried. A few strokes later, Allenthal began to push him back. He could beat this man. His optimism crumpled as, with a sick feeling in his gut, Allenthal watched Jaro raise his hand, sending the same dark lines swirling around to trap him. The strands of darkness appeared as light as air, but they surrounded him as strong and tight as thick iron bands. He couldn't move his arms or swing his blade, leaving him unable to defend himself. Jaro's blade sliced deeply along his side, leaving a trail of burning pain. Off balance, he sank to his knees. In Jaro's other hand was the deadly crystal. Allenthal struggled wildly, trying to free his limbs and stop his enemy. The mystic struck out, and the stone cut deeply across Allenthal's neck. Pain raced through him as he struggled against the unearthly bands holding him.

This was it. He was going to die right here.

The mystic lifted his sword, aiming for Allenthal's throat. Before the blow could fall, Kylith was there. His unexpected attack struck Jaro, knocking the smaller man down, causing the powerful crystal to fly from his hand.

Suddenly, Allenthal felt the bands around him release. He raised one hand to cover the wound on his neck, feeling blood pouring out from beneath his fingers. Kylith drove the mystic back, his swift blows forcing the man to retreat, but he didn't see another enemy coming to attack him from behind. The man lifted his blade.

Allenthal stumbled to his feet, raising his weapon. His hands moved slowly, his arm weak, but his sword managed to deflect the blow that would have killed Kylith. Instead, the point of the sword bit into Kylith's face from the end of his eyebrow, down along his cheek to his jaw.

Kylith turned, swinging his blade to strike the man down.

Green light swirled in front of Allenthal's eyes. He blinked, attempting to clear his vision. Through the cloudy haze, Allenthal saw Kyjia raising a sword to face Jaro. At the sight of her, the mystic started toward her. How had she even gotten here, into the middle of the battle, without being able to see? Jaro would kill her as easily as brushing away an insect, and probably just as thoughtlessly. Allenthal had to stop him.

CHAPTER 39

KYJIA

ER HEART POUNDING, KYJIA gripped the sword hilt in her sweaty hand, running into the battle. As a rider bore down on her, she drew the weapon and held it up to block his blow. The impact jarred her arm, but she kept running, and before he could attack her again, she moved out of reach, losing herself in the confusion.

Her stomach clenched as she saw Allenthal sink to his knees just a short way in front of her. This couldn't be happening. Her brother already lay on the ground, his tunic soaked in blood. Kylith was still battling, but how long could he last without any help? Already the sorcerer had gotten up from the ground to advance on them.

Kyjia had to stop Jaro before he killed them. He intended to enslave her people, to control all of Tyar. He had already cursed her. Why should she fear him anymore? She reached Terjan, sinking to her knees beside him. He was injured, unconscious, but not dead. As she watched, he blinked, opening his eyes to look up at her in confusion. He extended his hand to give her the golden tablet. Kyjia took it, gripping it tightly. She dropped her borrowed weapon to pick up the Sword of Kings.

She ran toward the mystic. "Jaro!" she screamed at him.

He turned to face her. "Battle is no place for a blind girl," he shouted. "You're only living now because of my mercy. Unless you want to die now, get out of here."

Allenthal moved toward Jaro, placing himself protectively between them. He was already injured, barely on his feet. Blood soaked his shirt from a wound on his side, and he covered another wound on his neck while blood ran out from beneath his hand. He raised his sword to attack Jaro.

The mystic exchanged a few blows with him, but Allenthal responded more slowly than usual. How was he still fighting?

"I won't let you hurt her," Allenthal cried.

"The poison will kill her anyway," Jaro snarled. "What difference does it make? Get out of my way."

He swung his weapon at Allenthal, who managed to block his blows. Their blades locked together, and Jaro used his free hand to strike a vicious blow to Allenthal's injured side. He grunted in pain and swayed on his feet, but he didn't give up. Instead, he slashed at Jaro, leaving a deep cut across his shoulder.

Jaro shouted in rage and stumbled back a few steps, gripping the wound, but it didn't slow him for long. He attacked again, and Allenthal barely managed to block him. Jaro shoved Allenthal's blade to one side and struck Allenthal's arm. The mystic shoved him off balance, causing him to fall to one knee.

Kyjia leapt forward, unwilling to allow the fight to go on any longer. No matter what happened to her, she had to stop Jaro before he killed Allenthal.

"You have already hurt too many people," she yelled at him. "No more! This is my kingdom. You will *not* rule Tyar."

Turning away from Allenthal, Jaro faced her. "No? And how will you stop me? That bit of gold is useless except to force loyalty from the people of Tyar. It's nothing more than a symbol. Karineth is dead."

Turning away from Allenthal, he strode toward her, his cold gaze fixed on her, raising his hand so that tendrils of darkness came from his palm, snaking toward her.

Fear nearly froze her heart, but despite the shaking in her knees, Kyjia stood straight and tall, facing Jaro. She gripped the tablet hard. It would be up to her God to help.

"I have no way to stop his dark magic, Divine Karineth!" she cried, as the darkness raced toward her.

He shall not have the power to harm you any further.

In her hand, the tablet glowed brightly, and the oncoming darkness stopped as if it had hit a solid wall. Jaro yelled in frustration. He raised his hand again, and this time, instead of darkness, light flew from his hand, a streak of shining fire that exploded from his hand directly toward Kyjia. She dodged to one side, the white-hot missile barely grazing her cheek, leaving behind a stinging pain.

No!

When Jaro aimed another blast at her heart, it fizzled into nothing before it reached her. She stared into his eyes and took a step toward him, holding up the Sword of Kings. He raised his own blade to protect himself. She held the weapon in her hand, but she was no soldier, and she had little experience with a sword. Yet, her God was with her, and she had to stop Jaro.

As Kyjia faced him, he raised his blade to strike her down. She swung the shining sword to block the blow. The shock as the weapons crashed together went all the way up to her shoulder. He aimed another powerful blow, their swords locking together. He shoved her back, causing her to stumble to one knee, dropping her sword. With her other hand, she held up the tablet. Jaro's eyes locked on the bit of gold, the ancient symbol of power in Tyar. He'd desperately wanted to possess the tablet all along. Back in the cave, he said he'd foreseen himself taking it from her hand.

Now he reached out to seize it.

You will not!

For a moment Karineth's voice rang in Kyjia's head before Jaro twisted the tablet from her hand and she couldn't hear Him anymore.

For a moment, a look of triumph grew on Jaro's face, before his features twisted in pain. His eyes widening in shock, he stared at his fingers clenched around the gold. His flesh turned black. He screamed as the darkness ran swiftly from his hand up his arm to his neck and face. A moment later, all his skin appeared as black as coal. He sank to his knees and then toppled to the ground, the gold tablet falling from his hand as his fingers crumbled to ash.

The tablet had fallen to the ground. Kyjia reached out, hesitant to touch it. When she did, it felt only slightly warm. As soon as her skin contacted the surface, she could hear the voice of Karineth.

Tyar will be safe now. You and Terjan must stop the fighting. No more blood should be shed this day.

Picking up the tablet and the Sword of Kings, Kyjia ran back to her brother. He blinked up at her, his jaw clenched and his hand gripping the wound on his shoulder.

"Jaro is dead." She helped him to his feet, holding out the hilt of the sword.

He took it and raised the blade with a shout, while Kyjia held the glowing tablet high above her head.

Terjan's voice rang loud enough to carry over the entire battlefield. "Jaro is dead. I am King of Tyar. I command all of you to stop fighting." He swayed on his feet, and Kyjia steadied him.

A sudden silence fell, shocking after the clamor of battle. For a long moment, the rushing water of the new river was the only sound. Slowly, the combatants moved apart from each other, every man on the field obeying their king's command. Zhandar's men lowered their weapons.

Kyjia stood beside Terjan as their mother came running through the confusion to reach them. She put her arms around them both for a moment before she began trying to slow the bleeding from Terjan's wound.

Where was Allenthal? He was hurt, and Kyjia needed to find him. She spotted Kylith, blood running down his face and neck from a long cut. As the fighting stopped, he bent over Allenthal.

She rushed to them and sank down beside Allenthal. He still moved, so he wasn't dead, but his body shook, and she heard his gasping breath. As she watched, his hand fell away from the ghastly wound on the side of his neck. His skin already had a faint green cast to it. As she applied firm pressure to the wound, the bleeding slowed a little, but the edges of the cut had turned a horrible dark green. Poison. Whatever dose of the deadly substance they had given her, this was much more severe. He wouldn't last long without help.

"Allenthal!"

He turned toward the sound of her voice, but he couldn't see her, couldn't answer.

"What can we do?" Kylith asked beside her. Desperation tinged his voice. "We can't let him die."

No, Kyjia couldn't let him die. She ran back to Jaro's fallen form, searching carefully through the pockets of his limp garments, the clothing now surrounding nothing more than a pile of dark ash.

"It must be here." She needed the cure. He had to have it with him somewhere. She searched again, and a third time without finding the small bottle. "Where did he put it?!" Maybe it was back in their camp. But she couldn't imagine Jaro leaving something so precious behind.

She spotted motion above her at the top of the dune. A lone man staggered over the crest, stumbled and fell, sliding part of the way down. When he came to rest, he lay still for a moment, before struggling to move. He tried to stand but failed. He began to crawl forward. With a shock, Kyjia realized it was Zhandar.

"Stay with Al," she ordered Kylith. He nodded.

She got to her feet and ran to the edge of the river, around the fountain of water, to the bottom of the dune. The deep sand slowed her steps as she hurried to reach him. She knelt beside him.

"Zhandar?"

His skin was deathly pale, his entire body shaking. A wound along his neck was crusted with blood, and the skin had turned an unnatural dark shade of green. Just like Allenthal.

"Kyjia?" he gasped her name, his hand reaching out desperately. Blindly.

She took his hand. "I'm here."

"It is you." He hung his head in relief. "I was afraid I'd never find you again. I can't see. Please forgive me." His voice was weak and scratchy. "I'm so sorry for what I did. I should never have trusted Jaro."

"Did he do this to you?"

He nodded. "I know I said I would try to kill all of you, but I was angry, and I shouldn't have said it. The more I thought about it, I realized I couldn't do it. There is no honor in such an uneven battle. When I ordered the men to retreat, not to attack you, Jaro was furious. I tried to stop all of it, but I was too late. Please forgive me for what I did to you?" His strength exhausted, he sank slowly to the sand. "I'm sorry." He murmured.

The shaking in his limbs ceased abruptly, leaving his body perfectly still. Blood spread all across his tunic, flowing down from a wound in his belly that she hadn't noticed at first. She held her hand above his mouth, listening for any sign of breath. She laid her ear against his chest. No heartbeat. Nothing. How would she find the cure now?

Tears welled in her eyes, and a sob escaped her. Looking down at him, she noticed Zhandar's hands, even in death, one still reaching out to her, the other closed tightly around something. When she pulled his fingers back, she saw the little vial. Relief flooded through her. The cure. In the end, he'd turned against Jaro. He could have swallowed the remedy himself, attempting to save his own life. Instead, his last action had been to bring it to her.

She took the precious bottle and ran back to Allenthal.

There was no choice to make. Not really. Allenthal now shared the poison, shared the curse. If she cured herself, removing the remains of the dark poison so she could live a long life, he would die today. There was only one thing she could do.

She found Kylith still beside Allenthal, holding a piece of cloth against the wound.

Kneeling beside them, Kyjia opened the bottle, pulled Allenthal's jaw open, and drop by slow drop, poured the white liquid into his mouth. Ripping a piece from the hem of her tunic, she took Kylith's place, holding it against the wound.

As she watched, the cure worked quickly. His skin gradually returned to a normal hue, though he remained pale with shock. She stayed where she was, holding the cloth against his neck. He had a cut across his arm, and another larger wound on his side. Kylith undid Allenthal's belt and lifted his tunic to look at it. He gathered several folds of the cloth and held them against the cut.

"How bad is it?" she asked.

"Pretty bad," Kylith admitted. "But it wouldn't matter without you stopping the poison. You saved his life today." His eyes met hers. "You could have taken the cure for yourself."

Kyjia felt tears running down her face. She shook her head. "I couldn't let him die."

"No," Kylith said, his expression grave. "Our people need him. Maybe he's never told you how much?"

With everything that had happened, she'd almost forgotten. "Divine Karineth called him Crown Prince Allenthal. Is it true?"

Kylith nodded. "We came from the Seven Rivers. In our land, we need our Goddess just as you need Divine Karineth. We share many things between our lands. Just like your family, our Goddess speaks to members of a single family. His father is King Valteron, and since the death of his brother..."

Her stomach churned. "He's the only child left of your royal family? And if he died without an heir, then—" She put her hand to her mouth in shock.

"I don't know what would happen. Maybe our land would become like Tyar has been with no connection to our Goddess. Maybe She would find someone else to speak with. We don't know for sure." Kylith reached out and grasped her hand, gratitude obvious in his expression. "Thank you," he said, meeting her eyes. "It was my duty to protect him, but without you, I would have failed."

Kyjia stared down at Allenthal. His features were still in unconsciousness. All this time, he'd never told her he was a prince. He had probably lived in a beautiful palace, in the middle of a land of shining waters. Why had he ever come to Tyar? He had nearly lost his life here in the barren desert. His breathing had grown deeper now, steady. They would take care of him, and he would be all right.

She loved him. How could she not save him? He had told her he loved her too, but why a prince from a prosperous kingdom should ever love a penniless girl who had grown up in the desert, she had no idea.

It would take him time to recover, but Allenthal would live. He would go back to the country of flowing water and live a long and happy life. Not Kyjia. Sooner or later, the poison would kill her. Tears welled in her eyes, not of regret. She would make the same decision again a hundred times. The tears were of sadness that they wouldn't have more time together. She loved him. Of course she did. She'd just given up any chance of a future to save him.

CHAPTER 40

CROWN PRINCE ALLENTHAL

ALLENTHAL OPENED HIS EYES to see the ceiling of one of the buildings near the city walls. He lay on a pallet on the floor. A burning pain in his side and another in his neck made it difficult to move. Jaro had stabbed him, and then he'd tried to prevent the mystic from killing Kyjia. Was she safe? Allenthal didn't remember what had happened after that. He needed to know if she was all right.

Looking around the room, he saw other injured men. A few were guards he recognized from his time with Raz Abbas, and Onar lay a little way off with a bandage on his leg. Allenthal's eyes fell on Tillian on the other side of the room. She bent over one of the injured, tending a wound on his shoulder.

Where was Kyjia? Had she been hurt? Had they found the cure? What had happened to Jaro? Gripping his injured side, Allenthal struggled into a sitting position, then dragged himself to his feet, his jaw clenched against the pain. Tillian glanced up, meeting his gaze.

"Is Kyjia all right? Did she take the cure?"

Tillian's mouth tightened into a grim line. Her eyes looked hard. "No. It's gone."

That couldn't be right. If they were all still alive, they must have defeated Jaro in the end. He shook his head. "What do you mean? Jaro had it. Surely there must be a way we can find it."

Her expression tight, she shook her head. "I mean, it's gone, and we can't get it back."

"How can it be gone?" he protested. "Where—"

Tillian's eyes focused on his. "She saved *you* with it."

Horror washed over him like a flood. Jaro had cut him with the poisoned crystal. Now, he was here, injured but alive, not burning with fever. His eyes functioned normally. He could see.

It all came back to him in a rush. Dark memories of burning pain and a toxic green light swirling in his eyes. He'd barely been able to see as he'd put himself between her and Jaro, trying to protect Kyjia. He'd been poisoned.

Kyjia had used the only cure to save his life. How could she have done that? He'd wanted nothing more than to find it for her.

Desperate to escape, Allenthal stumbled out the door, agony twisting through him. He leaned against the wall and vomited. The motion sent searing pain through his injured side.

It couldn't be true. It wasn't possible. There must be some other explanation. He stumbled through the gates of the city, away from the walls, staggering out into the sand. He fell on his face against the dune, pounding his fist into the uncaring sand.

After a few moments, he felt a soft hand touch his back. "Leave me alone," he groaned, his fingers still clenched into a fist.

She didn't leave. Instead, she sat down on the sand beside him.

Trying to calm the swirling storm of emotion inside, he couldn't speak again for a long time. Finally, he lifted his head, brushing the sand from his face to look at Kyjia.

"Is it true?"

She met his gaze directly, her beautiful, dark eyes locking with his. "Yes."

Another wave of despair washed over him. Then, distracted, he looked up at her again. She stared directly into his eyes. "Kyjia? Can you *see*?" He struggled back into a sitting position.

She smiled suddenly, and the sweetness and joy of it nearly broke his heart... again.

"How? When?" But his answering smile quickly faltered. "How could you do it? I would *never* have chosen my life over yours. You know I wouldn't."

She reached out to take his hand, softly urging his fingers to uncurl and allow her to slip hers between them.

"I know that," she said. "You showed love to me in a thousand different ways. I could tell how you felt. And so, when you were dying, I did what I had to do to save you."

"But the curse," he protested. "I wanted to get rid of it more than anything. I wanted you to be free of it, healthy, to live a long and happy life. This feels like what happened with Alvaren all over again. You gave up your life for mine."

She reached out to touch his face. "I know what you wanted, and I saw how you suffered because of what your brother did. But in the end, you chose to accept it. You must accept this too. I would rather live what time I have with you in my life."

He shook his head. "But how can you even look at me when I stole your only chance to regain your health?"

She looked at him sternly. "You did not steal it. I gave it to you freely, and I don't regret my choice. I know you don't agree, but the decision was mine to make, and I made it. Please don't be angry with me."

"Angry?" The word tore from his chest. "I've never been so angry!"

But tears welled in his eyes, and sobs choked his throat. She sat beside him and put her arms around him. He held onto her and cried.

Darkness covered the city. Everything was quiet. Kyjia and the others slept, but Allenthal couldn't seem to get comfortable on his pallet. He couldn't stop thinking about her. No matter which way he turned, the wound in his side ached. He needed to give it more time to heal. Finally, he got up and found a waterskin and took a long drink.

It felt good, and Allenthal was grateful for the life-giving liquid. For weeks, he'd been thirsty, and he knew the others had been too. He'd hated seeing Kyjia refuse to drink because they needed to conserve. It was better now. Since the day of the battle, they'd had all the water they wanted. The mysterious fountain of water had settled into a wide pool where pure water bubbled up from beneath the surface of the ground. The king's river continued to flow down through the valley. Already, green shoots sprang up all along its edges. This place gradually became more comfortable, but it would take time.

Stepping quietly so he wouldn't disturb anyone else, he walked to the door and out into the night. All was still. The wide sky spread above him in an arc of shining crystal stars. He drew in a long breath. When he'd begun this journey, he'd never imagined what it would be like.

He endured pain and danger, certainly, but he couldn't imagine his life without Kyjia now. She had no way of knowing how much her love had rescued him. She meant everything to him.

Moving a few steps away from the doorway, he saw Tillian sitting with her back, resting against the stone wall of the building. They still took turns on guard every night. Though her cloak was wrapped around her, her eyes were alert to everything, watching for any sign of danger.

As he moved closer, she looked up at him. "My watch is not over for two more hours. What are you doing up?"

He shrugged. "I couldn't sleep. If you'd like to go get some rest, I might as well watch."

For a long moment, she gazed up at him without speaking.

Finally, she nodded and got to her feet. "Are you worried about the future?" she asked.

"I'm worried about Kyjia, about finding a cure for the curse." He paused, turning from her to look up at the sky. Taking in a deep breath, he met her gaze. "What she did, it wasn't my choice. She made the decision."

In the starlight, Tillian looked at him sharply. "And I must accept it?"

He heard a measure of bitterness in her tone. He put his hand on her shoulder. "Yes. We love her and we must accept her choices, even if we don't agree."

A wave of sorrow swept through him as he said the words, yet he felt the truth of them. He bowed his head. If he could have stopped her from saving his life instead of her own, he would have. But he couldn't go back and change it now, and he still loved her. He raised his eyes to meet Tillian's.

"I will take care of her and search for a remedy for the curse."

She nodded, her jaw tight. "You must. Somewhere in the wide world is a solution. Promise me you'll find it."

Allenthal didn't hesitate as he spoke the words. "I swear I will devote my life to finding a way to help. I will do everything I can for her."

By morning, Allenthal knew it was time to face Kyjia. Pain still flared from his side every time he got to his feet, but it got a little better every day. The injuries to his body were healing, though the pain in his heart remained sharp. It was past time to talk to her. He wandered through all the buildings they had begun to use again without locating her.

He found a crowd of people surrounding Terjan, waiting to talk to him. The young king spotted him in the doorway. Excusing himself from the press of people, he came to stand before Allenthal.

"Are you looking for Kyjia?"

Allenthal nodded.

Terjan gestured toward the center of the city. "She said she would walk to the temple. You might find her there."

"Thank you very much, Your Majesty," Allenthal bowed. He looked up to see Terjan's ears turn pink. The young man would have to get used to it. All the onlookers appeared very impressed, and they turned eagerly back to Terjan.

With no one looking at him, Allenthal slipped quietly away, walking through the streets toward the temple. It would take many years to restore this city to its former glory. Now, it was silent and empty.

He passed the outer door and the courtyard to peek into the central chamber. She was turned away from him, facing the altar as she knelt in prayer, her long, dark hair tumbling down her back. Her head was bowed. The bright sun shone down on the white stone.

He took a step nearer.

"I hear you," she murmured.

He had thought his steps were silent.

She turned quickly to look; seeing it was him, she turned back to her prayer. He moved closer, seating himself on a fallen piece of stone beside her.

"You've been avoiding me."

She nodded, opening her eyes and turning to face him. "From how upset you were, I thought it wise to give you some time. I know you're angry with me, and I understand."

He was silent for a long moment before he tentatively reached out to take her hand. Her slender fingers felt soft and warm against his. "Please forgive me for being upset."

She looked up at him, her dark eyes searching his. "I forgive you," she said. "I told you, I understand. The real question is... can *you* forgive me for what I did?"

He took a long slow breath. "Can I?" He brought her hand to his lips and kissed it. "I have so many reasons why I think you shouldn't have done it. You gave up your future for me, and that's not what I wanted for you. I'm not worth your sacrifice. I would never choose to take something like that from you."

Her beautiful eyes held his. "And I have good reasons too. I couldn't watch you die when I could prevent it. Undoubtedly, you would have died that day, just like Zhandar did. Your people desperately need you to come back. And I need you." She took his hand in both of hers and held it against her cheek.

For a moment, her eyes closed, and a tear slipped from beneath her dark lashes.

No matter what else had happened to him, he had lost himself to her. "Whether I agree with you or not, I will love you forever." Leaning forward, he lowered his mouth to hers. Her lips were soft and sweet and entirely irresistible. He put his arms around her, drawing her closer. She answered his kiss, putting one arm around his neck and tangling the other hand into his hair, pulling him closer.

With her in his arms, he couldn't imagine being angry. With her lips on his, he couldn't think about anything but her. He trailed kisses across her jaw and slowly down the silken skin of her neck.

"Will you stay with me? When I return to my own land, will you come with me and be my wife?"

She gasped.

It wasn't clear if her reaction was to his lips at her throat or his words. He drew back and looked at her.

She met his gaze. For a moment, her eyes appeared dazed, but then her gaze sharpened on him. "Are you sure that's what you want? I have no fine clothes or jewelry. You wouldn't be embarrassed to introduce me to your family and friends?"

His brows lowered in concern, and he shook his head. "Of course not. They will welcome you. I will make sure you have everything you need."

She raised her eyebrows and stared at him. "Isn't there something *important* about your family that you might have failed to mention to me?"

He swallowed and cleared his throat awkwardly. Terjan said she already knew. He should have told her sooner.

She folded her arms across her chest, fixing him with a hard glare. "Exactly *when* were you planning to tell me that your father is the *king*?"

"I—" It had begun as a secret in order to keep himself safe, but then, they had just never talked about the details of his family.

He couldn't meet her gaze. "Forgive me. I didn't intend to keep it from you, we just never talked about it."

When she didn't answer, he raised his eyes to look at her.

She had bowed her head, allowing the dark waves of her hair to fall forward. Her thick lashes brushed against her cheeks. Her voice softened until he could barely hear her words. "Then it wasn't because you were ashamed of me?"

When he heard the pain in her voice, he pulled her into his arms. "No! Never. How could I be when you are the best person I know, the bravest, strongest, most beautiful woman I can even imagine? I would be proud to take you anywhere with me."

She held him tightly. "I'm sorry, Allenthal. I'm just worried that if we go back to your home together, I won't fit in. You grew up in a palace. I lived in a cave."

His arms tightened around her. "I'd move to a cave any day if I got to stay with you." He meant the words with his whole heart. "Don't worry about fitting in. You're stunning no matter what you wear, and you'll have the attention of every man in the room. And I've seen what you look like in an expensive dress. I couldn't take my eyes off you, and I only saw you from a distance."

"You saw me?" Her eyes widened in surprise.

He nodded. It wasn't a moment he'd ever forget. "Now that I know the brave, beautiful person you are inside, if I saw you up close, I would have gone to my knees right there and vowed to be your slave for life."

A slow smile crossed her face, a gleam of mischief in her eyes. "Is that offer still available?" she asked.

Heat flooded through Allenthal. That smile, and the quirk of one eyebrow made her even more irresistible. "Oh yes!" But instead of going to his knees, he kissed her. After a long moment, he drew back. "Will you come with me when I return to the Seven Rivers?"

She threw her arms around him. "I will."

EPILOGUE

KING ALLENTHAL

Present Day

THE GODDESS NAMRADILL, APPEARING in human shape, though infused with pure light, walked beside Allenthal as they followed a path through a meadow of soft, green grass. He was silent, his mind running through the experiences She had shown him.

Allenthal asked Her the question burning in his mind. "Divine Goddess, I have seen so many things during our time together. Why would you show me these memories?"

She turned her bright countenance to meet his eyes. "I am sorry, my son. Though there is much joy in them, I know they still cause you pain, even after so many years."

That was true. As usual, Namradill understood exactly how he felt. Though Allenthal had done his best to move on with his life, to raise his daughter, he had never really left behind the guilt or the pain. His time with Kyjia had been so happy. Their brief years together had been bliss. And Kyjia had given birth to a beautiful, healthy daughter, Tahlea.

In the end, the curse had claimed Kyjia's life. As days and years had passed, she'd grown ill. He had gone himself and sent his servants to search his kingdom for anything that might help her. Allenthal had returned without finding a cure. He stayed with her, every moment. He'd held her in his arms as she took her last breath.

Then, she was gone.

Namradill's words broke into the memories. "The time you had with her was filled with love. Not everyone is so fortunate. I have watched you through the years. You've been a good father to Tahlea. Now, she needs you. Because of Kyjia's sacrifice, Tahlea was born, and she lives to mother her own child."

"Tahlea's child?" Allenthal started in surprise. Was it possible? How long had he been here?

A slight smile lifted Her mouth. "Perhaps you and I have been together longer than you realize. Tahlea's daughter was born three months ago."

Joy flooded through him. "I'm a grandfather," Allenthal gasped.

"As you should be," Namradill nodded. "The time has come for you to return to the physical world. Only one thing remains. Come with me."

Allenthal nodded. Side by side they followed the path across the crest of a low hill and into a little valley where lush grass and flowers bloomed around them. He couldn't help but pause to inhale the scent of growing things. A towering stand of pine trees sheltered a cottage that stood near the shore of a crystal-clear lake.

"What is this place?" He looked around in wonder. He'd never seen anything like it.

Namradill gestured to the beautiful scene. "All those who depart from your physical world come to rest with me."

"Everyone?" Allenthal drew in a sharp breath. He should have realized it sooner. His parents, his beloved older brother Alvaren, and... Kyjia. He had thought of her every day since he had seen his first vision of her. How he'd missed her. It had been seventeen years since he'd seen her, and he'd never forgotten any of it. He wouldn't.

"Your time with me is ending," Namradill said. "As my gift to you, I give you this chance to reunite with her before you return to the physical world. Farewell, my son. We shall see each other again." Her glowing white form faded out of view, leaving Allenthal standing alone on the path.

He walked forward, toward the cottage. Someone stood in the garden just outside the cottage door. She bent to pick a bloom and then straightened, looking at him, her beautiful dark eyes wide.

She looked exactly as she had all those years ago, except that her porcelain skin now glowed with health. Her long, dark hair hung in loose waves. She wore a simple, white gown falling around her in graceful folds. He wanted to shout her name, but shock had stolen his voice.

A brilliant smile of pure joy lit her face. She dropped the flowers, gathered her skirts in one hand, and ran to him. He caught her up in his arms. She was real. He felt the warm, solid weight of her and her arms around his neck clutching him.

"Allenthal!"

He couldn't speak. He held onto her, determined never to release her again, burying his face in the satin skin of her neck. How many days and nights had he longed for her? The delicate spicy scent of her skin was exactly the same. Her voice. How many times had he woken, alone in the dark, thinking he heard her calling his name?

"Kyjia," he finally managed to say. "My love, I've missed you every moment."

"I missed you too." She pulled him close, holding onto him with all her strength. Eventually, she drew back to look up at him. "But you will have to go back," she said sternly. "It isn't time yet. Tally needs you. She was so small back then. Now, she's grown to be tall and brave, just like you. I wrote a letter to her and hid it in the bottom of my jewelry box. I intended to tell you, but then I was so ill. Will you please give it to her?"

"Of course, my love." His eyes moved from the silken darkness of her hair to her dark eyes and the delicate pink of her lips. He couldn't look at her enough.

She smiled.

The joy in her expression warmed a place in his heart that had remained cold all this time, waiting for her.

Her hand touched his jaw. "Don't be sad." She met his eyes. "Many years from now, when your time is finished, I'll be here, waiting for you."

Tears welled in his eyes, and he pulled her close again. "You can't ask me to leave you. I can't do it," he protested, his voice breaking. "I'm not strong enough to lose you again." He looked down at her.

Her expression became stern. "You *are* strong enough, and you know you must return." She pulled his head down against her shoulder. "Everything is just as it should be."

She was here, warm and real, and holding him. They stayed exactly where they were for a long time.

Finally, she spoke again. "Allenthal, I need you to do one more thing when you return."

"What's that?" he murmured.

She drew back to look directly into his eyes. "I know you so well, and I saw how it broke your heart that we never found a cure for my curse all those years ago. I remember how it hurt when your brother sacrificed himself for you, but eventually, you were able to move on from that. Now it's time to do it again. I need you to lay down your burden. Forgive yourself for what happened to me. Can you do it? For me?"

He felt the tears on his face, and he reached up to brush them away. "But you could have been cured! You could have been healthy and lived a long full life. You could have watched Tally grow up."

One corner of her mouth rose. "But if things had been different, there would have been no Tally. I would never choose to give up my strong, beautiful daughter."

He'd never really thought of it that way.

She brushed her fingers along his cheek. "There is no way now to change the past, nothing to truly ease the pain of our separation, except for you to remember that I am here, safe and happy, and I will see you again. I will see Tally again. You must go back to her, but when you do, I want you to leave your burden here with me. Let it go."

"But—" How could she ask that of him?

But her voice was stern. "Let it go."

Her words reminded him of those terrible moments when they had struggled to escape the cave. Without her, he wouldn't have found the courage to move forward. Taking in a long breath, he nodded.

She smiled at him, and he felt all her love in the expression. It sent a flood of warmth all through him.

"What a gift it is to be with you again," she exclaimed.

A gift.

It was. Like nothing he'd ever received before. He pulled her close, enfolding her in his arms. After a moment, she drew back, taking his hand to lead him toward the little cottage.

A voice came from a great distance.

"He moved. I think he's waking up."

Gradually, Allenthal became aware that someone held his hand.

"Father?"

The voice belonged to his daughter. Though he felt like he'd been away for a long time, he would know the sound of it anywhere. He blinked, opening his eyes to look up into Tally's familiar, beautiful face.

She smiled. "I missed you!"

Allenthal pushed himself up on one elbow, and she threw her arms around him. He managed to sit all the way up so he could hug her properly.

"Tally!" He had so much to ask, so much to say, he couldn't get it all out. For a long time, he simply held her. "I want to know everything," he said. "But first, tell me, am I a grandfather?"

She laughed, pulling back to exchange a significant glance with a dark-haired young man who stood behind her, a baby in his arms. "Father, this is my husband, Flint." She turned to meet his eyes. "We named our daughter Kyjia, after mother."

Tally looked happy. Even at a glance, Allenthal could tell that Flint adored her. He'd have to catch up on all the details later.

It felt like he'd left Kyjia in her cottage only a moment ago, but now, here was his room in the palace at Namradan, and Tally, with a new tiny person bearing Kyjia's name. Flint brought the baby nearer so Allenthal could see her. The little girl stared at him with round eyes.

"She's beautiful."

Allenthal got slowly to his feet. He felt a little stiff, but he'd expected worse. Had he really been lying there for nearly two years? It didn't seem possible, but it was clear much had happened while he slept.

He went to the chest of drawers and opened one, finding everything inside exactly as he'd left it. He took out Kyjia's jewelry box. No one appeared to have disturbed it. Lifting away the tray, he saw a folded piece of parchment. He hadn't wanted to feel the pain of looking through Kyjia's things, since it only made him miss her more than ever. He'd never realized it was there before. Her letter.

Allenthal turned back to Tally. "This message is from your mother. I should have told you more about her long ago. How brave and strong she was, and how much you have grown up to be like her. With your permission, we'll read it together, and I will tell you everything I remember about her."

Tally glanced toward the doorway, and Allenthal followed her eyes to see Tillian standing there.

His eyes widened in surprise. She hadn't been willing to speak to him for years. She looked older now, lines of care and sorrow etched into her face. She'd been so angry when he last saw her, and he hadn't blamed her. He had done everything he knew of to help Kyjia, but when she'd grown ill, he'd sent word to Tyar, and Tillian had come. She arrived in time to see Kyjia before the end. When it was all over, Tillian had been furious with him, consumed by grief. It was the last time they'd spoken.

They spent a long moment looking at each other. Allenthal wasn't sure what to say.

Finally, Tillian spoke. "I came to beg your forgiveness, Your Majesty."

He nodded. "There is no need," he reached out to take her hand. "I know how much you loved her."

At the words, tears ran down Tillian's cheeks. "I was wrong to blame you and to stay away so long."

He left a light kiss on the back of her hand. "You are most welcome here, Lady Tillian. You are part of our family."

She shook her head sadly. "I let my grief at losing Kyjia turn to anger. I should never have allowed that, not when you sacrificed so much to help us."

"I understand why you felt that way," Allenthal said. He bowed his head. "I blamed myself."

She stepped closer and stood facing him. "You must not." She looked up into his eyes.

It was exactly the same thing Kyjia had told him. She believed in him, whether he deserved it or not, and he couldn't let her down. He would use his life to serve his kingdom, his people, and his family, whatever came next. He would keep his promise to her.

ACKNOWLEDGEMENTS

Thank you for reading this book! Thank you family, friends and fans for supporting me during the creation process.

I cherish the opportunity to bring to life stories born in my imagination and share them. I hope you enjoy reading them and that we have many future adventures together.

About the Author

aj@ajparkwriting.com
www.ajparkwriting.com
Stay In Touch – Join my email list and download a FREE Story
https://BookHip.com/XKTAJDB

AJ Park is the author of several fantasy adventure books and has won multiple writing awards. She grew up reading everything she could get her hands on, and continues to cultivate her life-long love of stories.

When she's not working on the next book, she loves climbing mountains, being outdoors, and spending time with her family. She loves meeting new friends, being part of the local community, and works for a digital marketing firm that helps businesses grow.

POISONED SPLINTER

CHAPTER 1

BEING SMALL SOMETIMES CAME with advantages. No one saw Sam reach up to grasp the door handle and tiptoe out of the library, his lessons undone. Only a few moments later, he slipped through the door and down the steps to the dungeon, his small feet barely making a sound. Despite the oppressive stone walls and the gloom, he came here often. Grandfather hadn't locked anyone down here in decades, and it was the one space Sam could play undisturbed, his secret place.

Sooner than he expected, he heard the sound of footsteps on the stairs, and Sam darted to hide behind a stack of storage crates, fitting neatly into the narrow space. When he peeked out, he recognized a member of the royal court, Halderan, an older man with a long thin face and gray hair, dressed in formal robes. It was best to keep out of his way. Sam had never seen any of the important people in the dungeon before. Halderan wouldn't be looking for a small boy sneaking away from his lessons. There must be another reason he'd come.

Still hidden, Sam waited silently as a second person descended the stairs. At the sight of the tall form and familiar features of his uncle Adengo, Sam almost rushed out to greet him. But Halderan was still there, wearing an unpleasant look on his narrow face that informed Sam he shouldn't be bothered.

"Well?" Halderan asked. "Why did you ask me to come down here, Your Highness?" He looked around, his face pinched in disapproval. "The dungeon, of all places."

Instead of his usual easy smile, Adengo wore a serious expression. At his belt hung a dagger with a beautiful purple gem set into the hilt. Sam had seen him use it, only in practice, but Adengo knew how to fight. Sam wanted to be just like him when he grew up.

Adengo faced the older man. "I just received word that another two-dozen people in Kulin have fallen ill."

Halderan stared back at him, his heavy brows drawn together. "That is indeed unfortunate. We are all gravely concerned in these trying times."

Straightening his shoulders, Adengo faced Halderan, his eyebrows lowering in anger. "Unfortunate? How can you say that? You are well aware of the origin of this mysterious disease."

Halderan took a step toward Adengo, anger etched into the heavy lines of his face. "What are you implying?"

Adengo refused to back down. "It's you. They're sick because you're draining their hallan to increase your own power."

At the words, Halderan trembled with rage. "How dare you?" His eyes never left Adengo. "After all I have done for you? I came to Kulin specifically to instruct *you*, and now you claim that I practice dark sorcery?"

Hidden behind the crate, Sam shivered at the sharp malice in his tone, pulling himself even farther out of sight.

Adengo shook his head. "I didn't want to believe it. I hoped it wasn't true. But the more I learn, the more signs point directly to *you*. I haven't told the king yet. If you leave Kulin today, I won't say anything to anyone."

Halderan's complexion darkened in fury. "I placed my hopes in you. We could have accomplished great things together. It's been decades since I came across a student as talented as you are, and now you would betray me?"

"They're innocent people," Adengo exclaimed. "And you're killing them to fuel your magic!"

Sam's stomach clenched. He shouldn't be listening to this. Was Halderan really killing people? Sam should tell his father what he'd overheard. He would know what to do.

"You have *real* power," Halderan hissed. "Why should you care if a few of your unfortunate subjects fall ill? If you take a portion of their life energy, it's all for the greater good. Think what you could accomplish with the extra hallan!"

"But it's wrong. I'll never do that!" Adengo protested.

They stared at each other for a long moment. "Very well, Your Highness," Halderan said, lowering his eyes and his voice and stepping away from the other man. "There is no way we will reach an agreement over this. I will do as you suggest and leave at once."

Without further protest, Halderan turned and went up the stairs, leaving Adengo standing alone in the middle of the room, a frown of deep thought on his face.

Sam squirmed in his corner, accidentally bumping against the crate.

His uncle's gaze sharpened, focusing on his hiding place. "All right, Sam. Come out here."

Sam crept out into the open.

Adengo met his gaze. "What are you doing down here? You shouldn't have heard any of that."

Sam ran to Adengo, throwing his arms around his uncle's waist. "I'm sorry. I only wanted to play, and I didn't mean to hear. He scares me!"

Adengo hugged him, and then bent to one knee to meet Sam's eyes. "I'm going to make sure he doesn't hurt anyone else. Come on." Together, they climbed the stairs back to the palace. "Go to your mother," Adengo directed. "I'm going to see the king."

Sam ran through the marble halls of the palace, passing by the room where he was supposed to be working on his lessons, to the suite of rooms he shared with his parents. Ignoring the two guards watching over the door, he threw it open and ran inside. "Maman?" he charged into the sitting room. Finding it empty, he crossed the room to his parent's bedroom.

His mother lay crumpled on the floor in a pool of blood. Sam screamed, realizing a second later that his father lay just beyond her. Icy cold swept down his back, and for a moment, his entire body froze. He ran to his mother, dropping to his knees over her. "Maman!" he shook her shoulder, but she didn't turn to look at him. Her eyes stared up at nothing.

Two guards ran into the room, their eyes wide in horror as they took in the scene. One of them ran to Sam's father, searching for any sign of life. The other knelt beside Sam. He took in the still form of the princess, her staring eyes, and he placed his fingers under her chin, searching for any sign of a heartbeat.

More guards arrived a moment later. Sam heard his grandfather's voice in the hall. A moment later, he burst into the room, Adengo at his side. Both their faces were deathly white, and their eyes wide in shock. There was a moment of silence.

His grandfather, Hashoreth Algorian, King of Ischar, walked forward, kneeling beside the still form of his son. He took a crumpled scrap of parchment from his lifeless hand. His eyes widened as they scanned the few words written on it. "You will never rule Ischar." His gaze flew to Adengo. "It's your handwriting."

Shock froze Adengo's features. He struggled to speak, but no words came out. He took a deep breath and tried again. "I didn't write that."

Grandfather's eyes fixed on Adengo. "But your brother—it was in his hand. Is this about the *throne*? I never thought you were jealous of him."

Adengo's jaw clenched. "I'm not! I swear. No throne is worth losing my brother."

King Hashoreth bowed his head.

"Adengo didn't do it!" Sam cried. His strong, brave uncle would never harm his family for his own gain. In that moment, he felt sure.

Still bent over the body of his son, Hashoreth picked up something from the floor. He held up a knife with a purple gem on the hilt, the blade sticky with blood. Sam recognized the weapon immediately. Adengo's dagger.

Hashoreth held it up and turned toward his second son.

Adengo's eyes widened, all color draining from his face. "I didn't do this. Father, you have to believe me! I would never kill my brother!"

The king's eyes went to the empty sheath at Adengo's belt. "You had this knife with you?"

Adengo looked down at his belt. "I thought I did."

Sam stared at the empty sheath. Adengo had been wearing the dagger just a few moments ago in the dungeon, and now, here it was, covered with blood. Was it true? The king believed Adengo had killed Sam's parents.

"Seize him," King Hashoreth nodded to the guards, and they grabbed Adengo. The king nodded toward the door, and they dragged Adengo out.

"No! I didn't do it! Father, please! I didn't—"

In a moment, he was gone.

The king knelt beside Sam and put a hand on his shoulder. "Samanath."

Sam shook violently all over. He couldn't stop crying, and he clung to his mother, though her limbs were heavy and cold, and she didn't respond to him.

His grandfather gathered Sam into his arms and held him as he sobbed. "I'm sorry, Sam. So sorry." Sam clung to him.

The king stood up and walked toward the large windows. Outside in the courtyard, shouts and cries rang out. People looked upward, pointing at the sky. A shadow passed over the palace. From his place in his grandfather's arms, Sam caught a glimpse of an enormous dark bird. Wide wings carried it swiftly away. Only a moment later, it was gone.

POISONED SPLINTER

CHAPTER 2

19 Years Later

THE CARRIAGE JOSTLED DIA as it rolled over a stone in the road, startling her out of sleep. She straightened up abruptly.

Her younger sister, Lisenth, jabbed her sharply with an elbow. "How can you sleep? We'll be in Kulin in another hour, the home of the prince. In a few more weeks, we get to *meet* him. And you're sleeping." She shook her head in disgust.

Her sister's grumbling was so commonplace that Dia had learned to ignore it. Sometimes. Often, it was easier not to say anything at all than to argue with her. Dia tried to be patient. Before their father died, he'd begged her to take care of Lisenth, and Dia had promised she would do her best. She had no wish to bicker now. Instead, she straightened to sit taller in her seat and glanced out the window. Outside, thick, unbroken forest lined the road, as it had for hours. The afternoon faded into evening, and the light grew dim beneath the thick trees.

From the corner of her eye, Dia glanced at her sister. Lisenth looked elegant, even after a long day of travel. She appeared ready to meet her prince at any moment. Not a golden hair was out of place, and the ice blue silk of her veil draped gracefully from the crown of her head down around her shoulders. Sparkling gems hung across her brow.

Dia made a quick effort to smooth her own hair. But why should she worry? It's not like they'd meet anyone tonight.

Though dressed similarly, the resemblance between the sisters was distant. Dia was three years older, but shorter, plainer, more thoughtful, and much less ambitious than her sister. All facts that Lisenth took every opportunity to remind her of. Dia simply shrugged and glanced back out of the window. Her own goals were different.

Dia loved seeing new places. The unfamiliar scenery spoke to the place inside her that constantly searched for... something. She wasn't sure what it was, but she preferred to remain in the background while she looked. In contrast, Lisenth thrived on attention. Let her charm the prince if she wanted to. Dia had no intention of interfering.

As the sun dipped toward the distant purple horizon; the endless jostling paused and the carriage stopped. Roland, the footman who had been with their family for decades, opened the door and bowed. He was a plain-looking, sturdy man, his brown hair beginning to gray. "Ladies, would you care to stretch your legs for a moment? The view of Kulin is stunning."

Gratefully, Dia accepted his hand, allowing him to help her from the carriage. She straightened her spine and extended her arms, attempting to stretch the stiffness from her muscles. Lisenth alighted behind her. "You look ridiculous with your arms out like that."

Reluctantly, Dia lowered her arms to assume a more ladylike posture.

"Look at this!" Lisenth walked a few paces from the carriage to an opening between the trees. The last rays of sunset lit the green of the forest as it blended into open fields, a patchwork of crops. Central to the view was the city of Kulin, blazing with light. From this higher vantage point, they saw within the walls, all the way from small cottages at the outskirts to graceful towers in the center that could only belong to the king's palace. Kulin stood on the very brink of the cliffs that fell away around the edges of Ischar. Nothing could be seen of the precipice from up here.

"It's beautiful." Dia gazed at the city.

Lisenth sighed and placed a hand over her heart, looking at the distant towers. "When the prince falls madly in love with me, that will be my home."

If the prince behaved like any other man who met Lisenth, that would probably be his exact reaction. She was stunning, and by now, everyone expected that sort of thing to happen. Maybe it was inevitable.

"We're almost there," Lisenth said. "Let's go."

Dia wished for a moment of privacy to stretch again. "The view is lovely. I need just a moment more."

"But we're almost there!"

Her jaw tightened, but Dia drew in a breath, forcing the muscles to relax. "Only a moment."

Lisenth let out a breath of irritation and stalked back toward the carriage.

Enjoying the moment of solitude and the quiet, Dia took a deeper breath. The tight muscles in her neck loosened a little as she stood alone. Sunset lit heavy clouds with a touch of bright rose. Her eye caught a black shape moving along the horizon, silhouetted against the colorful sky. It circled the city before turning in their direction. A bird? The outline grew clearer as it approached. It had the shape of an eagle, except its wingspan was enormous. Even far away, it appeared big enough to carry off a horse if it wished. Perhaps because of the bright light behind, its feathers appeared black as night.

Dia's stomach clenched. If she truly saw what she thought she did, it had a name. Shadaroc. An omen of evil.

Before tonight, she'd never believed the stories she'd heard as a child of sorcerers who practiced magic and could change their form. When the Shadaroc resumed its human form, it could walk undetected among the people. If she truly saw one of them in Kulin, trouble would follow.

The dark shape of the mythical bird wheeled over the forest, drawing nearer every moment. Her hands tightened into fists. What could she do if it came to the clearing where she stood? She felt a sudden urge to flee and hide.

A moment later, it soared directly overhead, and Dia crouched instinctively as it passed. A sharp prickle raced over her skin, from the crown of her head to the soles of her feet. She couldn't breathe. The enormous dark shape turned and passed over her again. Frozen in place, she stared upward.

The great bird wheeled, flying lower to land nearby, out of sight among the dark trees.

It wasn't far from her. Dia needed to get away.

The sudden rattle of harnesses and carriage wheels brought her sharply back to the present. Drawing in a quick breath, she turned back to the road in time to see the carriage disappearing down the road.

"Lisenth!" Dia shouted in frustration. This wasn't the first prank she had been the victim of. The carriage quickly disappeared between the trees and silence fell.

She stood alone, staring down the road after them. They would come back for her. It was only a joke. Any moment now.

Roland and the driver had worked faithfully for the Ifereth family for many years, and they would never intentionally leave Dia alone in the forest. Her sister must have assured them she was already inside, ready to go. It wasn't their fault. When they discovered their mistake, they would certainly come back for her.

Thick silence covered the woods. A damp chill settled over Dia. The pale-yellow silk of her gown wasn't warm and her soft slippers had never been intended for walking in rough terrain. A few spatters of rain struck her. Lowering clouds quickly moved across the fading sunset, hiding any sign of the strange bird. It couldn't be too far away. Fear slid along her spine.

Darkness fell around Dia, and she shivered. Her sister had to be coming back soon. Letting out a breath of frustration, she stared down the empty road as rain began to fall. Clutching her arms around her body in an attempt to warm herself, Dia considered her options. She was alone. She had no light, no warm clothes, no transportation, and it was quickly becoming too cold to remain standing here. But they would be back any moment. Wouldn't they?

Lacking any other option, Dia started walking down the road in the direction of the city of Kulin. Maybe another traveler would come along and she could ask for help. As the rain fell harder, puddles formed, surrounded by patches of thick mud. She tiptoed around them in her yellow silk slippers.

The movement warmed her a little, but it was past time for the carriage to return. The darkness deepened around her, and the rain continued. Above the soft patter of raindrops on the leaves, she heard the howl of a wolf. Her body froze between steps, turning her heart to ice in her chest. A pack of hungry wolves would be happy to make their supper on a lost girl, defenseless in the woods. A second howl followed the first. After what she'd seen only a few moments before in the sky, she couldn't help but remember that, in the stories, wolves were loyal servants of the Shadaroc.

At the sound of another howl, Dia shook off her temporary paralysis and ran, leaving the road behind and plunging into the forest. Brush snagged at her long skirt. The fabric ripped as she jerked it free. Stumbling across a narrower path, she followed it. The howls grew closer.

Desperately, she searched the trees for one she might climb up into. When none of them had branches within her reach, she hurried on. She would have to take her chances on the ground. Wrenching the fabric of her gown free of the entangling branches, she pushed forward, emerging from the brush to find herself at the brink of a precipitous slope of bare earth and rock.

The world spun around her as she looked down from the height, and all her muscles clenched, but she couldn't pause. Branches rustled as the wolves pushed swiftly through the thicket behind her, leaving her no choice but to attempt the descent. Dia started down, her soft shoes slipping against the earth. On the wet soil, her footing grew worse every moment.

She shrieked as her feet slid out from under her, and she fell, tumbling and sliding down the long slope, finally coming to rest in the mud at the bottom. Pain raced through her arm and various other bruised parts of her body. Tears welled in her eyes, and for a moment, she didn't move at all, grateful to be still.

A howl reminded her that the wolves weren't far away. With a groan, she lifted her head and saw the black outline of one of the creatures at the top of the steep embankment. Hopefully, the animals had better sense than to follow her down the incline. Would they find a way around? Dia needed to move.

Dragging her aching body up, she got to her feet. Forest surrounded her in all directions. Which way should she go? Off through the trees, she glimpsed what might be an open area, and headed that way. Thick vegetation and brush attempted to block her way. She had several deep scratches on her arms before she stumbled out onto a road. If she followed it, perhaps it would join with the road to Kulin.

The distant whinny of a horse made the decision, and she followed the path in the direction of the city. She hadn't gone far when the square shape of a carriage loomed in the dark, its straight lines contrasting with the wild shapes of the trees. There was something wrong. Dia stared into the dim light for several moments, trying to piece together what her eyes showed her.

As she approached, she saw more clearly. The carriage lay awkwardly on its side. One of the horses must have broken its harness and bolted, leaving the remaining animal entangled, snorting nervously in its tethers.

Dia had no experience with horses. Was there a way to calm the frightened animal or even release it from the twisted harness? Putting that idea off for the moment, she turned toward the carriage. It must have carried someone.

Dia bent beside a shattered window at the back. Inside lay the crumpled body of a girl, her pale skin standing out against the darker interior, her skirts a tangled mass. A stain, black in the dim light, covered her neck and shoulder. Dia touched her hand. "Can you hear me?"

A faint groan was her only answer.

A howl from somewhere off in the forest reminded her that she didn't have time to linger. She shook the girl's hand. "Can you wake up? We need to get away from here before the wolves come."

"What happened?" the girl moaned.

"I don't know," Dia said. "But it's not safe to stay here. The wolves are getting closer."

That information appeared to motivate the injured girl. Dia used a branch to clear away the sharp pieces of glass remaining, and she helped the girl slide out. "How badly are you hurt? Can you walk?"

More howls came from the trees, closer this time. It was time to go. The horse might have helped them escape, but Dia didn't know how to ride, and she had no way to free it from the jumbled leather straps. There wasn't time to debate. She helped the girl to her feet, supporting her as they staggered away from the carriage.

"What's your name?" Dia asked.

"Carrina." The girl's features were tight with pain, her face white, and she held one arm cradled against her chest.

"I'm Dia, and we're going to try to find some help before the wolves reach us."

"Where's my father?" Carrina looked around at the dark trees.

"I don't know," Dia replied, "but we can't stay here."

Carrina started walking. They weren't fast, but at least they were moving. A little farther along, a dark shape lay in the road. With a cry, Carrina stumbled toward it, kneeling beside the still form of a man.

"Papa!" Reaching out with her uninjured arm, she shook him, but he didn't stir at all.

Dia bent down beside a middle-aged man in a fine tunic, now lying on his back in the muddy road. His skin appeared chalky pale in the faint light; his empty eyes stared upward. Dia shivered. She touched his forehead and found his skin damp with rain and icy cold. When she held her hand above his mouth, she felt no breath. He didn't move at all as Carrina cried and tried to rouse him.

What had happened to this family as they'd traveled? Had they been on their way to Kulin just as Dia and her sister had? Her questions would have to wait. She didn't want to tell the girl that her father was dead, but what choice did she have now?

She gripped Carrina's arm. "There's nothing more we can do now," she said, as gently as she could. "We'll find help and then come back."

Carrina nodded, accepting Dia's support as she got to her feet.

The chill rain still fell, soaking them both to the skin, and they shivered as they walked. Keeping the best pace they could, Dia realized it wouldn't be nearly fast enough. Where could they go? The trees on either side closed in thickly, but they were small, thin thickets here, nothing they could climb up to escape the wolves.

Would it have been safer to stay in the carriage? No. The wolves could have entered it just as easily as she had pulled Carrina out. Damaged as it was, it offered no real protection. Maybe if they could reach the main road again, they might find help.

They hurried on, exhaustion dragging at Dia's aching body as she tried to support Carrina. This evening had turned into a nightmare with no end in sight.

From the howls growing nearer, the wolves were quickly catching up. Dia looked desperately from side to side, looking for any means of defense. She picked up a sturdy stick, murmuring the words of a prayer to the Soul Mother under her breath.

Dia backed up until she felt the small trees against her back. Carrina huddled beside her, sobbing in fear. Several animals circled them, their eyes shining in the gloom. Her heart thudded in her chest. A growl ripped through the dark, and Dia clenched her jaw as she raised the stick.

This wasn't going to end well.

Continue reading in the full version. https://www.amazon.com/Poisoned-Splinter-AJ-Park-ebook/dp/B0DPLMY2CN